"We ___ d the dirty on us."

"Yeah," Jeff added. "How you snuck around and tricked us into whaling on each other. You taints sure stick together. You must have your own mutie code like us wag dudes have our bro code. High five, Ferd!"

"High five, Jeff! And the bro code says that now we have to make you pay. We're gonna stomp you good, and bust your filthy mutie bones."

Belatedly Jak made a move for the knuckle-duster hilt of his trench knife. He realized how that he'd drunk himself to the edge of oblivion. Under other circumstances, he'd already have sliced open Jeff's paunch, dropped his intestines onto the tops of his mud-splattered boots.

Instead his hand seemed to move, not like a striking sidewinder, but as if he were trying to punch somebody underwater.

But the fist that filled his vision first with a black moon and then bright exploding stars moved like nuking lightning.

**Other titles in the
Deathlands saga:**

JAMES AXLER

DEATHLANDS®

Hanging Judge

A GOLD EAGLE BOOK FROM
WORLDWIDE®

TORONTO • NEW YORK • LONDON
AMSTERDAM • PARIS • SYDNEY • HAMBURG
STOCKHOLM • ATHENS • TOKYO • MILAN
MADRID • WARSAW • BUDAPEST • AUCKLAND

Recycling programs
for this product may
not exist in your area.

First edition March 2014

ISBN-13: 978-0-373-62625-0

HANGING JUDGE

I am an American; free born and free bred, where I acknowledge no man as my superior, except for his own worth, or as my inferior, except for his own demerit.
—Theodore Roosevelt,
1858–1919

THE DEATHLANDS SAGA

This world is their legacy, a world born in the violent nuclear spasm of 2001 that was the bitter outcome of a struggle for global dominance.

There is no real escape from this shockscape where life always hangs in the balance, vulnerable to newly demonic nature, barbarism, lawlessness.

But they are the warrior survivalists, and they endure—in the way of the lion, the hawk and the tiger, true to nature's heart despite its ruination.

Ryan Cawdor: The privileged son of an East Coast baron. Acquainted with betrayal from a tender age, he is a master of the hard realities.

Krysty Wroth: Harmony ville's own Titian-haired beauty, a woman with the strength of tempered steel. Her premonitions and Gaia powers have been fostered by her Mother Sonja.

J. B. Dix, the Armorer: Weapons master and Ryan's close ally, he, too, honed his skills traversing the Deathlands with the legendary Trader.

Doctor Theophilus Tanner: Torn from his family and a gentler life in 1896, Doc has been thrown into a future he couldn't have imagined.

Dr. Mildred Wyeth: Her father was killed by the Ku Klux Klan, but her fate is not much lighter. Restored from pre-dark cryogenic suspension, she brings twentieth-century healing skills to a nightmare.

Jak Lauren: A true child of the wastelands, reared on adversity, loss and danger, the albino teenager is a fierce fighter and loyal friend.

Dean Cawdor: Ryan's young son by Sharona accepts the only world he knows, and yet he is the seedling bearing the promise of tomorrow.

In a world where all was lost, they are humanity's last hope....

Chapter One

"You, Jak Lauren, have been found guilty of the following crimes," the fat man on the scaffold intoned.

Marley Toogood wasn't talking to Jak, who stood on the trapdoor with the rough rope of the noose, still untightened, chafing his bare skin where it hung around his neck. The fat man stood to one side up at the front, addressing the crowd of spectators looking uncomfortable and unhappy in the periodic drizzle from low-hanging, leaden clouds. Jak's white hair clung to his head and neck, and the soaked-through shoulders of his T-shirt,

"Pillage, arson, murder, terrorism, treason, disorderly conduct..."

"Ooh, look at that one," muttered a woman in the front row, whose shapeless hat mirrored her shape in a rain-soaked dress made out of sacks. "He's so dangerous looking!"

"I don't know," the woman next to her whispered back. "I think he's good looking. For a mutie, I mean."

The woman was much the same as her companion, only a bit taller and wider. She smelled more strongly of onions, too.

Jak growled at her. Both women flinched gratifyingly. So did most of the other townspeople in the front row.

"...destruction of property belonging to the United States of America, and being a mutie." The fat man lowered the piece of paper from which he had been reading, now soaked almost to transparency, with a look of satisfaction smeared across his broad, wet, bearded face.

"Not mutie!" Jak snapped.

"And for speaking disrespectfully to authority," the fat man added.

He crumpled his paper and stuffed it in a pocket of his patched suit coat. It had been made for a man much smaller than he was, and the right sleeve was starting to come loose at the seams.

Jak didn't know nuke about tailoring, but his ruby-red eyes didn't miss much.

The fat man cleared his throat. Then, waving his stubby arms, he launched into a speech about the importance of the public watching justice in action and restoring the nation through displaying the awful majesty of the state.

Jak tuned him out. The noose was around his neck. His wrists were bound behind him with rough rope. It had been tied skillfully enough that all he got for trying to work his wrists loose was bloody, abraded skin. The U.S. Marshals, as the sec men of the ville named Second Chance liked to style themselves, clearly got lots of practice tying people up.

But it was not in Jak's nature to just give up. His every sense was wound tight to respond to the least clue—something, anything—that might lead to a possibility of escape.

Even if he failed, he would be content if he managed to take some of the bastards with him. That would be ace, too.

"What the glowing nukeshit is wrong with Toogood?" grumbled one of the men seated in the bleachers behind the scaffold and in front of the solid-built stone courthouse at the ville's center. "Why does he always insist on lowering himself like this? And why does he insist on going on so rad-blasted long?"

There were three of them together back there, Jak knew,

plus one empty chair waiting for the fat rich bastard when the speechifying ended and the hanging began. The four were the ville's leading citizens, main backers of the man who was the baron of Second Chance in everything but name.

"Wrap it up, Marley," a second man called. "Why do these events have to be made mandatory, anyway? It costs us all plenty in lost time from the laborers. At the very least, couldn't we cut the schedule back to once or mebbe twice a week, or better, just one big hanging party?"

"What's the matter, Mr. Myers?" a voice sounding like a crow's called from the stands. It came from Jak's left side. "You'd want to cheat the public of the moral lessons provided by regular public executions? With the country in its deepest time of crisis? You walk mighty close to sedition, there. But, by all means, keep talking—if you'd like to join this scapegrace with a noose around your neck!"

And he burst out laughing like a crazy man, which he was.

Only a crazy man would think of calling a sad little ville in the middle of a huge thicket of mutant thorn-bushes that was swarming with monsters "the restored United States," even if he had managed to conquer a couple of neighboring villes.

Judge Phineas Santee ruled his vest-pocket Deathlands empire with an iron fist. And the iron fists of Chief Marshal Cutter Dan Sevier, the tall sec boss whom Jak knew stood now at the Judge's shoulder—and the fists, truncheons and blasters of Cutter Dan's marshals.

The rich citizens shut up. Jak glanced over a shoulder. The one on the far right—Bates, his name was, Jak knew too well—was a skinny cuss, whose neck stuck up like a celery stalk from the sweat- and grease-stained, buttoned-up collar of his shirt. He hadn't said anything.

Instead, he was examining Jak's camouflage jacket, with the bits of glass and metal sewn into it. Like Jak's weapons, his many knives and his Colt Python .357 Magnum handblaster, it had been claimed as a prize by Bates. The man had tried to cheat Jak at his trading post outside town—and then called Jak a criminal when the albino called him on it. Bates turned his head and tossed the jacket back to an employee. The man fielded it gingerly; a couple of marshals who responded to the dustup at Bates's store had cut their hands trying to come to grips with Jak. They had grabbed the albino by the collar and had their fingers slashed by bits of razor blades.

Jak smiled at the memory. But briefly. If he got chilled here, his first regret would be not settling his score with that chicken-neck bastard.

The beefy hand of Santee's chief executioner grabbed the back of Jak's head and turned his face firmly forward.

"No rubbernecking, taint," the huge man rumbled. Jak swore to himself that he would let the guts out of that big belly, even if he had to come back from the dead to do it.

As Toogood's speech finally seemed to start winding down, the sound of hooves splashing in the layer of red water standing on the dense clay mud of Second Chance's main street reached Jak's ears. Accompanying that sound was the jingle of harness and the creak of a wooden wag.

He flicked his eyes to a pair of horses pulling a lightly built wag. It was driven by a man with slumped shoulders and a slouch hat turned down to let the rain fall off the brim before his face. The women were swaddled in black clothes and big hats. They wept and wailed loudly, their voices barely muffled by the huge bouquet of flowers each of them clutched to her face.

Jak knew those voices.

He kept the recognition off his face. He'd spent his life

having as little to do with other people as humanly possible. But the times he had dealt with others had taught him well to keep his feelings hidden. Even the past few years with his own companions, and they were the closest thing to family he'd really ever known, except for a brief interlude in the southwest that ended in tragedy.

The crowd noticed too. Elbows nudged; heads turned.

"What's this?" Judge Santee exclaimed. "Who are you people? What do you mean by this?"

"Stop there!" Cutter Dan barked.

The wag obligingly halted, roughly twenty yards from the crowd and the cordon of sec men that kept them cowed in place. A couple of marshals moved toward it as if to investigate.

"Spare this poor boy!" the taller of the women cried.

"Spare him his life," the shorter, stocky woman added.

"Not a chance," Santee called. His voice did carry, even if it more screeched than boomed, the way his sec boss's did. "The quality of mercy is not strained. And it has no place in the administration of justice!"

Jak could tell the Judge was smiling. Santee smiled a lot. He was well equipped for it: he had a face like a skull with a wet sheet shrunk to the front of it and giant teeth that he frequently showed off in a thin-lipped smile.

"And now, let justice be delayed no longer! Mr. Beemish, execute the sentence!"

The executioner reached his bare, burly arm toward the lever that would spring the trapdoor beneath Jak's feet and drop him until the noose brought him up short by snapping his neck. At least the Judge didn't believe in letting victims of his unique brand of justice dangle and strangle, like some barons did.

The shorter woman stood up in the wag box. "Not a fucking chance!" she shouted.

She hurled the bouquet as far as her strong arm could. It fell amid the crowd. Before the bouquet even hit, the other woman did the same.

Like the first, her bouquet left a trail of smoke white against the gray, leaking sky.

"It's a bomb!" Toogood shrieked in a high-pitched voice. He turned and dived off the back of the scaffold as the bouquets erupted in clouds of dense, choking smoke.

WITH A HEAVE of his shoulder, Ryan Cawdor yanked the quick-release lever J.B. Dix and his apprentice in mischief, Ricky Morales, had rigged for the horses.

As smoke boiled out of the concealed bombs, he glanced quickly back to see Krysty Wroth and Mildred Wyeth take their seats and hunker down, trying to make themselves the smallest possible targets in case any of the sec men got twitchy trigger fingers. They were both plucking at their dark, voluminous skirts, to prevent the fabric wrapping them up and interfering with their role in the next stage of the plan.

Which was escape. Ryan saw Doc Tanner pounding up the street toward them on an eye-rolling black horse. He led two more animals, saddled and ready for the women to ride out of the ville.

Ryan turned his head forward. He gathered himself and jumped onto the back of the right-hand horse that had, until a moment ago, been hitched to the front of the wag.

Screaming people rushed out of the smoke in all directions. They were completely freaked by the sudden, choking smoke. Following them were Santee's marshals, swearing and waving clubs and blasters, trying to corral them and herd them back to watch the hangings like good little citizens.

Ryan booted his mount, which lunged forward. Its companion came along, since Ryan held a long lead rein attached to its bridle. He urged the animals straight into the impenetrable wall of smoke.

A sec man lurched in front of him. He was trying to bat the smoke away with a hand holding some kind of wheel gun. His face was bright red, and he bellowed orders for the fleeing citizens to stop.

His blue eyes got wide as he saw Ryan and two horses bearing down on him. Ryan's mount knocked the man down to its left and kept on going.

The other horse trampled right over the screaming figure.

Ryan held his breath as he plunged into the smoke. He felt people bumping into him but no more went down.

The smoke thinned. Mildred had dropped her bomb in the middle of the crowd. Fortunately, Krysty, with her longer arm and greater strength, had gotten her loaded bouquet right on target: the base of the gallows, which was enfolded in its own thick cloud of billowing white.

None of the marshals remained at the scaffold's base. Whether they were off trying to chase down the audience, or shielding their lord and master with their bodies, Ryan didn't know nor care. They were out of his way.

He reined in the horses right next to the nearest leg of the gallows. Pausing only to tie the reins around the upright, he scrambled up onto the platform. The wooden planks boomed beneath his feet as he rose.

The smoke up there was thinner, it was still enough to tickle his throat and make his single eye water. But he could see through it. After a fashion.

Well enough to see a giant bare-chested executioner, choking and hacking, yank the catch for the trap beneath Jak's feet.

Chapter Two

Ryan sprang forward, already knowing he was too late.

But Jak wasn't standing on the now open trapdoor. Cunning as always, the skinny albino had sidestepped. The trapdoor had swung down and left him standing safe and sound.

The executioner goggled at him. Jak gave him a big grin, then he gave him a hard kick to the groin. The burly man bent over and staggered toward the back of the podium.

A series of thunderclaps boomed. Black-powder charges—big firecrackers—improvised by J.B. and Ricky had started blowing up in the wag bed. Krysty and Mildred had triggered them as they escaped with Doc.

A fresh wall of smoke rolled forward over the gallows. Through it, Ryan could just make out furious, confused motion in the viewing stand. He heard sec men yelling to one another to get the Judge to safety.

Not his concern. So long as they weren't paying attention to *him*. The executioner managed to start cranking himself back upright. Ryan stepped to him and gave him a straight right that squashed his already often-busted nose and splashed his slab cheeks and brutal mouth with blood. He toppled backward through the smoke.

Turning back, Ryan drew his big panga. He kept the broad blade honed razor keen. It parted the hangman's rope like rotted predark cloth.

Jak showed his teeth in a wolf's grin and bobbed his head in thanks. He was never much for talking.

Ryan jerked a thumb. "Horses," he said.

A big fist came out of a swirl of dirty-gray smoke right behind Jak and stretched him facedown on the planks. A man stepped into view. He was taller than Ryan's six-two by about an inch, and built along the same lines: lean muscled, wide across the shoulders, narrow across the waist and hips.

He frowned when he saw Ryan. He had a big square face with prominent cheekbones. His lips were thin, his eyes merciless blue. A red, white and blue armband was tied around his big right biceps in its faded blue shirt sleeve.

"What the nuke do you think you're doing?" he demanded. "Don't you know who I am?"

At Ryan's feet Jak stirred and moaned.

"You're called Cutter Dan," Ryan said. "You're a major coldheart in these parts."

The other man laughed. "Is that what the no-account trash drifters tell each other in the outlands? I'm the law, now—the Judge's strong right hand."

Ryan rushed him. The self-proclaimed marshal was wearing a piece, a heavy-frame Smith & Wesson revolver of some sort. But instead of drawing the blaster he whipped a big Bowie knife out of its sheath with his right hand.

He blocked Ryan's overhand cut with the flat of his blade. For all the one-eyed man's strength and the panga's greater weight, the sec boss held him off.

Cutter Dan's free hand snatched for the wrist that held the panga as the Bowie disengaged with a ringing hiss of steel on steel. Ryan jumped back, avoiding not only the grab but a gut-cutting sweep of the foot-long blade.

The sec boss sprang forward, slashing high and low, pressing Ryan hard. Though the panga's length made up for Cutter Dan's reach advantage, its relative heaviness meant that the Bowie was faster.

The bastard was good, Ryan realized. He feinted high, but before he could strike for Cutter Dan's left side his opponent launched another sideways cut of his own. Ryan sucked in his gut hard and bowed his back.

The Bowie's tip sliced a line of fire across his belly.

The smoke was clearing. He heard shouts from the grandstand as the sec men hustling off the bigwigs spotted something going down on the gallows. Time was blood, Trader used to say—and if it was, Ryan had just suffered an artery cut.

He launched the most savage attack he had in him, trying to power the taller man down as quickly as possible. Steel rang on steel as Cutter Dan parried every stroke. Ryan didn't dare take the long, looping cuts that would take maximum advantage of the panga's crushing power; the other man would cut him to bits. Ryan gave up little, if anything, in strength to his larger foe.

But big, bad Cutter Dan was wicked fast. He slammed the flat of his Bowie against the flat of the descending panga and steered the hefty chopper out and past to his own right.

He had opened Ryan to a chilling stroke.

Then he roared as if in surprised pain. For just half a second he froze.

It was all Ryan needed. He raised the panga and slashed Cutter Dan downward across the face.

As he followed through, he saw that Jak, still prone on the scaffold, had managed to sink his teeth into Cutter Dan's right calf above his combat boot.

The sec boss reeled back, his face exploding in blood.

With no more time to waste, Ryan kicked him off the back of the gallows. He reached down and yanked Jak to his feet by his left arm.

"Come on!" he shouted. He towed Jak to the front of the gallows where he'd hastily tied the horses. He swung down onto one. Jak sprang aboard the other. His hands were still tied behind his back, but he was a fairly skillful horseman who could steer his mount with his knees.

They rode hard eastward down the street.

SECOND CHANCE SURE was a sorrowful sort of dump, J.B. Dix thought, as frightened locals stampeded past him. He'd be glad to see the last of it.

The ville's buildings were mostly predark framed stucco, and only desperate and haphazard measures seemed to keep them standing against a century and more of bad weather and rot. The rest were shanties slapped together out of badly cut planks and random scavvied material. The only structure in the ville that didn't look like a hard look would blow it away was the gray stone courthouse, and the sturdy brick-and-block annex built onto it to house the population of prisoners that fed the ever-hungry gallows out front.

Lurking in a recessed doorway west along the street from the gallows, J.B. watched in satisfaction as the smoke billowed out from under the canvas that covered the wag bed. Doc was by the smoking wag on horseback, seeing to the getaway of Krysty and Mildred, who'd pulled off the diversion without a hitch. J.B.'s next job would commence directly.

The companions had had less than forty-eight hours from the time they'd watched a bruised and bloodied Jak being dragged out of a trading post on the ville's outskirts by a quartet of burly sec men—who weren't looking much better themselves—to whip together the makings of their diversion.

The wag had dropped into their laps as they withdrew into the nearby forest to regroup and plot in the gathering dusk. They'd hit a road where a six-legged catamount was still eating the guts out of the capacious overall-covered belly of the wag's former occupant.

Fortunately the big cat wasn't hard to chill. A quick shot from Ryan's Steyr Scout Tactical longblaster coupled with a blast of buckshot from J.B.'s Smith & Wesson M-4000 had knocked it right off its prey, snapping and hissing. A panga hack to the back of its neck had stilled it.

It had taken a lot of doing to make a plan and complete preparations to carry it out before the justice meted out by Judge Santee—whose fame had spread for miles around—took its speedy course. They boosted what they could from isolated farmhouses. Some things they simply walked in and purchased from the same general store where Jak had gone off by his stupe self and come to grief. At least damp brush, which served a key role in turning the wag into a giant smoke bomb, wasn't in short supply there in the Wild, as the locals called it.

Now, as Doc and the two women went racing back up the street unscathed, J.B. allowed himself a nod at a job of work well done.

He heard a powerful commotion from the other side of all that smoke, which totally filled the rutted dirt street and rolled over the roofs of adjacent buildings.

Suddenly a knot of grim-looking men wearing the red, white and blue armbands burst out of the smoke. A couple waved handblasters. Others carried clubs. They were all shouting at the fleeing ville folk to get back where they belonged.

Still staying half hidden in the doorway, J.B. pivoted

and fired a burst from his mini-Uzi from the hip. It kicked up splashes of rainwater on the packed clay soil of the street, where it had barely begun to sink in. Pink streaks appeared on the sec men's pants legs as they shied away from the impacts.

They threw up their arms in front of their faces. J.B. knew that was reflex, if triple stupe.

He fired two more 3-round bursts into the ground at their feet. That was enough for them. They turned and sprinted back into the dense smoke.

Ryan had told him not to chill anyone unless he had to. J.B. accepted that because of the dictum of his and Ryan's old boss and mentor, Trader, *no chillin' for the sake of chillin',* and because it made sound sense not to piss off the local sec men any more than strictly necessary.

He just hoped they didn't come to regret passing on the opportunity to thin the herd a little.

CROUCHED IN A narrow, stinking space between two sagging predark buildings, Ricky Morales watched Jak and Ryan ride past, east down the street and out of the ville. Residents fleeing the smoke bombs and confusion by the gallows scattered before them like quail.

Ricky moved back and held his longblaster behind his body in shadow. No point in getting spotted and ratted out to the sec men of the crazy man known as the Judge. It might seem strange to think of people disobeying the Judge's orders to look to do the man a service. But among the many things Ricky had learned since joining Ryan Cawdor's band and leaving his home island of Puerto Rico, high on the list was to be careful whom he trusted.

And strangers—especially strangers who might be looking to get back in the good graces of authority after disobeying in panic—weren't high on the list of trust-worthy souls.

Those thoughts flew fast through his mind by reflex—pure survival. At once his body flooded with a warm sensation of relief. His best friend, Jak, had been rescued from certain death!

A trio of sec men burst out of the smoke. One shouted, pointing after the pair of men rapidly riding away. Another threw a lever-action longblaster to his shoulder.

It was a stupe trick, Ricky thought, taking the shot, but Ryan had told him in no uncertain terms to avoid killing unless it was absolutely necessary.

Now he got a flash picture over the iron sights of his DeLisle carbine's fat barrel. His finger squeezed the light trigger, smooth and fast. The longblaster gave a cough and the buttplate thumped against his shoulder.

The barrel jerked to the side. Ricky heard a clang of copper-shod .45-caliber bullets on a blued-steel barrel. The self-proclaimed marshal yipped a curse and dropped the blaster as if it was hot.

The others stopped in their tracks and stared at him. "What?"

"I think somebody shot my piece!"

Ricky had immediately thrown the bolt to chamber a fresh round when his first shot went downrange. The smooth Enfield action and Ricky's long practice made it incredibly fast. He fired another bullet in front of the boots of the marshal closest to him, who had an impressive bandit mustache.

"Hey!" the third sec man shouted, pointing. "I saw something. He's in that alley!"

The first man was staring at his longblaster as if still trying to figure out what was going on. Ricky's shot might have bent the barrel. The other two immediately opened fire with handblasters.

Ricky ducked back into the narrow walkway as bullets sang by. A ricochet moaned by his ear.

Have I done enough? he wondered. Have I done my job? Ryan and Jak got away clean.

As Ricky hastily backpedaled, he slung the DeLisle and drew his Webley revolver.

A sec man appeared in the mouth of the passageway. Ricky shot him in the shoulder and he reeled back, yelling that he'd been hit.

Something hard hit the backs of Ricky's lower legs. He tumbled backward over it. As he fell onto the foul-smelling, slimy dirt, the mustached sec man sidestepped with his semiauto blaster leveled.

The only thing that saved Ricky from instant death was the fact that the marshal wasn't looking for a target on the ground. Ricky knew his reprieve wouldn't last. He tried to get his Webley up and around in time, but there was no hope.

From just beyond where he had fallen Ricky heard two quick crashing sounds. The sec man jerked and fell. Ricky saw a dark, wet patch already appearing on the front of his tan shirt.

"What the nuke are you playing at, boy?" Ryan demanded. "You eager to find out what it's like having dirt hit you in the eyes?"

Ricky managed to disentangle himself from the upturned wheelbarrow that had tripped him. Its wheel was missing. He scrambled to his feet.

"You told me not to chill anybody—"

"Unless it was necessary," Ryan finished. "I'd say not getting a faceful of lead is necessary."

"Is Jak with you?" Ricky asked as they headed toward the far end of the narrow alley.

"He rode right off into the weeds with his hands tied behind him," Ryan said. "Forget about it. Right now we need to power out of here so we don't wind up on the rad-blasted gallows ourselves."

Chapter Three

"Where the nuke did you go?" Ryan demanded.

Krysty looked at Jak. The albino had stepped into the circle of yellow glow cast by their campfire in a tiny clearing in the middle of a thorn thicket tangle in the Wild as casually as if he'd just gotten back from stepping away to piss.

"Got weapons back," Jak said. He was wearing his camouflage jacket once again. "What cooking?"

"Squirrel," Mildred said. "What's it look like?"

Jak shied away from the fire and the several small, skinned forms browning on spits over it.

"Squirrels not mutie?" he asked.

"Not as far as I know," Mildred said. "I know for sure that they didn't have two assholes each or anything like that."

The sturdy, black, predark physician was testier than usual this night. Everyone had been on edge wondering where Jak was and whether their elaborate and risky rescue plot had been all for nothing. It didn't help that Ryan had spent the hour since they made camp at the agreed-upon rendezvous site pacing like a tethered wolf.

Neither did it help that the night and the dense thorn-studded growth around them was alive with furtive motion, strange cries and the occasional glowing eyes.

"Answer the question," Ryan grated.

"Did," Jak said, sticking out his jaw mulishly. "Got stuff."

He meant his weapons, jacket and shoes, Krysty knew. He had cached his pack in a place where the others would be sure to see the special secret marker, before haring off on his own mission and getting himself caught by the Second Chance sec men. It was waiting for him beside the others' right now.

Ryan narrowed his eye.

"Where and how?"

Jak just glared at him.

"Jak," Krysty said. "Why not tell him?"

"Went to rich guy's store. Broke in, cut throat, got my stuff back. Paid bastard."

"Nuking hell!" Ryan said. "You left us waiting here while you pursued your personal vengeance. And if he was the one who was fondling your jacket by the gallows, he's one of the ville's big shits. If they weren't gunning for us before, they sure as burning nuke death are now."

"Easy, lover," Krysty told him. "I think we made enough of an impression on the Judge and his sec men that we need to be moving on to new territory soon, regardless."

Ryan shook his head. "Jak, what you've been doing for the past few weeks, ever since Heaven Falls, has really started sticking in my craw. You always want to head out on your own. Sometimes we've been on the firing line because of it."

"Restless, but look out for all," Jak protested.

Ryan strode over to Jak and got in the smaller man's face. "Is that what you were just doing?" he demanded, looking down on him. "Because it sure looks to me like what you were doing had nothing to do with keeping the group safe. You were making the situation worse."

"Owed rich guy," Jak said. "Paid."

"Mebbe if you'd consulted with the rest of us," J.B. offered, "we could have all come up with a plan together. We took some pretty hairy risks saving your skinny ass from that noose today."

"Not to mention putting in a big load of work," Mildred added.

Ricky rose to his feet.

"Guys, guys," he said, holding up his hands. "Please, can't we all just step back and calm down?"

Ryan and Jak turned to him and each shot out an arm tipped with an extended finger at him. "Back off," they said as one.

Doc put a hand on Ricky's shoulder.

"A valiant try, lad," he said, pressing him back down. "And see? At least you have induced a moment of harmony between them."

The two men returned to glaring at each other.

"However brief," Doc added sadly, sitting back in his own spot.

Krysty came up behind Ryan, deliberately cracking a twig under her heel. His senses weren't as inhumanly keen as Jak's, but that didn't mean they weren't better than most people's. As wired as he was right then, she did not want him to perceive that someone was sneaking up on him.

She placed a hand on his shoulder. He tensed as if to shake her off, but he didn't.

"Let's put this behind us," she said in her most soothing voice. "Or at least put it aside. We should be safe enough here tonight, but we're still in dangerous territory. And we're all in this together."

"That's the problem," Ryan said. "Jak's been playing lone wolf more and more as the days go by. As if he's too fast to run with the rest of the pack."

He glanced back at her.

"And we're *always* in dangerous territory. You know that."

Jak's face had been getting more and more twisted up, and his ruby eyes blazed redder the whole time Ryan spoke. Now he clenched his fists.

"You saying I not care 'bout companions?" Jak yelled.

Even Ryan took a step back at that. Mebbe not, Krysty thought, from the young albino's spittle-spraying vehemence, as much as the fact that Jak was so violently boiling-over emotional that he'd almost spoken a complete sentence.

But Ryan wasn't backing down. That was not what the man did.

"That's how it looks to me," he said, dead level. "That's the way you've been acting."

For a moment Krysty feared Jak would stab Ryan. Or try to.

Then she thought he was going to cry.

He shook himself like a wet dog. "All right."

Jak walked over to the backpacks, picked up his and shrugged into it.

"Gone."

He started to walk away, into the wild night.

"Wait!" Mildred jumped to her feet. "What's gotten into you two? You can't be serious about this."

Jak stopped.

"I'm serious as a ground burst," Ryan said. "I can't speak for Jak."

"Are you really talking about breaking up the group? Really?" Mildred pressed.

"I'm talking about doing what needs to be done to keep us alive," Ryan said. "Same as always."

"But—we're, we're like *family*. We look out for each other. That *is* what keeps us alive."

"Jak hasn't been looking out for us lately, in case you haven't been paying attention. He's been running off on his own, getting into trouble and dragging the rest of us in."

Jak pulled his head down between his hunched shoulders, but he stayed in place as if frozen.

"He made a mistake, Ryan," Krysty told him. "We all do that. We all have, we all will again."

"And you don't talk about throwing us out!" Mildred said.

Ryan scratched his cheek. "Nobody's talking about throwing anybody out. Jak's been separating himself from the rest of us. I reckon mebbe he thinks it's time to make that official."

"Well, Jak has gone off on his own in the past," Doc said. "Of course, he did rejoin us, after tragedy claimed his family in the former New Mexico territory."

"You're not helping, you old coot!" Mildred flared. "Anyway, New Mexico was a state, not a territory."

"Before that it was a territory," Doc said mildly. "And it's no longer either. QED."

Krysty noticed he finished on a vague note. In the firelight his blue eyes took on an unfocused look. Krysty guessed the mention of Jak losing his family had reminded Doc of losing his own and steered his mind toward wandering off through the mists of memory once more.

Mildred was glaring at Doc. Krysty decided that if she started yelling at him the emotional escalation was liable to do more damage than the distraction would help.

"Jak," she said, trying not to sound as urgent as she felt. "What about you?"

"Look out for companions," he said sullenly. "Scout. Guard. Eyes. Ears."

J.B. took off his glasses and polished them. "We've long since come to rely on Jak to recce, and that's a fact," he said. "We are pretty deep into unknown territory right now to cut him loose. And that's without taking the muties in this giant tangle of thorns into account."

"He's right," Krysty said.

"We got along ace without him before," Ryan replied. "We can do it again."

"Ryan, please," Krysty begged. "Get him to stay."

"Jak's been intent on walking his own road for a long time. I'm done with trying to stand in his way."

As the others tried to defuse the situation, Krysty had watched from the corner of her eye as Jak had lowered his head farther. Now he gave his head a quick shake and straightened.

"Fine," he said, still not looking back. "Want gone. Going."

He walked out of the yellow circle of the firelight and into the thorny embrace of the Wild.

With her heart sunk to the bottom of her stomach, Krysty stood staring at the place where he had disappeared.

No one spoke.

"Nuestra Señora!" Ricky yelped. "The squirrels! They're burned!" He grabbed both spits and waved the blackened carcasses in the air, trailing streamers of smoke.

Everyone had forgotten that their dinners were still cooking in the flames, even the vigilant and ever-practical J.B. To Krysty that underlined the seriousness of what had just happened.

"Burned or not," Ryan said, "they're still chow. And I'm hungry."

J.B. settled his round specs back in front of his eyes.

"Me, too," he added. "But I can't say I feel easy staying here."

"I agree," Doc said. Jak's departure had apparently snapped him back to the here and now. "Our enemies' ire has greatly grown. Or will, as soon as the merchant's death is discovered. We took a risk by tarrying here. Now that risk has been redoubled."

Looking glum, Mildred wrestled down one of Ricky's arms and pulled off a charred squirrel corpse with a handkerchief wrapped around her hand to protect her from the heat.

"So we're going to take off into a trackless tangle of briars, that's chock full of muties, in the dark," she said. "*Without* our scout."

Tension and grief had wound Krysty's hair into a cap of tight curls. She moved alongside Ryan, seeing his features harden.

For a moment he frowned, and his blue eye blazed with anger. Then the fire faded.

"No," he said. "That'd be stupe. We wait for daybreak. It's likely the Second Chance sec men will, too. If not, sooner or later everybody winds up staring at the stars."

"I'd prefer later," Mildred stated, crunching on a mouthful of squirrel.

Krysty slid her arm around Ryan's and laid her head against his shoulder.

It was all she could do.

Chapter Four

"It's anarchy!" the red-bearded man exclaimed, his high-pitched voice quivering with outrage. "Total anarchy loosed on the land!"

"Yes, yes, Mr. Myers," Judge Santee said dismissively. "Things fall apart. The center cannot hold. And so on. Nonsense! It is my sworn mission in life to hold the center—and to extend the circle of blessed order ever outward, until these American states stand united once again! Isn't that so, Chief Marshal Sevier?"

Cutter Dan nodded. He was already pissed off way beyond nuke red by the previous day's events. He didn't give much of an actual shit about Sonnard Bates getting his scrawny throat slit by random Deathlands scum. But coming on top of the fact that he had lost a prisoner straight off the gallows and had one of his own men wounded and another chilled, Bates's death was a personal insult to him.

The fresh cut along the left side of his face burned like a branding iron. He had stitched it up himself the afternoon before, once it came clear the criminals had made their escape and there would be no easy capture of them. By that time, Santee had ordered him to hold off starting pursuit until the Judge himself gave permission. Cutter Dan hadn't taken so much as a swig of Towse lightning to take the edge off the pain. He reckoned what didn't kill him made him stronger. An ache that fierce in his head had to be making him triple strong.

Cutter Dan was not a man to let shit like that *stand,* even if his job as sec boss didn't depend on it, as it surely did.

A smoky woodstove kept down the early morning chill in Santee's office in the courthouse. It had rained during the night, and the temperature had dropped considerably. A couple of kerosene lamps cast weak light on the pale faces gathered around a desk that had as many books piled on it as the shelves on the walls did.

"We need to devote our every resource to tracking these desperados down and bringing them to justice!" Myers said.

"Have you forgotten our plans, Munktun?" asked a small, obsessively neat man with receding black hair, sunken black eyes and a thin black goatee. Cutter Dan knew the neatness hid the fact that he wasn't particularly clean, even by the standards of the day. And the beard and hair were dyed to hide encroaching gray. "We've got to expand our foothold of order, which will in turn provide us the resources to sustain what we have."

"But how can we hope to hold on to what we have if such criminals are allowed to flout the law with impunity?" Myers asked. "Much less take over new villes. And restore them to order, of course."

"Let it go," the small man said. "So, they made us look bad. We still have the marshals to enforce our will. The Judge's will, that is.

"And if the marshals are all haring off into the Wild in pursuit of these phantoms? What then, Gein? Who will keep the peasan—the citizens of Second Chance in line?"

"Gentlemen," Marley Toogood said in an oily voice. "Gentlemen. We're all on the same side here. Let's remember our first principles."

"Get it while you can?" Myers asked.

"Never give a sucker an even break?" Gein suggested.

Toogood laughed. "You're both right, my friends," he said. "But the deeper truth—or higher, if you will—is that there are the rulers and there are the ruled. And the members of one class have everything in common with one another—and very little with those on the other side of the divide."

Santee emitted a cracked and whistling laugh. "But both kinds still strangle when they dangle at the end of a rope! You have that in common with your wretched underlings, gentlemen! If you don't remember that well enough, it may yet fall to me to remind you in the most vigorous possible terms."

That shut them up. Cutter Dan grinned outright in satisfaction. It tore like talons at the stitches in his face.

Toogood's smile got a little brittle, but then it came back strong. He was a fat, greasy bastard, but despite that he had at least a little steel in his spine. Cutter Dan reckoned that both the steel and the smarm accounted for why the Judge was willing to suffer Toogood calling himself mayor of Second Chance—when the only power in the ville that amounted to glowing night shit was Santee.

And, of course, his ever-expanding army of sec men. And their boss.

"Both sides are right," Santee said, after judging the three wealthy villagers had twisted in the wind long enough. "Just as Mr. Toogood said. But we must keep our priorities carefully in order.

"We must and we will continue extending the reach of the rule of law, until one day it extends clear across the Deathlands. But that isn't the work of a day, or of a year. And if want to extend the long arm of the law, we must above all make sure that its grasp remains inescapable and strong."

He paused, as if inviting comment. Nobody went for it. They just stared at him and began to sweat visibly.

None of these three could see a single hair past their own self-interest. Santee counted on that fact, as Cutter Dan happened to know. But not one of them was a feeb, either.

The closest thing to one, perhaps, had been Bates. Cutter Dan wasn't sure the filthy, red-eyed little taint bastard hadn't done them all a favor by slitting Bates's throat. The fact might even make Cutter Dan feel generous enough, when he caught up with him—and however long it took, whatever it took, he would catch him—to follow the Judge's invariant rule that captives had to be returned alive and relatively unharmed to stand trial so that they could be properly hanged. Rather than taking his own unhurried revenge on the coldheart. After all, a lot of things could happen out there in the Wild, beyond the reach of Santee's hell-black eyes.

Not that Cutter Dan felt comfortable crossing the Judge. He didn't have any evidence the old bastard had a doomie gift like second sight. Then again, he didn't have any evidence to the contrary.

"At the same time," Santee went on, "we cannot allow our grip to slacken on the home front—either in those areas we've restored to order or in Second Chance itself. Therefore, I will assign my Chief Marshal to take a picked squad, not to exceed twenty men, to pursue the fugitive Jak Lauren as well as his accomplices and bring them to justice. The rest of my sec men shall concentrate on their control and pacification efforts."

He looked to Cutter Dan.

"How long will it take you to prepare for your mission, Chief Marshal?"

"Give me two hours."

OUTSIDE, THE DAY was still cloudy but starting to heat.

Gonna be a muggy bastard, Cutter Dan thought. He took a long step to catch up with the three men who had just left their meeting with the Judge. They were talking among themselves in low, distracted tones.

"Gentlemen," the chief marshal said, laying a hand on each man's shoulder. Gein and Myers jumped.

"Just a friendly reminder for you. You might think of the Judge as just a crazy old coot. You have power here too. You're men of consequence, and Mr. Toogood, here, is even the mayor. But make no mistake. Santee is the law in Second Chance."

The two he'd grabbed hold of had turned their heads to look back at him. Myers's face was pale behind his beard, and his eyes were wide in fear. Gein was scowling and looked as if he had been on the point of lighting into Cutter Dan for having the nerve to lay a hand on him. Until the sec boss's little reminder let the air out of him.

"We understand, Chief Marshal," Toogood said. He shot a hooded glance at his companion. "And we know it's for the best. Believe me."

Cutter Dan gave him a big old smile. "Sure thing, Mr. Toogood."

His palm hovered by his violated face as he watched them split up and head for their respective homes. Along with the pain, the wound—and especially the stitches— were starting to itch like a bastard.

Cutter Dan dropped his hand to his side. He thought about the man who'd slashed him. He'd had a nasty scar down his face a lot like the one the sec boss was sure he was going to wind up with, though Cutter Dan hadn't lost an eye, as the coldheart had. Funny how things went like that.

It was going to be even funnier how this would end. He was going to find the one-eyed man and slit his throat.

After Dan made him watch him do things to his friends, of course.

"GREAT," MILDRED WYETH muttered. "Just great."

Slipping and sliding, she trudged miserably through rain and an endless hedge. Her lone consolation was that the thorns were so huge they were fairly easy to avoid and didn't stick into her as fast and deep as slimmer ones would. It seemed as if her whole world was Krysty's backpack ahead of her, and the gray-brown vines that seemed to writhe around her like diabolical tentacles with deceptive green leaves and silver spines.

And the endless drip of rain from a miserable bruise-colored sky.

They were somewhere northwest of Second Chance and not anywhere near far enough away. But they had to avoid the cleared areas around farms and such, especially the roads in and out, as if they were nuke hot spots full of deadly fallout. Those were the first places their pursuers would look for them. Instead, they were following what amounted to a game trail through the tangled, spiky, unnatural growth of the Wild.

"Any idea of where we're going?" Ricky asked. He was the last one in line, right behind her.

"Like Ryan would tell me," Mildred said. "But I'm guessing, away from Second Chance, mostly. Watch it, old man!"

The last was snarled at Doc, walking just ahead of her with Krysty. He had let go of a branch Ryan hadn't hacked from their path, and it had whipped back and almost nailed Mildred in the face. As it was, it sprayed water droplets on her cheek, which didn't do her any harm but still pissed her off.

"I am sorry," he said contritely. "I shall try to be more careful. The monotony has distracted me, I fear."

"Tell me about it," Mildred said.

Ricky said something from behind her. She wasn't listening close enough to make it out, so she answered with a grunt. He had begged Ryan to be allowed to take Jak's place on point. Ryan had shot him down in short order, insisting on walking lead himself.

She liked Ricky well enough, she guessed. He was just a kid, who should have been home with his folks and his sister on Monster Island. Except, of course, that coldhearts had chilled his parents before his eyes, and sold his sister Yami into slavery; he was still looking for her, with an obsessive devotion that might have been comical had it not been so tragic and doomed. He was an engaging little doofus, in his way, the fumbling, eager, perpetually cheerful adolescent instead of the snarly or surly-sulky kind. And yet, when the chips were down, he was surprisingly competent and bone reliable. And there was not a scrap of malice in him.

Sometimes he was in love with Mildred, or at least her boobs. Sometimes infatuated with whatever halfway-presentable woman crossed their path. And he was always totally hung up on the walking thermonuclear warhead of femininity that was Krysty. Lucky for him, Ryan was secure enough in his lead-dog masculinity not to get bent out of shape about it—or just didn't take a shy, awkward sixteen-year-old seriously as a romantic rival.

Krysty was Mildred's friend, who accepted and did not judge her, and would never think of using her beauty as a weapon against the shorter, stouter, plainer woman— "darker" didn't mean much in this here and now. Krysty never hesitated to use her looks against enemies—any more than any of them would hesitate to use any weapon that came to hand. She was as tough as leather and resilient as spring steel. But even though she could be as hard as need be to protect herself or a loved one, nothing ever touched her core of pure sweetness.

J.B. was Mildred's partner; the two were lovers of long standing. She knew he was anything but cold and bloodless, although he often came across to outsiders that way. He could be ruthless, with a cold practicality that sometimes eclipsed Ryan's. But she knew him as a good man.

Whatever that meant anymore. *She* felt he was good. Just as she felt that, down deep, they all were. It was enough.

It had to be.

Doc was a trickier case. The old coot exasperated her with his vagueness and his outmoded courtliness and sometimes otherworldly ideas. And yet she was uncomfortably aware—more than she had been in a long time— of the fact that his origin in time wasn't much further removed from her day than Mildred's was from the bizarre thrown-together family she and Doc now shared. And though she would, from a standing start, deny she could ever have much in common with his Victorian ideas, no matter how liberated they were for his time, the brutal fact was, the global devastation of the megacull and skydark created a far sharper and deeper disconnect than anything that separated Doc's day from Mildred's.

They were both strangers in this strange land. But because his attitudes were shaped by a far harder world to survive than the one she had grown up in, she might be the greater stranger here. And that, she realized to her acute discomfort, made her short with him. She, in a bizarre way, envied the tormented old man.

The real reason the family had split, of course, was that Jak and Ryan had clashed. Mildred wasn't even sure what the conflict was about, not really. She guessed it had to be one of those male things.

But questioning Ryan's judgment seemed the worst of alternatives to her. He was the force that held them together. He, more than anyone, had kept them alive.

And yet…he was the older of the two. He also hadn't spent most of his life running around the bayou like a feral child raised by the gators. Couldn't he have handled it a bit differently?

And what good had second-guessing anyone ever done for her, Mildred wondered? Even second-guessing herself? And what's more—

The boom of the stub-barreled shotgun stuck beneath the main barrel of Doc's gigantic LeMat revolver snapped her out of her tail-chasing reverie.

A shiny, leathery, many-legged horror the size of a flattened-out house cat flew through the air right toward her face, with giant insect mandibles open wide.

Chapter Five

Jak, crouched high off the ground on a gray-brown vine thicker than his arm, studied what his snare had caught him for dinner.

He wrinkled his nose in disgust. The thing thrashing in the noose that had trapped its hind leg was obviously a rabbit. Kind of. But no rabbit Jak had ever seen had been that shade of black, with gray streaks and rolling orange eyes. Nor had one ever had an extra orange eye, pushed up its head about an inch from the normal right one.

Mutie.

He looked left, looked right. There was no sign of danger in the tangle of thorn-studded vines with black-green leaves, just drizzle falling from a low-hanging sky and the low buzz of insects.

And the rumble in his stomach. He hadn't eaten for a couple of days now. The sec men in charge of Second Chance's well-populated jail hadn't wanted to waste food on a prisoner they were fixing to string up right away. And when he caught up with his friends—

He shook his head. No point thinking about that. Or them. They were part of the past. He was sadly walking away from all that, now.

But he couldn't outpace his hunger. He looked at the struggling rabbit and sighed.

Tainted or not, the creature's flesh wouldn't poison him. Hopefully.

AT THE SHATTERING roar from Doc's blaster, Krysty spun, drawing her short-barreled Smith & Wesson 640 as she turned.

She saw Doc pointing his LeMat off the trail—such as it was—through the thorn vines across his body to his left. Blurring motion drew her vision back, where she saw something about two feet long and shiny brown flying through the air at Mildred's face. Then Ricky stepped up from the rear of the file holding his longblaster by the barrel to whack the thing right out of midair with the butt.

From ahead of Krysty, J.B.'s shotgun went off with a less apocalyptic noise than Doc's.

"They're all around us!" she heard Ryan holler. "Close up, people. Watch each others' backs."

She heard a sinister rustle from close behind her and she whipped her head around.

A multilegged horror jumped at her. She batted it with the hand that held the blaster. It squealed and went cartwheeling away back into the tangle.

Dozens more of the things ran along the thick vines, flowing around the thorns, gripping with their many legs.

J.B. closed up with her, blasting a jumping centipede into a viscous yellow spray.

"Cease fire," Ryan said from right behind him. "Got more bugs than we got bullets."

Krysty looked at the snub-nosed revolver in her hand and winced. It carried five shots. Even with the speedloaders uncomfortably sitting in the pockets of her worn jeans, it took a relatively long time to recharge it.

"What do we fight with?" she yelled, kicking away a pair of the monsters scuttling toward her legs.

"That works," J.B. said.

"Not well!" shouted Mildred, stamping on one. "Shit! They're hard to kill!"

Ryan hacked away a three-foot section of vine that had six-inch thorns but no leaves. He handed it to Krysty.

She accepted it, hefted it, gave him a grateful grin. Spinning, she whacked a centipede that was rearing off a vine and was preparing to strike at her head. The weapon felt like a good ax handle and worked the same way, cracking chitin with a crunch and spinning the thing into the thicket.

"Circle up!" Ryan snapped.

The companions shifted to put themselves back to back, shoulder to shoulder. Krysty knew intuitively and at once why: it made it hard for the horrors to get on their flanks—or worse, behind them.

"Are they poisonous?" Ricky asked, clutching his De-Lisle by the fat suppressor that enclosed the barrel.

"Try not to find out," Ryan said. He was dividing his attention between hacking the centipedes into writhing, goo-oozing segments and cutting branches like the one he'd given Krysty. He threw one to Ricky. It bounced off the boy and landed at his feet.

"Don't screw up your blaster, kid," he called. "It's for shooting, not hitting."

"Not mine," J.B. said with a wicked grin. He was holding his M-4000 by the barrel, the same way Ricky held his weapon. The synthetic stock already dripped with yellow gore. "Made for this kind of fandango."

Mildred caught her section of vine just in time to close her eyes and take a mighty home-run swing that knocked two leaping monsters away. One broke apart into three segments, its hooked legs waving frantically as it vanished into the thicket.

"What about fire?" she yelled.

"Rain!" Krysty and J.B. shouted back in unison. It had slowed to a faint drizzle that brushed Krysty's face with deceptively gentle cool, scarcely more substantial than fog. But it had been falling for an hour or two this day, and there had been plenty more over the past few days. The thicket was well soaked, even the ample number of obviously dead and dried-out strands, which continued to do their part for the plant colony's collective defense with their still-wicked thorns.

Except it didn't take Krysty's special connection with Gaia the Earth Mother to know there was nothing remotely *natural* about this giant jungle of thorns.

In a moment everyone had a clubbing weapon—or in Ryan's case, a knife whose fat chopping blade could double as a club. For a few moments there was nothing but the sound of grunting and impacts.

The attack slackened, not because their losses had discouraged the giant centipedes, but because for a moment the supply ran low.

"What now, lover?" Krysty asked Ryan.

"We move."

"Where?" Mildred probed.

"Keep heading the way we were going," Ryan said. "Until we run into something better."

"Down"

It was Doc.

"This unnatural vegetation prefers the higher ground, you will have noticed."

"Yeah," J.B. said. "He's right. When we come in the stuff was all on top of the ridgelines. Made the whole place seem less of a mess than it is. But we're on the flat right here, Doc. Where's 'down'?"

"Water," Krysty stated.

Her companions didn't dare take their eyes off the surrounding vegetation, where occasional glimpses of shiny, flat brown forms scuttling along vines showed that the mutie centipedes hadn't forgotten about them. But they all gave Krysty a fast, puzzled glance.

"It runs downhill," she explained, nodding downward. "Look."

The slow rain had fallen long enough to outrun the dense clay soil's capacity to absorb it. Water had begun to pool around their boots. Red-brown water trickled off to the right of the way they had been heading when the horrible creatures attacked.

"Right through the thickest part of the vines," Ryan said. "Ace."

He turned and began hacking at the strands with his panga.

Instantly the tangled growth came alive around them with racing, many-legged forms. "Here we go again," Mildred said.

Krysty moved to put herself as close to Ryan's left shoulder as she could without interfering with his attack on the vines. She glimpsed J.B. doing the same on his right. Mildred came up alongside him and Doc was next to Krysty. Finally, Ricky completed the circle.

Only just in time. Dozens of the enormous centipedes swarmed them. High and low they struck at the embattled humans.

For a timeless moment all was sweat, gasping for breath and effort. And always the elemental, gut-twisting fear of giant bugs and of the unnatural.

Krysty and her friends held off the two-foot-long arthropods, but just barely. She felt her own strength flagging, her arm speed slowing.

A centipede leaped for her face. Wielding her club with both hands, she was just too slow to slap it away. She had to duck her head to the side. Her sentient, motile hair was taut against her head, keeping the creature's many waving legs from snagging in it as it flew past.

The mutie landed on J.B.'s backpack and promptly began to slither upward toward the brim of his battered fedora.

Biting her lip, the redheaded woman reached her left hand, grabbed the centipede near its tail-segment, and hurled it far off into the thicket.

"Krysty!" Ricky yelled, his voice breaking in panic.

She already knew what provoked the boy's scream. She could feel the pinpricks of sharp, chitinous legs as the monsters ran up the legs of her jeans.

"Fireblast!" she heard Ryan grunt at the same time.

She had to use her hands to rip the quartet of centipedes away. One of them bit for her hand with two-inch mandibles. It missed, but she imagined she could see drops of venom glistening like dew from their tips as she backhanded the creature off her and stamped it furiously with her boot.

"What's wrong?" J.B. asked Ryan.

"Vine's too thick and too green. Won't cut."

"There seem to be a lot more of them closing in on us," Ricky reported nervously.

There was also the problem that the mutie centipedes were hard to chill. Stomping them, however hard and often, seemed only to slow them for the length of time it took the creatures to extract themselves from the mud. Even cutting them in pieces didn't always work: large segments attached to a head could still run—and bite.

But Ricky was right. The thicket around them rustled and twitched with bodies rushing on many hard, crooked legs. It was just a matter of time until one of them bit somebody.

And then not much time before lots of them started biting *everybody*.

"Everyone down," J.B. said. As usual the Armorer didn't raise his voice. But it had an extra edge to it.

"But—" Ricky was frozen, confronting a carpet of the awful arthropods on the ground right in front of him.

Doc tackled him from behind. The two went down with a splash of red-brown water and a compound squeal of centipedes squashed by their combined weight.

Krysty was already flopping down. She gritted her teeth as she felt claws digging through her hair as a centipede scaled her head. She felt actual pain as well as horror; her hair, unlike normal hair, was alive and contained nerve endings.

A savage crack stabbed her ears. Accompanying it came what felt like a line of hard force passing over her fast from right to left. The centipede's legs plucked futilely at her hair as the unseen force plucked it away.

She recognized the sound of a high explosive detonating; the force was the shock front of its dynamic overpressure expanding over her. Apparently it had hit the low-slung creature just right to carry it away—probably rearing up to look for exposed skin to strike.

Through the loud ringing in her ears she heard Ryan roar, "Up! *Go!*"

She thrust herself up out of the muck, despite the combined weight of her well-muscled body and the well-stuffed pack on her back. She got a boot under her and sprang to her feet. Then she reeled and just managed to catch herself. The shockwave had affected her inner ear and scrambled her balance.

The first thing she saw was Doc, his white hair standing out wildly from his head, helping to drag Ricky to his feet by a handful of his rucksack. Though he looked to be in his sixties—and was around a century older than that, to go by his birthday—Doc had lived roughly the same number of years as Ryan. But the whitecoats' experiments that had trolled him from his own time had also prematurely aged him—and affected his sanity, though sporadically these days.

But despite his feeble appearance, Doc was fairly strong and durable.

The centipedes had fallen back again. Krysty glanced toward Ryan and saw several lying on their backs waving their innumerable claw-tipped legs in the air. Apparently they didn't like the shockwave.

Ryan had pushed between the shattered ends of the main vine. She saw at once why it had resisted all his massive strength, determination, and hyper-adrenalized fury. It was at least as big around as one of his thighs.

Now he was whaling two-handed with his panga at the spiky growth beyond the gap. As Krysty looked he vanished from sight.

"Everybody follow!" J.B. shouted, then he vanished, too.

Because Mildred happened to be closer to the gap, she beat Krysty through it despite her shorter legs. But just barely. Then Krysty plunged between the splintered vine stumps and the hastily cut-up tangle beyond.

The ground suddenly sloped away beneath her. The thin top layer of clay mud acted like oil beneath her boot soles. She lost all purchase, fell on her rear and slid down into a gully they hadn't even seen was there, thanks to the exuberant growth of the vines that had hemmed them in.

At the bottom ran a thin trickle of a stream. Ryan was on his feet; J.B. bounced right up beside him. He still clutched his inevitable fedora to his head with his right hand.

He helped Mildred up as Krysty slid down into the tiny stream with a splash. "What the hell did you do, John?" Mildred demanded.

As Krysty stood, still a little dizzy, she saw the Armorer give Mildred a quick grin.

"I happened to have a quarter-block of C-4 stashed away in case of emergency," he said. "I always say, there's few problems in life that can't be settled by a proper application of high explosives."

Doc slid down on his heels, surprisingly nimble, his stork legs bent and the black coattails of his frock coat flapping. Ricky followed far less gracefully, sliding on his belly, raising quite a pink-slurry wave.

"Tsk, tsk," Doc said, bending down to grab a strap on Ricky's backpack and haul him sputtering out of the water. "Young people these days have so little fortitude."

"It's not fortitude," Ricky said, spitting out water. "It's bad luck. I tripped, okay? *Nuestra Señora!* Cut me some slack, here."

Krysty took quick stock of their new surroundings. As they had seen before, the narrow gulch was clear of the thorn vines. It ran down, none too steeply, toward her left, when her back was to the blown-up section. Vaguely northwest, she reckoned.

"Uh, guys," Ricky said. "We got a new problem."

She turned to see the youth pointing a mud-dripping arm up the small ravine.

Up toward the top of the cut, not thirty yards away, a gigantic hog stood glaring at them with enraged red pig eyes and shaking a head full of tusks like rusty sickles.

Chapter Six

"Nothin', boss," Scovul called. The black marshal was riding his black gelding back down the road through the thicket. Its white-stockinged feet were kicking up geysers of thin red mud at every step.

"No way they took the road," the chief deputy marshal said. "We'da caught 'em up by now, sure as shit."

Cutter Dan grunted. "Ace."

His two trackers were half Choctaw and Wild raised. They had confirmed that the scumbags who rescued the white-skinned mutie from Judge Santee's justice had headed west initially. But they hadn't made it away with enough horses to carry all of them; Mort and Old Pete had found several of the animals grazing near an old burned-out farmhouse that the thicket hadn't reclaimed yet. The wag was abandoned there, too. They might've piled the extra perps into it, but would never have been able to outpace the swift mounted pursuit they surely knew would follow.

He turned back to the miserable cluster of people standing in the rain by their horse-drawn covered wag with their hands up.

"Can we go now, Marshal?" the older man asked. "Whoever you're looking for, you gotta know by now we had nothin' to do with 'em."

In a way it was a relief they had headed off into the Wild. Had they had enough horses and just kept riding west down the road, they'd've cleared the mutie thicket in a day or two. Then the odds of Cutter Dan and his sec men ever catching up with them would have become small, indeed. Bashing through the thorn vines would take them days.

It was a pain in the ass following them, of course. Old Pete and Mort would pick up their trail eventually. But Cutter Dan's posse couldn't move much quicker than they could. If they could even go as quick.

"Marshal," the bearded wagoneer said. "Can we please be on our way? Or at least let us put our hands down. My arms are getting tired. And the womenfolk are bound to catch their death, standing out here in the drizzle like this—"

Without even a glance his way, Cutter Dan drew his huge Bowie knife, flipped it into the air, caught it by its tip and threw it. Hard.

He heard a *thunk*. The wag dude's words trailed off.

Cutter Dan looked at him then and nodded. The fat blade had caught the bearded man right in the chest, with enough velocity to punch through his sternum and cut his heart in two. The trader coughed once and collapsed like an empty sack.

The women screamed. The younger man yelled, "Pa!"

He jumped to cradle the older man's head in his lap, plopping his skinny rear right down in the road mud. The older man's eyes were rolled up in his head. Instant chill.

"You still got the touch, C.D.," his deputy drawled.

The women clung to each other and screamed. The younger trader raised a reddened face running with tears. His mousey hair was plastered to his head. His features were all knotted up like a gaudy-man's bar-rags.

"You bastard!" he shrieked at Cutter Dan. "You murdered my pa in cold blood!"

In a wave of reddish spray he hurled himself off the roadway at the sec boss, his fingers clawed. Cutter Dan met him with a hard boot heel to the chest. The younger man flew backward, landing in an even bigger splash within a foot of where he'd started out.

"Assaulting an officer of the peace," Cutter Dan said, shaking his head. "That's a capital offense, you taint."

"We take him back for the Judge to string up, Dan?" Hammer asked.

"Not this trip. We travel light. We gotta catch these coldheart pricks."

A gunshot cracked. The kid's head jerked to the side as a dark spray gushed out the temple. He fell across his father's cooling corpse.

"Why'd you go and waste a good round on the taint, Yonas?" Cutter Dan asked the marshal with the eye patch, and a smoking Ruger Old Army .44 in his hand.

"It's just black powder, C.D.," Yonas said, gesturing with the handblaster.

"Bullets cost jack," Cutter Dan said. "So do caps and even the powder. Oh, well, smokeless or smoke-pole, can't ever get the bullet back in the blaster."

Like their now-deceased menfolk, the two female captives showed an age split that hinted strongly they were mother and daughter. Oddly enough, the mother was the better-looking of the two, with dirtwater blond hair streaming like waterweeds down her back and big jugs in her homespun dress. She was sturdy in the hips but not any kind of sow. The daughter had a crossed eye and a hint of black mustache, though otherwise she was put together pretty decent. She was slim built but clearly hadn't missed many more meals than her mother. Apparently being traders had worked out well for them.

Until today, anyway.

The mother had been hanging on to her daughter as if holding her up out of the mud, while they both carried on. Now with her left arm still circling her daughter's sob-convulsed shoulders, her right hand dived inside her voluminous skirts.

It came up with a dingy-looking Davis .380 hidie hand-blaster, which rose to aim square at Cutter Dan's broad chest.

But the first motion had triggered the sec boss's bow-string-taut danger sense. Before her little pistol came to bear his Smith & Wesson 627 slid out of its holster and spoke first.

She reeled back as the .357 Magnum jacketed hollow-point slug took her in the chest. Because she didn't go down or drop the piece right away, he shot her twice more. Her knees finally gave way.

Shaven-headed Belusky stepped up behind the girl and caught her in a bear-hug from behind before she could collapse all over her chilled mom.

"Who's wastin' good ammo on road trash now, Cutter Dan?" he asked, grinning beneath his blond mustache. "And modern smokeless cartridge, too."

"Shut your pie hole, Belusky. I already used my knife. As you would've noticed if all the blood hadn't run to your two-inch hard-on."

The sec man's grin never flickered. "Might not be long, Danny boy," he said. "But wide? Lord, is it wide!"

"You call yourselves lawmen!" the daughter screamed from his unfriendly embrace. "But you're nothing but a bunch of murdering coldhearts!"

"Yeah, well," Cutter Dan said, emptying the cylinder, with its three spent casings and three live rounds, into a palm. "We are the law hereabouts, see? So the law's what we say it is."

"Us and Judge Santee," Scovul called from the back of his horse, which was so used to blasterfire it hadn't even reacted to the shots, loud as they were. The two plugs hitched to the wag were sure tossing their heads and rolling their eyes, though. But with the handbrake set, they weren't going anywhere. "And since he ain't here—"

"See, the boys'n'me have suffered an emotional blow, recently," Cutter Dan told the distraught girl. "And we're naturally frustrated because the criminals who wronged us have so far managed to elude justice. So it's just natural we need to let off a little steam."

"And you had to go and chill the better-looking snatch, C.D.," Hammer said. "Even if she was an oldie."

Dan laughed. "Not like the bitch left me much choice there, did she? But I tell you what. Just for that you can take your place last in line."

"But why are you doing this?" the cross-eyed girl shrieked.

"Some folks're resisting the rightful restoration of law and order under us and Judge Santee," Dan said, stuffing both the loose cartridges and empties in a pocket and reloading his handblaster from a speedloader. "So we gotta provide 'em object lessons in the terrors of living under all this anarchy."

He snapped shut the cylinder of his beefy stainless-steel blaster. Then he smiled at the girl.

"Just think of it as doing your patriotic duty. Everybody's gotta make sacrifices."

Holstering his blaster he began unbuttoning the fly of his jeans.

"Today is yours. Get her stripped and bent over the wag box, boys. Time to dispense some justice, American style!"

"FIREBLAST," RYAN SAID.

The giant hog glared blood and death at him and gouged deep grooves in the red dirt of the stream-bank with a sharp black hoof. It stood a good four feet high at the peak of its back, which was topped with bristles like tenpenny nails. Its body had to be as long as Ryan was tall or longer. Its jowly head was the size of a beer keg, and it brought back memories of the horrible hogs they had faced a while back in Canada.

All of the companions had blasters, but Ryan's Steyr Scout was the only one in the bunch with a lost child's chance in a scalie nest of dropping the monster in a single shot. It was slung across his shoulder, and he knew that those huge feral porkers could move like a high-power bullet when they dug in and launched themselves.

As one this old and bad and mean surely would, the instant its little bloodshot eyes saw any of them make a move.

Ryan had just resolved to draw his SIG Sauer P-226 and try for the hog's beady eyes anyway when he saw a stirring in the leaves of the vines near the immense creature.

A living wave of scuttling shapes boiled from the vines at the top of the cut. They closed on the hog from both sides. The centipedes climbed up one another's segmented bodies, forming a sort of living pyramid.

Too late, the hog realized the danger. It began grunting furiously. It shook its massive head and stamped with its hooves. Its jaws and tusks shredded the many-legged creatures and sent parts and yellow ichor spraying in all directions.

"Well, now, that's a mite unusual," J.B. observed mildly.

The hog began to squeal like a steam-train whistle as the monster arthropods' mandibles began to find ways through its dense fur to rip into its hide.

Ricky raised the fat barrel of his longblaster to aim at the beast, now all but completely invisible beneath the surging brown bodies. Ryan promptly grabbed it and twisted it skyward.

"But I was going to put it out of its misery!" the youth protested.

"Not this time, son," J.B. said. "The fact it's fighting back is mostly what's putting those little monsters out of *ours*."

For a moment the Ricky's dark eyes blazed rebelliously, then he swallowed and nodded.

"Right," he said hoarsely.

Ryan let go of the blaster. Ricky obediently turned it to the side, making sure the muzzle never covered his friends on the way.

"Compassion always loses to survival," Mildred said. "Welcome to the Deathlands, kid."

"Time to haul ass downstream," Ryan told them. "Those bastards aren't our only problem."

Ricky yelped shrilly. Ryan turned to see a giant centipede that had apparently decided it was too late for the raw-pork feast and jumped down from the vines on the bank above, clutching Ricky's right arm with its hundred talons. It sank its huge hooked jaws into the exposed skin of his forearm.

"Oh, my God!" Mildred yelled.

Ricky whipped his arm to the side. The centipede flew away, to hit the bare clay slope on its back. As it slid down, J.B. destroyed its head with a blast of buckshot from his M-4000.

Ryan didn't say a word to his friend about the ammo expenditure. J.B. was the Armorer. He was more sensitive about all things blaster than even Ryan was. If he thought this merited a shell, it did.

Mildred sprang for the stricken youth.

"Hold still," she said, her voice surprisingly calm despite her burst of frantic activity. "Hold your arm down by your side."

Numbly Ricky obeyed. He continued clutching the DeLisle's foregrip with his left hand. His olive face had already gone an unhealthy ashy-yellow.

"Going down," he said.

His eyes rolled up in his head and he collapsed into Mildred's arms.

Chapter Seven

Jak ran with the pronghorn, filled with exhilaration.

After several moments the yellow, antelope-like creatures left him quickly behind, bounding across the flat Deathlands plain with graceful bounds.

He slowed to a stop, laughing, as he bent, panting, with his hands on his thighs. He watched the pronghorn bounce up and down as they dwindled across the vast flat. The red soil had begun to dry and fracture in the sun after just a couple of days without rain. Tufts of green grass sprouted from the fissure lines, as did a few white-and-yellow Deathlands daisies.

He might not be able to keep up with the beasts, but it felt good to run. And run free.

He was a child of the Louisiana bayous. He had grown up wild and hard, a feared and successful freedom fighter—or terrorist, depending on which side you viewed it from—from childhood on. And this flat, arid land was no more similar to the environment he'd grown up in than the rubble-choked streets of some urban nukescape.

But he felt at home here. Or almost, anyway. He felt alive when he was on the loose in nature. He often felt confined in villes.

Being able to run and be free of responsibilities and rules lifted a tremendous weight from his shoulders. It made him feel as if he could breathe again, for the first time in a long while.

He felt a twinge, somewhere inside him. He decided he was just hungry.

Jak's T-shirt was soaked through. He stripped it off, then laid it across his white shoulders to keep them from burning. The pronghorns' butts disappeared into the heat haze on the far western horizon.

He glanced up into a surprisingly cloudless sky whose blue was without pity, though not as threatening as the orange and yellow clouds that usually took it over. The sun was past zenith but still plenty high. He had lots of time to hunt or gather food before dark.

Even if this wasn't his sort of country, Jak just seemed to have a knack for living off it.

Laughing softly, he turned and began walking back to where he'd cached his jacket and pack.

Life was good.

"Our life sucks," Mildred said.

Even though Ryan, Krysty, J.B. and Doc were bearing the brunt of Ricky's deadweight as they carried him, his blasters and backpack down the cut, the physician's short legs made it hard to keep up with her friends. She was busy holding up Ricky's arm to examine it, without raising it as high as his heart, to try to keep the mutie centipede's venom as localized as possible. But she still had to examine the wound, because in a case like this seconds could count.

If it wasn't too late already. She felt her face flush and the sweat roll down her back—not just from all the frenzied exertion in a humidity-drenched atmosphere that was starting to heat up despite the clouds and rain, but at the prospect of losing another member of her small and tight-knit family.

From behind came sounds too terrible to describe as

the huge black jaws of the swarming centipedes devoured the hapless monster hog.

"Is the lad still alive?" Doc asked anxiously.

"So far," Mildred answered. "Still breathing, still got a pulse. Both pretty strong."

Ricky's arm was completely relaxed in her grasp. The other hung loosely, hand dragging in the tiny stream underfoot as they splashed downhill.

"He just seems to be unconscious," she stated.

"All right," Ryan said. "I think we can stop here."

The other companions did so with minimal awkwardness. Mildred glanced up to find herself and her friends at the bottom of a ravine. The walls were maybe fifty or sixty feet high and steep red clay. They were crowned with the dense tangles of the Wild.

The bottom, though, widened considerably from what they'd first come down. They had reached a small canyon, of sorts. There was enough room to get out of the stream, which had widened and deepened considerably from other gullies feeding into it, as the runlet they had followed did.

Gratefully, Ryan and the others set Ricky on a relatively flat, grassy bank. The rain had stopped completely, though the sky was still the color of bullets overhead. Mildred relinquished her grasp on the poisoned boy's arm long enough for the others to extricate him from his backpack and slung rifle. Then they rolled him onto his back, and she knelt at once beside him.

Ryan came and hunkered across him from Mildred. "What have we got?" he asked.

She thumbed open the half-closed lids of Ricky's brown eyes. "No dilation of the pupils. Strong, steady respiration, same as before. Pulse still strong. Temperature seems normal."

She took her fingers from his neck and stretched his

wounded arm out from his side. Then, bending close, she examined the bite.

"Huh," she said. "No signs of inflammation except a little bit around the actual puncture wounds. No discoloration."

She looked up at Ryan. The others had gathered around, as well, in a circle of concern.

Except the Armorer. She frowned in sudden irritation with the man. The kid was his apprentice, so to speak, and he couldn't even be bothered—

Then she caught him in the corner of her eye. He was standing to the side, his Smith & Wesson shotgun in his hands, keeping a lookout while the others focused on their injured friend. It wasn't lack of concern for Ricky that kept him apart. It was concern for his companions.

"Mildred, what is it?" Krysty asked in alarm. "Is he—"

She shook her head. "I think he's fine," she said. "Like I say, he just seems to be out cold."

"What about the venom?" Ryan asked.

"Beats me," she said. "I gotta warn you, I'm not a toxicologist. But there are certainly none of the gross signs of hemolytic toxin present. Nor of neurotoxins, though I'm on way shakier ground here. At least, not the sorts that cause death or serious nerve damage."

"His eyelids are fluttering," Doc said, bending over with his hands on his skinny thighs.

"Does that mean he just fainted?" Ryan asked.

"Don't be too hard on him, Ryan," Krysty said, laying a hand on his shoulder. "I'd be triple upset if one those things bit me."

"I'm pretty sure there's more to it than that," Mildred said. The supine boy was beginning to stir. He moved his head slightly. "He didn't seem freaked out or anything. Not enough that he was going to faint from fear.

He seemed mostly taken by surprise and then—boom. Out like a light."

Ricky's lips moved. No sound came out. His jaw worked.

"Let's get him some water," Mildred said, reaching for a canteen.

"Are you sure that is wise, in his state?" Doc asked.

"No," she replied, unscrewing the lid. "Like I said, I'm not a poison specialist. And neither are you, you old coot. I don't see any reason to let him get dehydrated, here. Help me hold his head up so we don't choke him, Krysty."

With the redhead's help Mildred trickled a few drops of water into Ricky's barely open lips. He coughed, spit, shook his head vigorously. His eyes shot open.

"What?" he demanded. He looked wildly up at the others. "What are you all staring at?"

"Seems like it'd be pretty obvious," J.B. said from the side.

"What? Oh. Sorry." Ricky sat suddenly upright. "*Nuestra Señora,* that thing bit me!"

"Yes, it did," Ryan said. "And you keeled right over like you'd been shot."

"I—I did? Wait—where are we, anyway? What happened?"

"Someplace safe," Krysty told him.

"Safe enough," Ryan said. "For the moment."

"What did you feel?" Mildred asked.

Ricky asked for more water. Mildred held the canteen up to his lips for a swallow, then let him take hold of it and drink some more.

"Well, it stung like a bast—like fire," he said when he'd drained half the container. "It kind of gave me a jolt. And I felt like there was something else, like an *edge* to it, almost. Like when you get stung by an ant, you can tell you've been poisoned, if only a little, you know?"

"Yeah," Mildred said. "Go on."

"Well, my arm started to go numb. And I started feeling really cold. My stomach got woozy, my head started to spin, my vision seemed to get dark around the edges. Then, well, next thing I remember was waking up here on the grass."

Ryan stood up. "Reckon he's gonna live?" he asked Mildred.

"Afraid so," she said.

"The centipede's venom must produce some kind of soporific effect," Doc said.

"Like some sort of knockout dose," Ryan suggested.

"Seems so," Mildred said. "Pretty fast acting, though."

"Muties," Krysty stated simply.

"I guess."

"How do you feel, kid?" Ryan asked. "You fit to fight?"

"Don't really know," Ricky said thoughtfully. Then he grinned at Ryan. "But I bet I can walk and carry my pack. That's what you're really asking, isn't it, Ryan?"

Ryan grinned. "Reckon so."

He leaned down and, gripping Ricky forearm to forearm, pulled him to his feet.

"And that's what we need to do," he said. "Move. For one thing, there's no way of knowing whether some of those bastard centipedes might've missed out on the pork banquet and decided to come looking for us. Plus, while this gives us a nice handy route to try to get clear of this damn mutant thorn tangle, it's also a natural highway for everything else big and bad."

"Including our friends from the ville," J.B. said.

Mildred and Krysty helped Ricky get his pack up and onto his back.

"Speaking of that unfortunate swine," Doc said, looking speculatively back up the way they'd come, "I cannot help wondering…if the outsized centipedes' bite produces instant unconsciousness, why did the hog continue to struggle and squeal for so long?"

"Don't ask me," Mildred said. "I'm barely a people doctor, in the way I so often need to be. I'm certainly not a bug doctor."

"Dear lady, while those creatures are unquestionably arthropods, they are, equally unquestionably, not of the class of *Arthropoda* that constitutes the insects."

She fixed him with a furious glare. "They have nasty, segmented chitinous bodies, too many legs and they bite," she said. "They're bugs."

"Less talking," Ryan admonished sternly. "More walking."

"Yes, sir," Mildred said.

"How far does this thing go on, anyway?"

At the question, Krysty glanced back over her shoulder at Ricky, who bringing up the rear. He was staring up at the heights above the tangle of miniature canyons by which they made their way through the Wild.

"How would I know?" Ryan said from the lead. "Not like we got any reliable maps of this country."

"Rumor in the last ville we stopped at before Jak's adventure says the thicket's expanding," Krysty said. "Or trying to. The cook I talked to at the eatery said it keeps running up against the drought and acid-rain-prone belts of the Deathlands. So far, they're winning. But it's double big."

"If we could take the roads we could be clear in a day," Mildred grumbled. "Two, max."

"We'd be hanging by the necks in front of Judge Santee's courthouse before sunset the first day," J.B. said.

"Aside from that."

She glanced up again. The thorn vines showed no signs of thinning, either up the walls of the ravine or ahead, as far as the eye could see.

The route they were taking was fast only in comparison to creeping along snaky game trails through the Wild or trying to hack their way through by main force. It wasn't a practical thing to do for very long, in any event. The ground underfoot was muddy and mucky, and it clutched at Mildred's boots despite the grass roots holding it more or less together.

"Shit," she murmured, mostly to herself.

"I know," Krysty agreed sympathetically.

"I know it's stupid," Mildred said, still keeping her voice way down, "but still I can't help wondering if we'd be having quite this much trouble if, well, you know...."

"How can you say that?" Krysty asked. "You know Ryan does all he can—all *anyone* can, and then some—to keep us alive!"

"Yeah, I know, Krysty. Sorry. I don't know what I was thinking."

But I do, she thought, more miserable even than before. I was looking for someone or something to blame for us being in shit this deep. But it's nobody's fault. Except the asshole politicians and whitecoats who blew up the world and made this mess.

She heard Krysty sigh gustily.

"I'm sorry, Mildred. I shouldn't have bitten your head off like that. The fact is, deep down—I wonder too, sometimes. And that's why I reacted the way I did. Overreacted."

"We all have our skills, but Ryan can do anything," Mildred said. "At least, it feels like he can. Anything we've ever needed him to do to pull us through, he's done."

She shook her head, setting her beaded plaits to swinging.

"But, well—"

"He can't do everything at once," Krysty admitted. "And even he'd admit, Jak's a better scout than he is. Just as J.B.'s handier with blaster-smithing. Though I wouldn't try to pin down Ryan on the whole Jak thing just this particular instant—"

"Look out!" Ricky screeched from the rear of the procession. Belatedly he added the useful part. "Ryan, *down!*"

Chapter Eight

"And the only possible sentence is death!" Marley Toogood finished, making his voice ring.

Though the day was dreary, with more low, gray clouds spewing a miserable drizzle, his heart soared. Something about being able to proclaim those words, loud and proud, to the assembled citizens of Second Chance and Judge Santee's nascent empire, and hear the moans of despair and the increasingly desperate pleas for mercy from the four condemned men and women standing with nooses around their necks, just made a man's heart naturally soar.

He heard the creak and grind as the hangman threw the lever. Four traps snapped open under four sets of feet.

"Oh, please, no, not my baby, too—"

The sound of necks snapping was like the ripple of blasterfire from a firing squad, which was also a satisfactory way to send off evildoers, Toogood thought. But it cost more money, even for black-powder blasters. And also the Judge was a traditional sort of man, with a strong fondness for the gallows as a symbolic statement of community principles.

And, of course, a way of making sure that anybody who disagreed with him too strongly on pretty much any subject at all sooner or later found himself swinging from one.

The crowd issued a joint sigh of sorts. Toogood looked around sharply. The sec men on duty monitoring the area didn't seem to notice any particular offenders.

The louts get slack when Cutter Dan is out of the ville, he thought. Ah, well. We can hardly recruit men of higher caliber to do what is, after all, a menial chore.

Santee pushed himself out of his chair, stood to his full skeletal height and shambled inside. He moved with a purpose. Knowing a little about the state of his internal affairs from the Judge's house servants, whom Toogood was careful to bribe just the right amount, the mayor suspected Santee's bowels had been struck with the sudden urge to make one of their infrequent and irregular movements. It wouldn't do for a man of Santee's dignity to soil his trousers in front of the whole ville, after all.

"So, how long will it be before the chief marshal catches those coldheart scumbags and gets back to his real job, Marley?" asked one of his fellow town fathers. They had risen from their seats on the dais and stood beneath umbrellas.

"You're asking the wrong man, Gein," he said. He pulled out his handkerchief to wipe sweat and rain from his broad expanse of forehead—broad, signifying a powerful, *thinking* brain behind it, of course.

"You know everything that goes on in the courthouse," the fussy and diminutive man said.

Toogood laughed. "You give me far too much credit, my friend."

"I'm worried," said the sturdy Myers, frowning beneath bushy red eyebrows at the crowd, sullen as the ville folk ambled away to get back to their daily duties under the watchful eyes of a dozen sec men. "We're spread too thin. If only we had let the coldhearts and the filthy mutie they stole from justice get away scot free, instead of weakening our sec force! Just look at these shiftless scoundrels. They're just waiting for the opportunity to pull us down like wolves and tear us apart."

"Why else do you think I just sent off a foursome at once, gentlemen?" cawed a familiar voice from behind them.

They snapped their heads around to see Judge Santee sheltering inside the open door of the courthouse and silently laughing at them.

"What better way to remind them who's in charge, eh?" the Judge said. "Make an impression! Justice is not to be denied!"

He smiled unpleasantly. It occurred to Toogood to wonder if he'd ever seen the man smile any other way.

"Perhaps you gentlemen would be wise to take such lessons to heart, before you walk quite so perilously close to sedition. Wouldn't you agree?"

And cackling openly he turned and vanished into the darks depths of his lair.

Myers's bearded jowls shook as he vented a shuddering breath. "Brrr. The man's unnerving sometimes."

"We, of course, appreciate fully how fortunate we are to find ourselves in Judge Santee's strong and capable hands," Toogood said loudly. "Of course, none of us harbor any thoughts but those of complete loyalty to our Judge and his vision!"

He winked one eye furiously at his fellow grandees.

"Of course!" Gein piped up. He nudged Myers in the well-padded ribs with his elbow.

"Oh, very well," the stockier man said. Then more loudly, he added, "Of course I know that the Judge's decisions are wise!"

"Better, gentlemen," Toogood said, nodding and beaming vigorously.

"The real shame is that this snipe hunt is slowing up our schedule for restoring the rule of law to nearby villes," Gein said, in far more subdued tones. "Once we start consolidating our grip—that is, consolidating the rule of law and of the United States—we'll have no trouble bringing in enough recruits to keep the rabble in their proper places."

"For now, we must agree to disagree, Donnell," Myers said.

He turned to Toogood. "What's the next ville due for reintegration into our United States, Marley?"

Toogood frowned as he thought about the question. "I'm not privy to strategy," he said, and officially that was true. "That's for the Judge and Cutter Dan to decide. But I believe it's the ville of Esperance, to the southwest."

"Ugh," Myers said. "A real nest of vipers and freethinkers. I know we rely on trade with them. All the more reason to bring them to heel. I can't say I'll be sorry to be able to free my employees from their pernicious influence and example."

"See, Munktun?" Gein proclaimed. "We'll make a believer of you yet!"

"Perish the thought," Myers said.

THE FACT THAT Ryan only had one eye severely restricted his peripheral vision. But, as he marched in the lead of his companions, he kept his head constantly turning, like a one-eyed tomcat in a ville back alley. Even before Ricky shouted his warning, he'd spotted the missile arcing toward him from the dense mutie growth atop the high wall to the left.

His mind registered that it was a spear. Then it passed through the place where he would have been walking and embedded itself in the red clay bank to his right.

He threw himself forward into the stream. He had been carrying his Scout longblaster. Now he held it up as he belly flopped clear to the bottom of the shallow running water. Then, rolling rapidly to his right, he brought the weapon to his shoulder and pointed toward where the spear had come from.

He saw a creature gazing back down at him from the edge of the braid of thick, spiky vines. At first he thought it was another mutie animal, an outsized lizard of some sort, or mebbe a bird. It was about four feet tall, with a black-banded gray face and an off-white, streaked belly. It had a crest of turquoise feathers. He couldn't see more of it for the growth.

Then he noticed the thing had something like a bandolier slung across its chest. It looked as if it had bags and pouches attached to it, and a knife in a beaded sheath.

A second one appeared, with an arm cocked back to throw another spear.

By this point Ryan had his longblaster pointed in the right direction. He caught a flash picture through the ghost-ring iron sights mounted beneath the scope and gave the trigger a compressed speed break. The lightweight rifle bellowed and bucked. When Ryan pulled it back online, both inhuman faces were gone.

"They're on both sides!" Ricky shouted. "What are those things?"

"Trouble," Ryan yelled, rolling on his back in the stream and jackknifing to stand back up by the sheer power of his gut muscles. "They're not just animals! They got hands and weapons."

Muzzle blasts buffeted Ryan's ears as his friends opened up. He hoped they were picking their targets. They couldn't afford to just bust caps, lost in the Wild like this.

He got his boots beneath him and, first things first, quickly sidestepped. It got him out of the stream, onto soft and slightly slippery, but still more reliable footing, and also shifted him out of the target zone for any other arm-launched missiles that might heading his way.

The vines atop both walls rustled with a seethe of drab-colored bodies, as the lizard muties appeared to throw stuff and duck back out of sight. After the first one missed Ryan, few spears seemed to be coming their way. The muties seemed not to want to waste their prime weapons. Mostly what came raining down on Ryan and his companions was hefty chunks of vine, many with long thorns still attached, tumbling end over end.

He slung his Scout and drew his handblaster. Now that the enemy knew he and the others could hit back he wasn't going to get many good shots. If he was going to waste ammo he preferred to burn the lighter, easier-to-come by 9 mm than the 7.62 mm his Scout used.

To his relief the others had stopped their brief flurry of fire as they realized they were just busting caps. Now they were concentrating on spotting objects thrown their way, ducking and dodging, or batting them aside.

Ryan looked quickly around. When in an ambush, he remembered, Trader always advised the best thing to do was assault right into it.

The problem with that was, the most obvious way to do it in this case was to charge straight up one of the steep and wet-slick clay walls of the little canyon, which would almost certainly turn into a particularly grubby and arduous type of suicide. Likewise, charging straight ahead the way they'd been heading might send them straight into the heart of the nest. Or whatever the lizards lived in.

"Back the way we came," he yelled. "Triple fast! J.B., take the lead. I got the rear."

With his short, bandy legs, the Armorer was unlikely to set a pace that any of them couldn't keep, and risk falling behind—fatally. Even Mildred could keep up with him.

"What about the centipedes?" Mildred demanded.

"Let's all try to stay alive long enough to get back to them," Ryan called back. "We can sort that out then."

For the first few moments, as Ryan trotted along the stream bank, he thought their attackers would be content to let them just back out of their domain. The hail of vine chunks tapered off rapidly.

Then he had to yell a warning as another spear came zipping down from the right bank.

Chapter Nine

"Why would we help you?" one woodcutter demanded.

Cutter Dan stood facing the two men, rubbing the side of his face. Then he snatched his hand away. The cut the coldheart bastard had given him had far from truly healed, and it itched like blazing blue death.

"Fair question," he said.

He turned slightly, drew his big handblaster, and shot the man's partner through the belly. He fell, clutching his ruptured guts, screaming and kicking at the bare red dirt yard of the ramshackle shack.

"Now," Cutter Dan said, turning back to the first man, whose sandy-bearded face was slack with shock and white behind its soot and grime. "I sure hope you know the Wild hereabouts better than this gentleman, my friend. What's your name?"

The man's thick, callused hands quivered in the air by his shoulders as he looked down at his black-bearded companion. The man's screams had turned to a visceral bubble of pain and sorrow.

Cutter Dan cocked his handblaster with his thumb. "I asked you a question."

"Uh, Torrance. Sir."

"All right, Torrance. Now you see why you should help us, right? If you do, I don't shoot you in the belly, too. Painful way to die. Believe me, I've seen it happen a lot."

He tapped the often-broken bridge of the man's nose

with the muzzle of his Smith & Wesson 627. The man's pale green eyes blinked rapidly at the still-stinging heat of the blaster barrel.

"And since I'm in such a generous mood," the sec boss went on, "I'll even put your friend here out of his misery as a bonus. But only if you help."

The man drew in a long, shuddery breath.

"All right," he said. "I'll help you. Now, please. Take care of poor Elliott."

"Right. Wise choice, Torrance."

He was a man of his word. A man was nothing if he wasn't as good as his word. He holstered the Smith & Wesson and drew his trademark Bowie knife. Stooping, he cut the wounded man's grimy, stubbly neck to the backbone with a single swift cut.

Torrance fainted. Maybe it was the arterial spray of his best friend's blood splashed across the shins of his faded jeans.

Cutter Dan wiped his big blade carefully on the chill's black coat. As he straightened, he sheathed it again.

He looked down at the prostrate form of their new guide and shook his head.

"I hope he's not going to be such a lightweight on the hunt," he said.

"Mebbe he just don't like the sight of blood," Scovul stated.

"Well, that could be a problem, too. Seeing as the object of this expedition is the shedding of blood. Though not too much, at least when it comes to our fugitives. We need to take 'em back to the Judge in presentable shape and not too drained out."

Yonas laughed. "Well, if he does turn out to be a weakling, you can always chill him, too, boss."

Cutter Dan shook his head.

"We got severely limited time for these kinds of games, fun as they are," he said. "Now, somebody throw a bucket of water over this simp and rouse him up. Those scofflaw coldhearts aren't going to hang themselves."

RYAN SPOTTED ANOTHER mutie standing up out of the thicket on the left. It held a spear poised to throw. Ryan snapped two quick shots at it from his P-226. He mostly intended to make it duck and spoil its aim. But he saw blood squirt from the left side of its narrow chest. It dropped the spear and fell squalling into the green tangle.

"Ryan!"

It was Ricky, shouting from right behind his back—meaning, ahead of him in line. By sheer reflex Ryan jumped left and forward into the shallow brook.

A spear brushed his pack. Another mutie uttered a gargling cry from atop the bank to Ryan's right. Then it came half tumbling, half sliding down the bare red slope.

As Ryan watched it fall, he heard the clack-clack as Ricky threw the bolt of his silenced DeLisle. It really *was* silent—the action working was far louder than the actual shot had been.

That was old news. Ryan was far more interested in the creature descending toward him in an increasing tangle of limbs. It was bigger than he thought. The body was the size of a big dog or a small man. Its tail was about as long, bringing it to roughly nine feet in length, total. The reason he'd thought it smaller was that it seemed built to carry its body horizontally, not upright like a human.

Its body wasn't bare skin or scales, either. It was covered with what looked like small feathers, judging from the way the mud made it spike up. The creature came to rest with big taloned feet in the air. The feet did have scales, yellow ones, and each sported a single, much bigger claw higher than the rest. The open mouth was full of knife-tip teeth. The wide-open eye staring Ryan's way was yellow.

"Wow," Ricky breathed. "With teeth and claws like that, why would they even *need* spears?"

He yelped as Ryan hopped toward him and caught him with a powerful sidekick in the hip. It threw the boy sprawling in the wet grass.

"Why'd you—?" Ricky began to yell in outrage even before he stopped sliding on his side. Then his eyes got big and his mouth shut as another spear stuck into the grass right where he'd been standing.

"They need spears to throw at stupes like you who stand there making targets of themselves," Ryan said, turning and loosing a shot. The spear caster ducked out of sight. "Now, move!"

The shower of hurled objects continued as J.B. led them back up the ravine, less dense, but containing more of the metal-tipped spears. Ryan saw flashes of the strange lizardlike creatures moving fluidly through the growth at the tops of the walls. He suspected their powerful, clawed hind feet gave them the ability to run along the thicker vines.

He could hear them chirping and screeching at one another. It was like being hunted by a cross between a wolf pack and a flock of crows.

The companions couldn't outrun their mutie pursuit, it seemed. But they were thinning it out. The pursuers were getting strung out along the cliffs. And the companions were popping occasional shots their way to make things as rough on them as possible.

Ryan guessed that was likely why the muties had started throwing their precious spears again—to keep their prey from getting away. Those that missed—all of them so far, anyway—they could easily come back and retrieve later, when this was done one way or another.

"We're going this way, Ryan!" he heard Mildred call.

He looked around. J.B. was leading the group up a gully that joined the main line from the northeast. To his relief he judged they were still well shy of the place where they'd left the monster centipedes to devour the wild hog alive.

"Right," he said. He turned and started running to catch up to his friends, who had pulled away. Watching their back trail was suddenly no longer the top priority.

Seeing that their prey had veered away from half their pursuers, the feathered-lizard muties chittered in rage. J.B. suddenly stopped and turned to his left, his Uzi in his hands.

"Up the bank," he called to the others. "Lay down some righteous cover fire."

He ripped three quick bursts into the vines on the northwest gulch bank. Ryan doubted many of the dispersed pack had caught up yet—that was their only real shot at getting clear, in fact. But he heard a squawk, followed by thrashing among the thorn-laced leaves.

Krysty, Doc and Mildred obeyed. This bank sloped at a more shallow angle than the walls of the canyon they'd quitted. But the slick red surface was treacherous, with only a few sprouts sticking out to give them something to grab on to. And they were heavily loaded down by their weapons and the backpacks, and the soles of their boots were well caked with wet clay that reduced purchase to near zero.

But they were strong and they were motivated. They were survivors. They made their way up, painfully and haltingly, but steadily.

And now they had Ryan to protect them, as well as J.B. He paused a few yards up the new cut to point his hand-blaster with both hands at the northwest bank.

A mutie reared out of the growth, ready to throw a

spear. Its head was a big target from the side so he aimed for that. His first bullet punched through its snout behind its nostrils. As it whistled in agony the second bullet hit the membranous patch behind the yellow eye that Ryan guessed was its ear and blew its brains out the side of its narrow skull. The spray of blood and chunks looked black against the lowering sky.

J.B. ripped another burst into the vines. Then Ryan realized Ricky wasn't following the others. He was standing a little way up from Ryan, pointing his fat-barreled blaster at the far bank.

"Get going!" Ryan shouted.

"But—"

"But nothing. Move!"

Ricky faltered. He lowered his weapon, not seeing any targets, anyway.

It was a good thing that he did. A spearhead thunked into the wooden stock just ahead of his trigger finger. The shaft was painted in bright rings and a clump of feathers shook behind the steel head. Ryan couldn't identify them; they looked too long to have come from one of these muties.

J.B. fired a 3-round burst. Ricky yelped. He ripped the spear out of his weapon with a frenzied heave. Then, resourcefulness winning out over triple-stupe childhood heroics and terror alike, he dropped the blaster to hang by its sling, turned and used the spearhead to dig into the clay slope and help him scramble up to join his friends disappearing into the vine skein above.

Ryan turned back. A mutie was sliding down the other bank with blood spurting from its chest and a feather-furred arm. It looked as if J.B.'s jacketed 9 mm bullets had rendered it not much of a threat.

But more of the lizard creatures had arrived. They set

up a clamor like a bunch of crows disturbed from sleep in an abandoned attic. A shower of spears and pieces of vine the size of Ryan's arm came cartwheeling toward him and J.B.

The one-eyed man sidestepped a spear, batted away a spiked wood chunk, then ducked another. J.B. ripped the growth with full-auto fire.

"J.B., go!" Ryan called to him.

The Armorer didn't hesitate. He turned and rabbited up the bank, as well. Following his apprentice's clever example, he let the machine pistol hang from its sling and used the synthetic buttstock of his M-4000 scattergun to help him up the slippery slope.

Flashes stabbed from the tangle above, bright yellow in the gloom. Blasterfire pounded Ryan's eardrums. The three companions who'd gone ahead had found cover and opened up.

Ryan turned to climb the slope. He'd just have to trust to the big bulky pack hulked up over his shoulders to protect him from a spear in the back. It left his legs exposed, but that was life in the Deathlands, where the only certainty was that it would end with you staring up at the stars.

He stuffed his SIG hurriedly away and pulled out his panga. Its heavy, broad blade wasn't meant to be used as a razor, and anyway he could always hone it—if he lived. He started jabbing it into the thick, heavy clay to help him make his way up.

Before he'd gone a third of the way, he sensed something scrambling up to his left. He turned his head to see a lizard mutie overtaking him, climbing on all fours, using his long, curving, birdlike claws to help. The thing might have been lucky or bastard smart, Ryan thought, coming up on his blindside like that. Given the craft with which they made their primitive weapons and the way the pack communicated, he reckoned it was the *smart* thing.

The creature whistled in fury and snapped at his face. Its face was the size of a big timber wolf's and was filled with teeth and malice.

Ryan's panga was in his right hand; its blade was buried in the dirt. He jerked his head right. At the same time he launched a left-hand punch that was half hook, half uppercut. It caught the side of the mutie's wide-open lower jaw. Ryan felt bones crunch as the creature's head torqued to the side.

But it wasn't done. Screaming shrilly, the mutie turned back to him with his jaw askew. It slashed at him with the claws of its left hand.

Ryan jerked the panga free and swung it hard. The fat blade caught the feathered limb midforearm. Skin, flesh and bones parted, easier than a human's would have. The thing was built light.

But it was a predator and extremely tough. Despite its broken face and blood-spurting stump, it dug in its remaining three limbs and hurled itself at Ryan. He could hear its pack mates trilling triumph now; all it needed to do was slow him up another heartbeat or two.

"Nuke that," Ryan grunted, as he swung the panga overhand to meet its rush. The blade caught it at the left-hand juncture of neck and chest and caved its ribs in as much as cut into it. The mutie collapsed with a ghastly whistling wheeze.

Ryan's blade came free easily, though coated in gore. He plunged it back into the clay and went up the bank fast.

Not fast enough. Just as he saw the green profusion of the thicket erupt a few feet from his face—a welcome sight despite the wicked thorns all those leaves hid—a heavy weight landed on his back.

It slammed him, face first, into the mud. The muties might have had light bones, but they were still big. It was as if a man had jumped on him.

He felt a pain in his left side. The bastard thing was raking his short ribs with its long claws. He suddenly realized the purpose: in a matter of seconds it'd be tearing his guts out. He tried to push himself up, turning his head to stare rage-filled defiance into a pair of triumphantly glaring yellow eyes.

One of which suddenly vanished in a spray of blood and aqueous fluid. The sound of the handblaster going off not far from Ryan's head was thunderous.

With half its head blown off, the mutie fell away. Ryan, ears ringing, launched himself in a final furious spasm of effort.

He hurled himself toward a reaching, pale-skinned hand—and the world's most heart-stoppingly beautiful face.

"Come to me, lover," Krysty said. "I got you."

Chapter Ten

Why not? Jak thought.

The ville on the edge of the Wild was small but neat. Neater than Second Chance, anyway.

Not that that was saying much.

The evening was coming down under a sky that had largely cleared, except for big black-and-bloody bands of sunset clouds to the west. He watched from the shadow of some trees as lights came on in the settlement. The ville lay on the north edge of the Wild, where the freakishly wet weather conditions that allowed the mutie thorn thicket to grow in such insane density gradually gave way to the drier climate of the hard-core Deathlands, what Doc and Mildred said used to be called the Great Plains.

Apparently people in the transition zone around the Wild fought robustly against the encroachment of the mutie thorn plants, incursions by the mutie wildlife that thrived inside them and raids from the coldhearts and the desperate people who wandered there, outlanders who sought a better life. The payoff was high: all that extra rain provided good growing conditions.

Jak could see that the borders of the Wild were packed tight with farmlands, already well filled with green crops even though it was only spring. The number of obviously derelict homes, burned-out shells he sometimes spotted while inside the thicket, told Jak that the settlers didn't always win those fights.

This ville clearly benefited from all that produce, as well the fact that it lay on a road that led directly through Second Chance. But he also knew full well that that was as much a curse as a blessing. During his brief captivity in the ungentle hands of that crazy Judge Santee's self-proclaimed U.S. Marshals, he had heard them joking about how someday soon they'd add that ville to their list of conquests. They seemed to look forward to it. Only the fact that it was relatively far away had held them back, he gathered.

Why do this? a voice asked inside his head. Why not stay free?

He shook his head. He hated that voice sometimes.

"*Am* free," he muttered under his breath. "Run where want, when want." He saw no more purpose in wasting words or even syllables than he had when running with… his former pack. In fact, it was growing up a lone wolf that gave him the habit of saying as little as possible to achieve communication and often less.

Anyway, it wasn't as if he was lonely. Not him. Not the White Wolf of the Louisiana bayous. Nuke fire, he'd hardly been gone from his former companions a couple days.

But he did have some ammo in his pocket for trade, and a growling hunger in his belly that, until he learned the local edible plants and the local game and its habits, he was going to have to check out the ville.

Plus, he had a thirst for something other than water.

Jak stepped out from behind his sycamore tree. His pack was cached somewhere safe and dry, of course. He'd be able to bolt if trouble happened, and vanish in the woods where no ville rat would find him. And if trouble got too pushy, he had his camouflage jacket sewn with sharp bits of glass and metal to encourage people to keep their hands to themselves, his knives to carve himself an exit. And the big Colt Python blaster.

The blaster was strictly for emergencies. He did love to use his knives. Feeling an enemy's blood gush hot over your knuckles as you did him was the essence of what being a human predator was all about.

He squared his shoulders and—despite the disquiet that stirred in the recesses of his flat gut whenever he approached civilization—strode toward the yellow lights of the ville as if he owned the place and was coming to collect back rent.

"It's a matter of justice, Your Honor," the man in the khaki overalls said.

Judge Santee sat in his gloomy cave of an office in the bowels of the courthouse. Toogood saw him drum his spidery fingers on the surface of his book- and document-cluttered desk. Once. Twice. Then he crossed a long leg over the other.

"Justice is my business," he said in his dry rasp of a voice. "Explain yourself, if you will, Mr. Down."

His pale blue eyes met the Judge's squarely and without flinching. At least, so far as Toogood could see, standing behind Santee's shoulder. Not many could do as much, he had to admit. Down was a technician of some sort for Gein: a solid blond man of middle years.

"The people feel that simple justice demands that the laws that govern us be made public," he said.

"Which people, Mr. Down?"

"*The* people, Your Honor. The citizens of Second Chance. And I do, as well."

"And by what right do you and these...people see fit to level your demands on me?"

"Not on you, Judge. On justice. If we can pay with our

lives for violating the law, at least we deserve to know clearly what the law is!"

The Judge settled his gaunt frame back a little more deeply in his chair. Toogood was aware of Lovato and Keynes, the two sec men on duty in the office, lurking in the darkness by the shelves of jumbled, dusty books.

"If you're not doing anything wrong," Santee said, in a perfectly reasonable-sounding voice. "You don't have anything to worry about. Do you, Mr. Down?"

Toogood felt a droplet of sweat break free from his hairline, sadly in retreat, to run a tickling trail down the right side of his forehead. Judge Santee was taking this apparent defiance far more calmly than Toogood ever could have anticipated. It almost seemed he respected the millwright for having the courage to present his case to his face.

Rad-blast the man for his unpredictability, he thought. He really is cracked.

"But what is wrong?" Down asked. "When a citizen steals something, or attacks someone, that citizen is put to death, regardless of provocation."

"It's acts that matter in this world," the Judge said. "Not excuses. Crimes."

"Yet when one of the bosses sends their henchmen to take something that belongs to a citizen by force—or when they beat a laggard worker so severely that he dies—they never seem to be punished. Why is that?"

Santee's shoulders hunched. Toogood could tell that he was frowning.

"What are you doing here, Down?"

It was the voice of the small, fussy Gein, striding into the office. Toogood let out a long, slow breath and secretly smiled.

"I came as fast as I could, Your Honor," the mayor's

fellow leading light said. "Is this man bothering you? I apologize if he is. He'll be dealt with most strictly!"

"Mr. Down and I are discussing the abstract concept of justice," the Judge said. "He was raising some most interesting points...."

"Justice? But justice is a flexible concept, Your Honor. Perhaps you can see your way clear to leniency in this case—"

"Justice!" Santee slammed his hand down on his desk so hard the stacks of books jumped fractionally off it, and a cloud of dust rose up. "Flexible?"

He shot to his feet.

"The very nature of justice is that it be inflexible," the Judge thundered. "Not swaying this way and that, like a willow in the wind. What this tormented land requires is nothing but the most rigid form of justice to set things right! Is that what this is all about? To try to weaken my justice, to make it bend? Never!"

He was almost trembling with wrath as he turned to Down.

"Guards," he said. "Take this man out and hang him straightaway. We will show him how unyielding the true justice is!"

The two looming marshals pushed away from the musty shelves, grabbed the blond man and marched him out of the office.

"Your Honor, please!" Gein said. "How am I supposed to run my mill without him? What about the grain?"

"You'll find a way, Mr. Gein," Santee said with brittle humor. "Men like you always do. Or are you questioning my justice as well?"

"N-not at all, Judge Santee! I'd never dream of such a thing."

Toogood came around the desk to lay a comforting arm on Gein's shoulder.

"Come on, Donnell," he said. "I'll buy you a drink."

The little man looked at him, then nodded almost convulsively.

It's the least I can do, Toogood thought, behind a smile that widened quite genuinely, after your timely arrival forestalled a most inconvenient outbreak of rationality.

Toogood intended to be the only power of consequence in this new empire, after only the Judge himself. So he worked, subtly, step by step, to undermine his rivals. He almost felt grateful to that skinny little albino mutie for solving the Bates problem for him at a stroke.

It would have been a shame if all the time and effort he'd devoted to persuading Down to approaching the Judge had come to nothing.

I do so hate waste, Toogood thought.

Chapter Eleven

"Can't stay here too long."

"Why not, John?" Mildred asked.

The Armorer stood looking out the window of the former living room of what she would have considered a modern ranch-style home. Perhaps a tract home—although, if it had been part of a development, the Big Nuke and the Wild had long since devoured all other remnants of it. The glass had been broken out so completely that no trace remained, in the frames or even on the concrete floor. The carpet had long since rotted away except for some dried and sorry-looking clumps here and there.

"We've got water and food," Ricky pointed out. He sat with his back against the wall, cleaning his DeLisle, which he had stripped down on a small tarp in front of him.

J.B. turned away from the window. Outside the shadows of sunset had pretty much overtaken the small clearing that remained outside the house as the Wild claimed it.

"Somebody's going to find us here," he said. "Sooner or later. Emphasis on sooner."

"Affirmative," Ryan agreed.

He bit the word off even shorter than usual. He was pacing a groove in the concrete floor. Krysty had insisted not just on taking her solo turn on watch outside, but on actively patrolling the perimeter. Ryan was a little concerned, not because Krysty was incapable of staying alert to potential trouble, but because of all the muties they'd encountered. There was a possibility that if they attacked she would be overwhelmed. He'd wisely kept his mouth shut.

"It seems not unlikely the lizard creatures already know where we are," Doc said. "Even though we saw no signs of pursuit once we discouraged them from chasing us across that ravine, they might readily have shadowed us here. Or tracked us after the fact. We are not that far from where last we saw them."

Ryan grunted.

"Tactful, Doc," Mildred said.

He looked at her with genuine puzzlement. "What did I say?"

"So, what do we call them?" Ricky asked, a little too loudly and brightly.

Everybody looked at him. He blushed and dropped his eyes.

"I mean, those feathered muties. They were like lizards and everything. But they weren't scaly."

"They do have scales," Ryan said. "On their feet, anyway."

"They look like those velociraptors from the Spielberg movie, *Jurassic Park,*" Mildred said.

"I saw that vid, once, home in Front Royal," Ryan said. "But those were dinosaurs. They had scales, not feathers."

"I say we call 'em dinos anyway!" Ricky said. "Dino muties!"

This time he didn't flinch when everybody looked at him.

"I loved dinosaurs when I was a little boy," he said, a little defiantly. "Tío Benito made me toy ones of wood, based on the picture books we had. They do look like little dinosaurs."

Mildred shrugged. "Good as anything."

"Dino muties, lizards, scalies." Ryan shrugged.

"Whichever way, it doesn't load us any blasters. Call them what you want."

The house looked as if much of it had fallen down or been otherwise destroyed before its most recent set of occupants. Before them, Mildred mentally amended. It was a typical late twentieth-century frame stucco house. She was surprised it hadn't melted away entirely, given the abuses it had to have endured, particularly heavy downpours, lashing winds and the occasional acid rain. What remained showed signs of repeated patching and shoring up, with everything from warped planks to sheets of corrugated metal to lengths of what had to be Wild thornvine trunks. Or whatever you called the central stem of a vine. She wasn't a plant doctor any more than she was an entomologist.

The roof had a few holes in it that hadn't been patched. Most likely, she reckoned, they'd happened after its last inhabitants had abandoned it for whatever reason. A few bullet holes in the walls of the three usable rooms suggested one possibility. But the gaps in the roof didn't seem to make much difference. The rain had stopped, and a warm northwest wind had blown steadily since they forted up here the day before.

"Seems like we should stay as long as we can," Mildred said. "Water well still works."

It also showed so sign of pollution that their severely limited means could detect. Ryan's and J.B.'s rad counters had detected no signs of fallout.

"Plus there's the game trail nearby." Ricky had bagged a young whitetail buck not thirty yards from the house the previous day. The meat was hung bagged in a plastic sheet down the well to keep it cool. J.B. and Ricky had rigged up a drying rack on the roof where animals couldn't get at it, so they could try to make some of it into jerky. Mildred thought that was pretty optimistic. She suspected the guys did too. No doubt there were flying predators around. But it was better than not trying, no doubt.

"If they do find us we can defend the place, easy," Ricky said enthusiastically.

Wordlessly, his mentor and idol J.B. pointed to the bullet holes in the thin walls. Ricky's face fell and his shoulders slumped. He looked so doleful Mildred was torn between feeling sorry for him and the urge to bust out laughing.

"He's not wrong, though," Ryan said. He was still pacing the floor like a caged wolf. "Leastways, not all the way wrong. Better to shoot from concealment without much cover than from none. And it's a better grade of both than we'd get out in the brush."

He scratched his jaw. The fast-growing blue-black bristles of his beard crackled audibly.

"Anyway, if those birds or lizards or bird-lizards or whatever the nuke they are had anything better than spears to shoot at us, they would have. Walls'll give us some protection against those. Even walls like these. And the muties are smart enough not to like what happens when they try wading into blasterfire."

"Yeah," Mildred said. "I wish stickies were that smart. Or smart in that way, anyway. They can be pretty damned cunning sometimes."

"'Sufficient unto the day is the evil thereof,'" Doc quoted. "Let us neither think of nor invoke those vile creatures, until and unless they too arrive to afflict us."

"You afraid that if we speak their name they'll appear?" she asked, laughing. "Come to think of it, they pretty much are devils, aren't they? Or close enough as may be. So it seems you got a point for once."

"Those sec men from Second Chance have blasters," J.B. said. "Unless you reckon they've given up chasing us."

"Zero chance," Ryan replied. "And the longer we stay here, the more likely it is they'll stumble onto us."

"You think they get out in this awful stuff often enough to get that familiar with the Wild?" Ricky asked. "They seem way too ville-bound for that. Like they're just typical sec men, no matter what fancy name they call themselves by."

"We know they get out on the roads," J.B. said. "We had to hide from them once or twice when we were fixing to spring Jak, in case you've forgotten that little detail."

"Well, sure," Ricky replied. For all his overt hero-worship of J.B.—and Ryan—and general shyness, the youth could be pretty brash sometimes. Usually when he thought he was right about something. "But that's not the same thing as being willing to go out and get poked by thorns."

"The lad has a point," Doc said.

"Yeah," Ryan agreed. "But that doesn't mean they can't rustle up local folks as guides."

Ricky looked shocked. "But who'd help them? Nobody likes the marshals. We could tell that even without talking to anybody."

"People they paid," Ryan said. "People they threatened.

"People whose loved ones they got held hostage," J.B. added. He stuck a hand up under his fedora and scratched his head. "It's a bad old world we live in, boy. You've still got a lot to learn about that."

That struck Mildred as a trifle excessive, given that Ricky had seen his mother and father murdered literally before his eyes. But the youth sighed and nodded.

"I know. Everyday I think about poor Yami. I try to imagine what's become of her and I—well, I just can't."

"Perhaps that's just as well," Doc said, a faraway look

coming into his pale blue eyes. "Perhaps you'd be wiser not to try at all."

"Then why stay here, Ryan?" Mildred asked. "I mean, if they're going to find us anyway."

"We could use a rest," he said. "Whatever we can store up before setting out again, I judge we need to do so. And along with making for halfway-decent defenses against the lizard muties, if and when they do decide to try us on again, the walls and roof give us a pretty safe place to sleep. Make it hard for random muties or natural predators—presuming that's what eats those whitetails—to come on us and started gnawing on our faces while we sleep."

Mildred thought about the glistening, venom-dripping mandibles of the giant centipedes biting her face and shuddered.

"So long as we don't get trapped inside here," J.B. pointed out.

"Yeah," Ryan said. "Well, that's another reason not to stay longer than necessary. And yeah, I know I just said we need to stay a spell. And we got no way to know for sure when not enough becomes too nuking much."

"You never know the difference between too little and too much until it's too late," J.B. stated.

Mildred looked at him quizzically. "Did Trader say that?"

Trader was a legend in his time, but he was an aphoristic son of a bitch, too, as Mildred knew from the brief spell they'd run with him when he turned up years after he'd vanished. Ryan and J.B. were always quoting one saying of his or another.

But J.B. just showed her a puzzled frown. "No, Millie," he said. "I did. Just now."

"Problem is," Ryan went on, "I'm not eager to just go

wandering around this rad-blasted living barbed-wire fence at random. We got some idea what kind of unfriendly wildlife calls this shithole home. The natives we run into don't love us, either. And we don't know what kind of territory they claim, or even where it is—we might've just been spotted by scouts, who called for reinforcements to bushwhack us. Nor do we have any idea where the Second Chance sec men are. I don't like the idea of leaving such shelter as we have here only to blunder right into more of that kind of trouble. Not to mention kinds of trouble we don't even know about yet."

"You mentioned scouts," Krysty said, opening the front door and walking in. "And that's what it sounds like we need."

Ryan grinned at her. "Thought you were on patrol. You eavesdropping on us?"

"There's no glass in the windows," she said sweetly, "and your voice carries, unless you make an effort for it not to. Mebbe you feel a little more secure here than you should?"

"Mebbe. What were you trying to say about us needing a scout?"

"We need someone to recce. You yourself were complaining about the lack of it, a moment ago. We need to go out and see what's out there. Some of us, or all of us."

"But how's that different from, you know, blundering around until we run into something big and bad that wants to eat us?" Ricky asked. Then his eyes got round and he blushed, realizing that he might have said more than he should. Again.

"That's why I suggest *some* of us should go," Krysty said. "It's easier to stay stealthy when it's not all sev—all six of us traipsing through the undergrowth together. So mebbe two of us need to start heading out on recce patrols."

"I don't like splitting us up like that," Ryan said, jutting his jaw mulishly. "Not when we got two sets of enemies hunting us, could snap on us together like jaws on a trap at any moment. We've been unlucky enough."

Krysty looked him dead in the eye. "What alternative do we have, lover?"

In the silence that followed, Mildred got to her feet.

"Sooo," she said, drawing her ZKR 551 target revolver and opening the cylinder to check the load. "Looks as if it's my turn on sentry duty. Y'all have fun."

And ignoring a strangled protest from Ricky—whose turn it really was—she walked out the door into the early evening.

Chapter Twelve

"He's not a mutie." the Last Resort's stout proprietor, Meg, said to the burly, boozed-up customer across the bar from her. "He's an albino. Dumb ass."

Jak smiled slightly as he walked away from the bar, carrying his mug of bitter local brew.

The Last Resort was above average for a gaudy, the way Esperance was above average for a ville. The plank floor was covered in sawdust, which helped Meg's efficient staff keep the grosser messes scraped up, including the odd drunk who wound up passed out on it. You could pass out on a table, but if you flopped on the floor, out the door you went.

You might find yourself propelled by the oil-drum-shaped gaudy owner and chief barkeep herself, or by her main bouncer, a colossal Osage named Bo with a scalp lock and a propensity for scary red face paint. They also enforced the establishment's strict no-fighting policy, with or without the aid of a lead-loaded truncheon or two. In the two nights he'd been drinking there Jak hadn't seen any blasters drawn at all, though plenty of the patrons openly carried them, including Jak. That suggested to him that anybody brandishing a blaster got squelched even faster and more finally than brawlers did.

That was fine with Jak. He preferred to use his own .357 only when he had to.

He sat at what he'd quickly picked as his customary

table. He put his back to the corner and sipped his brew. The place didn't smell too much like puke or piss, which was saying something to a man with a nose as keen as Jak's.

It wasn't well lit. That suited Jak fine. He wasn't eager to be seen, which was why he picked the darkest, most obscure corner he could find. While he wasn't completely hidden here, he could see pretty much the entire barroom. The shadows and his own lack of size, plus his ability to be quiet in more ways than not talking, helped him avoid drawing attention to himself. As fond as he was of stealth, being able to see was even more important than not being seen.

While he gathered Santee's so-called marshals weren't exactly welcome in Esperance, and especially not in the Last Resort, he reckoned he was cutting it close enough, appearing in public right up the road from the place that'd tried to hang him so recently.

It was a decent crowd, perhaps half the chairs were taken. It was loud but calm. Such outbursts as he'd seen appeared to be caused mostly by outlanders, starting beefs with each other or the locals. Being on a well-used road, as Esperance was, that was a normal state of affairs. If they weren't coldhearts themselves—or even if they were—the men and women who traveled the Deathlands roads certainly had to deal with coldhearts on a regular basis. They tended to have a greater need to blow off steam than locals did, at least in a relatively well-off ville like this one.

He savored the taste of the beer. In part because it tasted of defiance. He'd once had a little trouble handling his liquor. Since then his companions—*former* companions—had been on him all the time to not drink too much, if at all. Krysty had been worst of all, mebbe because of her mother-hen instincts—and mebbe because Jak couldn't say no to her; few men could.

Meg had been fairly jazzed to pocket the .22 rounds he'd bartered with. They were originals, not reloads. But at the prices Meg charged he'd eat up his ammo credit double quick. That didn't concern him much. He could get by. For one thing, Meg was always looking for fresh meat and other victuals for her head cook, Cho, to fix in her kitchen. The gaudy served a lot of meals, and they weren't any worse than the alcohol, maybe better. He knew if you approached the pronghorns the right way—from downwind, to start—they'd actually stand there and let you walk right up to them. He could sell meat here, enough to pay his bar tabs.

And if not, he reckoned he didn't have to drink. Though he had to admit, he did enjoy the way the warmth flowed through him, even after just a little beer. That showed how little head for alcohol he had.

He felt comfortable here.

Jak frowned and shoved that feeling ungently down. These were manmade surroundings; he could never feel at ease here. Another night, maybe two, with gaudy rentroom walls around him to decrease the risk, let him rest and build up, then he'd be gone. Like the wind, blowing away across the wide, free lands, leaving humanity's works, the ugly little joke they called "civilization" and, most of all, his past behind him.

He was thinking about ordering a plate of beans and bacon when a disturbance drew his eye to another, even more obscure corner of the gaudy—well away from the bar and out of its direct line of sight, though not double far from the kitchen door.

It was the kitchen girl. She'd caught his eye a couple of times, though she was quiet and seemed to try as much as possible not to be seen herself. But since she was always scuttling in and out of the kitchen, cleaning tables, carrying spent bottles and mugs and crockery, and, with her water-pail, coal scoop and sawdust bucket, cleaning up the messes not massive enough to require Bo's intervention.

Also, she interested Jak because she was as black as he was white—a midnight, almost blue-black color that he'd frankly never seen before. Her hair was straight and cut relatively short above a high, gleaming forehead. Her eyes were bright, alert and aware. She was pretty in an unconventional way, tiny, and looked to be no older than fourteen, too young even for him.

But she hadn't been quick or furtive enough to escape the attention of a couple drunken louts. One was tall and burly, with a curly brown neck beard. The other was shorter and leaner, with straight hair and slightly bugged eyes. By their dress and their smell, which he could pick out from all the other smells crowded into the gaudy even at this range, they were drivers and handlers for a horse-drawn wag. Or maybe a local stable, though something about their manner suggested they were the passing-through types.

"What we got here?" asked the taller man, leaning over the much smaller girl, bracing his left arm on the wall over her head and crowding her with his gut in its stained linen shirt. "You sure are shiny. You sure you ain't a mutie?"

"Nobody's that dark and shiny," his partner said, "'less they got the taint. You must be a mutie, girl." He stood to the taller man's left, helping back the kitchen helper in a sort of nook in the irregularly shaped barroom.

She shook her head resolutely. "I'm not a mutie," she said. "My parents were just like me."

The two bullies traded a look and a booze-heavy laugh.

"Then yer folks must've been muties, too," the big man said.

Though Jak's face was turned to the gaudy's center, and carefully kept as blank as the sheet of paper its color suggested to so many, his eyes were fixed narrowly on the pair hemming in the diminutive girl. They had his interest now.

Skin color wasn't much of an issue in the Deathlands. He only knew that it had been at one time because Mildred talked about how different things were back in her day, like, all the time. Unfortunately, what did make a difference was the prevailing fear and hatred of *mutation,* and anything that smacked of it.

That was a prejudice Jak shared, though one of his closest friends for years had been Krysty Wroth, a mutie herself. Because of her, largely, he had at least learned to keep a leash on it. But it was hard, specifically because the most dreaded and dangerous accusation that could be leveled in the Deathlands—that of bearing the mutie taint—was often thrown at him.

Stay out, he told himself sternly. Not business. Can't draw attention.

"Lookit the little mutie," said the taller goon. "Pretending to be a real live norm and all."

He grabbed the girl's pretty face and squeezed so hard the obsidian skin of her cheeks turned gray.

"Got a purty little mouth for a inhuman monster."

She tried to bat his hand away. "Let me go!" She didn't say it loud. Out of the whole gaudy, only Jak heard.

"Ooh." Her two tormentors exchanged looks.

"The mutie done attacked you, Ferd," the shorter man said.

"That she did, Jeff."

"I was only defending myself," the girl said, her voice

still venomously low. "Now let me go and nobody gets hurt."

"Mutie scum ain't got no rights, like natural people have," Jeff said. "So you got to pay for your crimes. How we gonna make her do that, Ferd?"

Jak found himself on his feet and sauntering casually toward them. Fixated solely on their victim with a predator's typical tunnel vision, they had no clue he was approaching. Of course, he was careful to walk up slowly, from behind as well as from the side.

His mind spun furious schemes. Bare-handed brawling could end in disaster. Attacking the two with weapons would be starting trouble, in a way he knew Meg would crush rapidly and with extreme prejudice—and, likely, with no questions asked up front.

And say he successfully bled out both of these bastards—what then? His travels with the companions had taught him about the ways of ville life and justice. Or rather, its injustice, of which his narrow brush with death in Second Chance had been only a relatively minor example, major though its consequences had almost been—and he stepped hard on the lump rising into his throat at the thought of what his companions had done to free his neck from the chafing of the noose.

Even if Meg backed him for helping out one of her people, as for a fact she seemed the sort to do, the local authorities would automatically tend to assume he was wrong and guilty. Especially since they'd no doubt take him for a mutie, too.

But Jak hadn't earned the dreaded name of White Wolf as a mere child by taking on bigger, badder enemies directly. He smiled and made his moves.

Like all the best plans Jak's was simple. Coming in on the men's blind side, he steeled himself, rolled the fingers of his left hand into a stiffened spear and, coming closer than he liked to a man who smelled like that, reached around to poke Jeff in the right buttock. The inside—as if it came from his left.

He turned his head to his pal.

"What'd you wanna go and do that for, you asshole?" Jeff demanded.

"Do what, now?" Ferd sounded totally perplexed.

"You goosed me, you freak. Don't try to pretend you didn't!"

"I dunno what you're talking about, you feeb. Here now, see? You distract me, you're gonna let this little bitch get away afore we can break her in right and proper as a gaudy slut—hey!"

The last came out explosively as Jak glided past behind the drunken pair, boots noiseless on the sawdust-muffled floorboards, and delivered the same stroke right-handed to the inner part of the cheek of Ferd's ass.

For men like this—whether drunk or not—there was usually only one way to settle a dispute. Barely remembering to push off from the wall slightly so he didn't collapse against it face first, Ferd balled his left hand and delivered a surprisingly credible hook right to the bridge of Jeff's nose, which broke with a loud snap.

Jeff didn't go down. He took a step away from Ferd, his eyes glaring bloodshot outrage. He reached up to his lip, then looked down at a hand dripping with the blood fountaining from his violated nose.

"You nuke shit no-account Hoosier cocksucker!" he yelled. He launched himself at his larger partner with a fury that sent them both reeling toward the kitchen door.

And the fight was on, rolling, kicking and eye-gouging in beer-fueled rage and general stupidity. Until hands the size and general color of smoked hams grabbed both men by the backs of their jackets, hauled them bodily upright and slammed their heads together. Both immediately went limp.

By this time, Jak had slipped into a chair at the vacant little table closest to the kitchen door and sat watching with the sort of mild amusement that might be expected if he'd just been sitting there all along, a totally innocent bystander.

The girl had slipped away the instant Ferd's attention was diverted. She crouched with her back against the wall next to the recess, panting like a dog on a hot summer day.

A dazed Ferd gurgled and then puked. Most of it went down the front of his shirt. Most of the rest wound up spattering his moaning, head-rolling partner. None at all got on the enormous bouncer, who, well seasoned at his trade, had correctly read the warning signs and shoved them both out to the length of his bare, impressively brawny arms.

A cupful or so slopped onto the floor.

"You nuke-withered assholes!" the girl hissed. "I have to clean that up."

"Fit, little girl?" Jak asked as the unspeaking Bo dragged the combatants to the door by their collars. Jak was reminded why gaudies traditionally had swinging doors when Bo was able to blast them wide open with Jeff's and Ferd's faces without needing to free up his hands to work a knob or anything.

The girl frowned furiously at him a moment. Then her brow smoothed in comprehension. If not much less irritation.

"Yes, I'm okay, thank you. And I'm not a little girl. I'm nineteen years old."

"Huh," was the only thing he could think of to say. It was more than he usually would have, but these were special circumstances.

The fact that she wasn't the child he'd taken her for was making his cheeks unaccountably warm.

"And I'll have you know I could've taken care of them myself!" she snapped. "I was just about to, before you—horned in."

He had to laugh at that. A low laugh, a wolf's laugh that reminded him of Ryan Cawdor.

Even as he felt his brow furrowing at the thought, she met his eyes. Hers were the same gleaming black as her skin.

After a couple heartbeats she giggled. "Though I got to admit, those were some pretty slick moves. Long as you wash your hands up double careful!"

"Chally!" Jak glanced reflexively over his shoulder at Meg's disinterested but bull-voiced shout. "Clean up, girl."

When he glanced back, the girl was gone.

Chapter Thirteen

Ryan came instantly awake. He sat bolt upright in the bedroom with his 9 mm blaster in his hand, blinking his eye at a blackness just slightly diluted with gray before he knew what had wakened him.

Bootsteps were flying across the clearing toward the half-collapsed house. Somebody was coming fast, and making no effort not to be heard by those inside.

He heard a whistle from the living room. That was J.B., letting Ryan and Krysty know he was alert.

Ryan was at the door in a single step. It was already open. He had his jeans on—he'd slept in them after doing his turn on sentry duty some time before.

Ricky was on watch now. The teen yanked open the front door and nearly stumbled inside, clutching his De-Lisle carbine by one hand. His cheeks were flushed, his dark eyes wild.

"They're coming!" he said.

Ryan nodded satisfaction that the kid still had the presence of mind enough to say it quietly.

"Who?" Mildred asked muzzily. She was still sitting on the makeshift pallet of clothes she'd shared with the Armorer, who was on his feet, fully dressed, boots all laced up and everything, with his glasses in front of his eyes and his fedora on. He held his Uzi in both hands and looked speculatively out into the darkness past the front window.

Ricky stared at her as if she'd just landed in a flying saucer. "Marshals."

"How many in the house?" Cutter Dan asked. He ran a thumb down the new scar that marked his face from brow to jaw. It seemed to be healing nicely, but the itching drove him crazy.

Payback's coming soon, One Eye, he thought. Hope you like reaping what you sow.

He and his United States Marshal posse were hunkered down in a more-or-less clear patch of thicket. Around them the vines stirred with unsanctified life, and things that weren't crickets and things that might once, generations ago, have been birds chirped and croaked to greet the coming dawn.

"All of 'em," answered Mort, the younger tracker. He had on a battered black hat with an eagle feather stuck in the band, though in this light, or absence of it, the main reason Cutter Dan knew that was memory. The Choctaw knelt on the springy turf with the butt of his Winchester .30-30 grounded beside him.

"How many is all of them?" Cutter Dan asked, reminding himself to stay patient and keep his tone civil. Indians could be mighty touchy cusses. And Second Chance was nowhere near powerful enough to go pissing off their head man. Especially not since they were currently all buddied up to the Osage Nation, the most powerful of regional tribes.

"Six," Old Pete said. Cutter Dan knew he had a face made up mostly of deep seams and deeper ones beneath his turban, the same way he knew Mort had a dark face or that the oldie wore a Navy Colt replica stuck into the front of his belt. He preferred to use the one-piece drop-forged scavvy steel hatchet in its beadwork holster by his hip, though.

"They all inside?"

"No," Old Pete said. "One's out walkin' around. The Mex kid with the funny-lookin' longblaster."

"C.D., it's darker out than twelve feet up a coal miner's small intestine," said tall, gawky Edwards. "How can he see a thing like that?"

"I trust the wrinklie old bastard," Cutter Dan replied. "The kid, now, he's gotta prove himself. But Old Pete, he knows and I know that Chief Billy Feather of the Choctaw doesn't want to piss off Judge Santee, any more than we want to run afoul of him. Right?"

Old Pete grunted. If Mort objected to the Chief Marshal's statement about him, he gave no sign.

"I was hoping the mutie woulda met up with them again by now," Scovul said. "So we could scoop 'em all up at once like mouse turds in a dustpan."

"Life's a bitch, sometimes," Cutter Dan pointed out.

"He did join up," Old Pete reminded him. "Night after they broke him loose from your four-holer hanging tree. But he turned and walked right out of their camp. That's all the trace we seen of him."

He shook his head. "Can't hardly track that one. He's like a ghost."

"So we get what we got," Cutter Dan said. "We're gonna surround the house first at a distance, then move in, catch 'em in a nice neat bundle. If they got any sense, they'll surrender and save us all the trouble."

"I hope they don't surrender," Edwards said. He was clearly feeling his oats.

"Ace in the line," Cutter Dan told him affably. "I hope you enjoy explaining to Judge Santee subsequently how fired up with happiness you are that we were unable to comply with his clear directive we bring them all in more or less intact."

Edwards swallowed audibly and took a step back. Scovul caught his boss's eye, not an easy trick in this gloom. He nodded at their not-really-willing guide, the woodcutter, who stood nearby twisting his wool cap in his hands and tried not to quiver too visibly in his boots. Scovul's eyebrow crooked a question.

"We may still need him," Cutter Dan said. "In case some bastards get away. Gag him, tie him, leave him."

"In the Wild? You can't do that!" Torrance told him, his spoiled-egg green eyes practically popping out of his face. "The muties'd get me. Or a catamount. Guess it don't rightly make me no nevermind which of 'em eats me."

Cutter Dan gave him a brief, unpleasant smile. "Then you better hope we wrap this up quick, huh? All right, everybody, let's get split up in our parties and move like we got a purpose! We pull this off, we can be back in time to enjoy a well-deserved tall, cool one with our lunch."

"I WAS OFF in the thicket a ways," Ricky said. He wouldn't meet Ryan's eye.

"What were you doing out there, boy?" J.B. demanded. "You were told not to do any brush patrolling by yourself."

"I was taking a leak. I'm sorry. Anyway, I just got done and buttoned back up when I heard something scrape, and then somebody said a bad word under his breath."

"You have got to be the only person on this entire planet who ever makes a conscious effort to avoid cussing," said Mildred, who was dressing as fast as she could.

"Cache it," Ryan ordered as he laced up his boots.

"Then somebody else hissed at him, something like,

'You feeb, Edwards.' And I came back as fast as I could and still be quiet."

"Ace," Ryan replied.

"I think they're surrounding the house!" Ricky said.

"No kidding." Ryan stood up.

"We're going to break away in the opposite direction from them—west," he said. "We need to get out and get deep in the thicket ASAP."

"But that's right back at the lizard-muties! Or dinosaurs. Whatever they are," Mildred protested.

"One problem at a time. Plus, I like my odds winning a shootout with them a lot better than with Cutter Dan's bunch, from what we heard about him. We'll try not to have to do any of that."

He knelt, shrugged into his heavy backpack and stood. He hefted the Steyr in his hand.

"Reckon I'll just hang back here and hold them off while the rest of you get clear," he said.

"Ryan, you can't!" Krysty cried forcefully.

""No!" Mildred said at almost the same time. "We can't afford any self-sacrificing heroics right now."

"Or ever," Doc added solemnly.

"Well, I'm not planning on getting chilled—" Ryan began.

"No, you're not," J.B. said, "because you're not staying. I am."

He held up his Uzi and grinned. "But don't worry. I'm not planning on dying, either. Not today, anyway. This baby ought to make them stand back."

"Right," Ryan said. "Everybody ready? Time to go. We'll got out through the side door. Ricky, you'll take point."

"M-me?"

Ryan grinned and clapped him on the shoulder. "Don't worry, kid. I'll be right behind you."

RYAN PRESSED RICKY's shoulder from behind. "Go," he said.

Bent way over by the weight of his pack and responsibilities, Ricky set out across the yard at a lumbering run. Outside it was dawn, if not much of one yet. He could see where he was going in the dismal gray light, pretty much.

Ryan jogged right behind. Any closer and he'd have stepped on the kid's heels. He had his panga in his hand.

The ideal was for them all to get away into the Wild and signal J.B. to follow them without ever being noticed. Let Cutter Dan spring his trap on an empty house. Slightly less unlikely was the prospect that they'd be able to beat the closing jaws of the trap, or at least wedge them open and hold off the sec men moving in from both sides to close the ring until J.B., having slowed up the rest with some full-auto fire, could blast his way out to join them.

Worst possibility was that they were already caught in an unbreakable noose of steel. In that case, all that was left for them to do was get ready to die.

Ricky made it across the brief open ground and into the vine tangle. Thorns plucked at Ryan's pack as he followed. At least they'd had time to recce quick escape routes away from the house—a first-day priority no matter how tired everybody was. Their hunters would have to pick their way through the maddening labyrinth of strong, intertwined, spiky vines.

He didn't look back. He just trusted Krysty, Mildred and Doc to be following at a safe distance. They knew what they had to do.

They'd all been together long enough—except maybe Ricky—to function as a well-oiled machine, even if it was missing one of its parts.

Ricky had slowed the moment he got in among the thorn vines. Though speed was vital, going too fast would only make noise. If they attracted attention too soon, that'd all be chilled.

Then he stopped dead.

SKULKING IN THE derelict farmhouse's dark easternmost room, a few feet back from the window so he'd be invisible from outside, J.B. watched his would-be chillers creep through the thicket by the faint light of dawn.

They were spaced out wide. At least, the ones J.B. could see rustling the leaves were. He was far too cagey an old tomcat to assume that nobody was there just because he didn't see anybody.

But it suggested that the attackers had to spread out to surround the place. And that made sense; there were pretty severe limits to how much manpower Second Chance's sec boss could spare to chase the fugitives. The ville maintained way too many sec men on its roster for a settlement of that size to support, which told Ryan—and J.B. agreed—that they were draining resources from the other villes under their control in order to support the so-called marshals.

And also that they needed that many sec men. Not just to expand their little vest-pocket empire, but to keep the subjects they already had under close control. So, even though they had a power of blasters, they could still only release a few of them to go chasing through the Wild. No matter how badly Judge Santee and his sec boss wanted to see Ryan and his friends swing.

J.B. hoped that meant his friends could make it through the closing circle without detection. He had heard them leave the rubbled west side of the house, headed for shelter in the Wild.

His scalp began to prickle as he began to catch glimpses of actual hunters through the vegetation—a patch of sun-faded jeans, an oval blur of face. They were coming on pretty boldly, plainly to get in fast as much as to get in quiet.

Ryan had left it to J.B.'s judgment when and whether to start the party.

"Showtime, boys," he said aloud.

He raised the Uzi and raked the thorny tangle with a long, shuddering burst.

RICKY HAD HUNKERED down behind a turn in the narrow deer path through the dense growth. Right up the winding path, barely twenty-five feet away, a man wearing the armband of one of Santee's ersatz U.S. Marshals was approaching the house, bent low over a bolt-action rifle, which meant he was heading directly toward Ricky and Ryan.

The teen glanced back. His eyes were as round as saucers. Ryan nodded once, briefly.

Hurry, kid, he thought. This is why I put you on point.

Timid and tentative though he could sometimes be, especially confronted with a member of the opposite sex, Ricky was capable of acting calmly and decisively in combat. Once Ryan had reassured him it was ace to take the shot, there was no more hesitation.

He raised the rifle, which he had held with the steel buttplate poised just below and ahead of his right shoulder, into position and pulled it back snug. From the slight motion of his pack Ryan could tell he was already drawing in a deep breath as he pointed the weapon toward the target.

He got a fast picture over his iron sights. The sec man's eyes spotted something. Ryan saw them go wide in the piss-poor light. He was that close by.

The fat 230-grain slug, leaving the barrel well below the speed of sound, made little more noise than a spit. The DeLisle kicked up.

The sec man went down with a hole punched directly over his left eye.

Ricky had already jacked the action, chambering another round. Ryan tapped him on the shoulder again, as a sign of a job well done. Then he pointed forward.

Bent low, Ricky slipped around the bulge of thorn vine and walked up the trail. He barely glanced down as he stepped over the corpse of the man he'd just chilled.

Ryan gave him a once-over as he came up on him. He had fallen with his longblaster's stock beneath him. The one-eyed man paused long enough to stoop and pull it soundlessly out. Then he stood, stepped over him and followed Ricky forward.

The kid didn't show much taste for looting his chills. Not enough, truth to tell; that was one of the better ways to survive.

In this case, though, the reluctance had served him well enough. Time was the only thing that mattered now, except for stealth. Loot didn't do a person any good when dirt was hitting him in the eyes. Ryan, more experienced, had been able to snaffle the longblaster while barely breaking stride. If it was the same caliber as his Steyr, he'd empty the magazine for the Scout. If not, he could always shoot it until it was dry and save his own precious ammo. Plus, a working blaster was some of the primest scavvy there was; they could always trade it for a good price down the line.

Or ditch it if they had to lighten up to flee. Whichever. Ryan would do one or the other without a second thought. Even passing up valuable scavvy wasn't near as stupe as getting chilled for it.

When they'd gone another ten yards along the narrow path past the dead man, Ryan gave a single short, low whistle. Ricky stopped and turned back. He held the blaster ready and his eyes scanned the vines that coiled and twined all around.

Ryan came up and gestured him to shove in among the leaves for concealment.

"Thorns," Ricky said.

"Won't chill you," Ryan replied. Following his own directive, Ryan shifted into cover on the left side of the game trail, looking back toward the house.

It wasn't visible here, from the turning of the path. But the place where Ricky had taken the shot still was. Ryan reckoned they were outside the closing cordon now. It was time to hold position, get ready to provide cover for Krysty, Mildred and Doc.

And hope like hell J.B. could get clear, as well.

As if summoned by the thought, Krysty came into view, bent over with her short-barreled blaster in her hand. Mildred followed right behind, holding up her ZKR in both hands. Doc brought up the rear, glancing frequently over his shoulder.

Ryan spotted something that turned his blood to ice in his veins.

It was another sec man coming up on them from Ryan's right—Krysty's and the others' left. By a fluke of the Wild, the three companions couldn't see him. They wouldn't until he stumbled right on top of them.

Nor could Ricky, the only member of the group who could shoot him without bringing the enemy down on them like yellow jackets from a busted-open nest.

Ryan could only watch in helpless horror as the whole escape rotted into ruin before his eye.

Chapter Fourteen

J.B. gave the bastards a full 30-round magazine. It was a lot to pay, but he had a plan. He reckoned it was worth the price.

He got no indication he'd hit anything other than leaves and thorns and branches. It was light enough in the yard that he could see a few of the lighter blown-apart fragments floating down onto the bare ground. He saw no thrashing and no bodies fall, didn't hear any screams of agony.

That suited him fine. For a rare once the Armorer had expended ammo, and a power of it, without caring whether he hit anything or not.

From back in the thorns came shouts of confusion and alarm. Off to his left some bold soul fired a shot at the house. A single shot, from a high-powered longblaster by the pitch, and not a 5.52 mm, either.

Another shot came from almost dead ahead, from where he'd spotted a sec man a moment before.

From off to J.B.'s right—the south—somebody else cut loose with a semiauto handblaster. And now other voices joined the blaster chorus.

"Go for it," he said out loud, as he stuffed the spent magazine into the belt of his cargo pants and slotted a fresh one home. It wasn't as if anybody could hear him in the sudden ruckus that had wrecked the dawn stillness. Neither was it as if he cared at this point. "Burn up that ammo, shooting spooks. Be less to carry with you when you're chasing us through these bastard brambles."

He turned and ran through the living room and out the west door of the farmhouse, following the path his friends had taken.

FULLAUTO BLASTERFIRE blew apart the early day's deceptive calm.

Ryan saw the sec men freeze. He was on the other side of a snaking line of head-high thorn vine from Krysty Wroth. Another step, two at the most, and the sec man would have seen the trio.

From the south a voice shouted, "The house! Close up! Don't let any of the fuckers get away!"

The sec man turned smartly right and began making his way toward the farmhouse, away from Krysty, Doc and Mildred.

More blasterfire erupted from the far side of the house, and there was more to Ryan's left. He had no idea what those sec men thought they were shooting at. It sure wasn't coming their way.

Ricky crouched low but kept scanning for targets. The other three, meanwhile, picked up their speed toward where he and Ryan waited.

As they came up close, Ryan whistled. He didn't want any startled reflexes pulling triggers and causing heartache. Or just holes.

Krysty slowed the pace. In a moment she and Ryan were sharing a brief and passionate hug.

"What about J.B.?" Mildred asked, looking worriedly back along the trail.

"I'll go help!" Ricky piped up immediately.

"You won't," Ryan said decisively. "You'll stay right here and keep your eyes skinned. Just like the rest of us.

If J.B. isn't with us in two minutes, or if it sounds like he's run into trouble, I'll go back and do what I can for him. Alone."

Ricky opened his mouth to protest. Then he saw the look on Ryan's face.

"Yes, sir," he said.

J.B. RACED ACROSS the clearing as fast as his legs could carry him, clamping his fedora on top of his head with his left hand. His right held the Uzi by the pistol grip.

The backpack jogged on his shoulders and banged his kidneys. He barely even noticed it. It would've had to hurt ten times worse to make him think about anything but shaking the dust of the derelict house from his heels as fast as possible.

He couldn't afford to be cautious. He could hear shouts and random shots closing from the west—the very direction he was headed. All he could do right now was blaze ahead full speed, and trust in his firepower and fast reflexes if he ran into trouble.

He started to relax once he got into the sheltering arms of the Wild. He'd scarcely run a dozen paces, however, following in the steps of his companions, when a sec man in a red bandanna stepped out onto the trail not ten feet ahead of him.

The man's blue eyes went wide in his black-bearded face. His double-barreled shotgun came up.

J.B.'s Uzi was already leveled. He gave the man two quick bursts, three shots each, the recoil kicking the stubby barrel up and left.

The first burst punched red holes in the left thigh of the sec man's jeans and a thumb's width above his steer-horn silver belt buckle.

The second burst planted one an inch above that and

blew a chunk of short rib out of the man's right side, three inches higher.

The sec man's clutch reflex blasted off both scattergun barrels, but too soon and wide right. J.B. would've been lying, though, if he said he didn't feel the wind of the passing double buckshot charges slap against the left leg of his trousers. Or, at least, he imagined that he did.

He never broke stride, but he took his hand off his hat long enough to swap out the partially depleted mag for a full one.

Fortunately, the fedora stayed put.

Firepower and fast reflexes, he thought in satisfaction as he coaxed a bit more speed out of his legs. Never want to rely on them. But when you need them, there's just nothing better.

"Don't shoot!" Ricky Morales called excitedly. "It's J.B.!"

"No shit, kid," Mildred said. "It's not like we all can't see him."

The Armorer was making no attempt to sneak up toward them, and no wonder. All hell was breaking loose behind him.

"That went better than any of us deserved," he said, puffing as he jogged up to them and slowed, practically stumbling to a halt. "Whew. Let me just catch my breath, here."

"Glad you made it, J.B.," Ryan said. "Run into a little problem on the way?"

"No," the Armorer said. "The marshal had the problem. He hasn't got any at all, now."

"Ace in the line."

Ryan started moving west again, keeping to the narrow trail as it undulated between the courses of thorn-studded vines. He didn't say anything to the others about it. It was as if he just assumed they'd follow.

They did.

J.B. waved Ricky ahead. "I got trail," he said. "Biggest threat right now's those boys running up on us, though it doesn't seem likely they'll do it any too soon. They seem happy enough having a firefight all by their lonesomes— it should keep them occupied for a spell."

"We can't assume that, though," Ryan said from the point position.

"Of course not," J.B. said cheerfully. But Ricky thought his mentor was right. The Second Chance sec men were burning a prodigious amount of ammo shooting up an empty house.

And, if the fugitives were lucky, each other.

"So where to now, kemosabe?" Mildred asked. She sounded almost cheerful for once. Ricky guessed she was still hyped up by the sudden onset of danger and their hair-thin escape.

"I'm going circle us southwest," Ryan said.

"But that's—"

"I know."

Ricky saw Mildred glance doubtfully over her shoulder at Krysty, who was walking behind her. Doc came next, between the redhead and Ricky. The teen saw Krysty shrug.

"It is a pity we had no chance to explore for a clear path out of the Wild," Doc said.

"I'm thinking about all the nice deer meat we had to leave drying in the shed back there," Mildred said.

"Bullet won't ever come back, once it leaves the blaster, Millie," J.B. called. "We've left better behind."

"I know," Mildred replied, now back in a more characteristic mood. "I hope the damned sec bastards choke on it."

A high-pitch crack sounded just to the right of them. The thump of a blastershot a beat later confirmed what Ricky's educated ears had already told him: a high-powered longblaster bullet had just busted through the sound barrier on its way past them.

"That was fast," J.B. remarked, still casual. He turned, held his machine pistol up over his head with both hands and triggered a burst back up their trail.

"That ought of remind them what they have waiting for them," he said, lowering the piece.

"All right, everybody," Ryan called. "Time to power out of here." He took off running into the Wild.

THE FRESHLY CHILLED deer lay on her back by the brook with her legs in the air. Expertly Jak cut her belly open from butt to breastbone. Then he set about field dressing her by removing her innards. It was slippery, bloody work, but work he was well accustomed to. He had stripped off his jacket and shirt before getting down to it.

She was a small whitetail doe, about ninety-five or a hundred pounds. The weight was manageable for dragging back to Esperance, where Cho's kitchen staff could hang it to skin it, finish cleaning the body cavity and butcher it proper. Assuming Meg bought it off him, which he reckoned was a good bet, indeed. It was prime quality venison. The gaudy owner did enough restaurant biz she'd recognize that as well as he did. Or, at least, her cook would.

He didn't have to make a second cut in the windpipe; that had been how he'd taken her, waiting for her and the small herd to come to drink, confirming she had no fawns with her, stalking close and springing. It was surprisingly easy to chill a deer with just a knife, if you knew how to do it. Jak had been doing it since he was a pup.

The secret was in the stalk, and that was just what he was best at. Not even Ryan had the skill to get close enough to a wild, awake deer to grab it and slash its throat, Jak knew.

He widened the incision. Reaching in, he pulled out the liver and heart. The lungs he tossed into the vines along with the steaming guts. The predators and scavengers in the Wild needed to eat too, and he was in no position to choose whether that was muties or natural creatures like coyotes. It didn't really matter to him. It was the way things were, the way the world worked. The parts needed to come out fast after the chill, or they'd quickly turn the meat so rotten foul no one would touch it. Not unless the person wasn't much shy of Death's open door, anyway. He sure wasn't going to drag the not-inconsiderable mass of offal along with him back to the Last Resort.

He took a special watertight cured-skin pouch out of his belt, where he was carrying it this day, and placed the liver inside to eat later. The heart he set aside on some clean grass. He'd eat that raw on the march. It tasted good and would give him strength and energy to drag the carcass.

That done, he washed the knife in the stream. He quickly splashed his arms and upper torso to get most of the blood off. He hated the sticky way it felt drying on his skin. He put away the knife and pulled his shirt and jacket on again.

Finally, he took a length of rope from his belt. He tied the doe's hind feet together. He recovered the heart and set off for Esperance.

He took a big bite. Blood ran down his chin, still warm from the whitetail's recent life.

Nothing like the first bite of fresh, warm heart to cap off the natural satisfaction of a successful hunt.

Chapter Fifteen

"Argh!"

Krysty turned back at Ricky's strangled call.

"It's those nuke-withered things again!" he shouted, waving his left arm furiously. A wide, flat shape a foot and a half long flew off end over end into the Wild, frantically waving its many hooked legs. "No! You can *not* bite me again, you puke!"

"Great," Mildred said. "I knew this would happen. I tried to tell you, Ryan. You were heading us right back to these slithering little bastards."

Still trotting in tail-end Charlie position, just behind the still half-panicked Ricky, J.B. chuckled.

"You reckon he didn't know that, Millie?"

Ryan held up a hand for attention and slowed his pace. Krysty narrowed her eyes. He had deliberately kept them to a rapid trot out of consideration for the slower members of the party, especially Ricky and Mildred. Longer-legged Krysty could keep up at full speed. Surprisingly, given his ancient and battered appearance, so could stilt-legged Doc Tanner. J.B. was no sprinter, but he could keep up the fastest pace he could muster, well past the point where even Ryan's tongue was hanging out.

Mildred and Ricky were audibly puffing. They'd been fleeing at least an hour from their enemies. Krysty felt sure the pace Ryan had set them had thinned the ranks of active pursuers. Santee's self-proclaimed marshals didn't seem the type who got much aerobic exercise in the course of their daily duties of terrorizing and oppressing beat-down ville folk and farmers.

But there was a hard core hanging close behind them. Too close. At the last twist of the path between the vine skeins they were currently following, Krysty had caught sight of the man who ran at the head of the pack, not forty yards behind J.B.

She'd never seen him before, but she recognized him right off from Ryan's description: Cutter Dan, the Boss Marshal himself. He was built along the same wolf lines as Ryan, with long muscled legs, narrow waist, and broad chest and shoulders. And from the grim smile she'd made out on his square, not-unhandsome features—below the long scar Ryan's panga had left—he seemed to be made of similar stuff to the man called One Eye Chills in campfire tales across the length and breadth of the Deathlands—and beyond.

He could've taken a shot at them then, maybe even hit someone if he was a steady enough hand with his big revolver. Or, for that matter, could've been carrying a long-blaster.

The fact he hadn't, and wasn't, had implications that Krysty tried hard not to think about.

"Sweet suffering Christ, Ryan!" Mildred almost hissed. "Why're you slowing down? They're going to be all over us. Oh, not you little fuckers, too." And she broke off to stomp furiously on a pair of the giant mutie centipedes that had scuttled out to scrabble at her boots with their pincers.

Ryan looked back over his shoulder and grinned.

From too close behind them Krysty heard a sudden deep-voice exclamation of surprise—and anger.

"OH, FOR FUCK'S sake, no!"

They leaped at Cutter Dan from a spot on the game

path where thorns gouged his wide shoulders from both sides. What seemed like dozens of the mutie centipedes waved their horrible feelers and held their sideways jaws wide open.

He tried to bat them off as he ran. He could hear Mort's boots drumming not far behind him. The oldie Choctaw tracker had bowed out of the chase. Cutter Dan knew some of his marshals had dropped out, too. He was lucky if he had half a dozen more close enough to do any good when he got into a place he thought they could pounce on their prey with maximum chance of taking them alive and at least relatively unpunctured.

He was going to have a few choice words to say to the stragglers after these coldhearts were caught. The possibility they might not catch them was something he refused to let into his mind.

But though he was what the stern Deathlands granny who had raised Cutter Dan would have called *more back than leg,* the younger Indian kept up with the longer-limbed chief marshal.

Cutter Dan shouted in disgust as a mutie bug landed on top of his head. He felt its claws scratching his scalp and tangling in his hair. He reached up, grabbed it by the revolting butt, which managed to feel both leathery and slippery at the same time, peeled it off and threw it blindly away.

The sec boss had heard stories of the monster centipedes, of course. He hadn't been sure whether to believe them. Travelers in from the wasteland told some pretty tall tales, no matter which wasteland that happened to be—Cutter Dan had knocked around a goodly portion of the Deathlands himself before discovering his true destiny as Judge Santee's strong hammer hand. But he knew as well as anybody that the Wild harbored some strange things, of which the fabled outsized centipedes were far from the strangest.

He had to slow down for fear he'd trip over a root or stray thorn branch and fall. That'd be fatal right off, he knew well. The sec boss tried to bat the things away from his arms, chest and legs. He kicked the many-segmented bodies flying when he could.

Then he felt a sharp sting on his left wrist.

He brought the heel of a clenched right fist down hard on the horror that clung with dozens of claws to his other forearm, its mandibles sunk into his flesh. Its ugly, venom-laden mandibles. Yellow juice and goo and a sort of squeak were squished right out of the monster by the impact. Its legs spasmed mindlessly and released their death grip on his arm.

The chief marshal's head suddenly began to spin, as blackness swallowed up his vision from outside to in.

"Fuck me," he said, as the world went away.

RYAN HEARD SHOUTS of consternation from behind. Too close behind.

The sec men were running unencumbered by packs. He took for granted they'd be carrying nothing more than blasters, bullets and water. As he'd told Cutter Dan that day he'd cut his face for him, he'd heard the name before. He had a reputation as a stoneheart of brains and skill as well as guts. He would have had his troops cache their packs before he deployed them to attack the half-decayed farmhouse where he thought he'd run his quarry to ground.

By contrast, Ryan and company were struggling under the full weight of their gear, and they weren't all prong-horn fleet at the best of times. The Second Chance sec men should have run them down and blasted them half an hour ago.

That they hadn't confirmed Ryan's surmise: the crazy old Judge who ruled the ville, Santee, had given orders they be brought back alive. Ryan had a fair idea what sort of threats he backed those orders up with, too. The man was clearly single-mindedly obsessed with hanging as many human ornaments as possible on his gallows tree.

Not that Cutter Dan's reputation made him out to be any better to cross.

So the chief marshal had closed on his intended victims, waiting for the inevitable moment he could jump them and capture them.

That was, of course, why Ryan had decided to take his companions back to revisit their many-legged old friends, the centipedes.

He turned promptly along the next break in the vine wall to his right. He'd try to pick a path north, hopefully clearing the feathered mutie lizards' territory, and make their way out of the Wild by the shortest route he could find.

He heard more yells, and at least one voice screaming in pants-shitting panic, from the pack on their heels.

Ryan grinned into the wind of his passage and the hot dry breeze that blew through the thicket, rustling the thorn branches and starting to make the dead vines and fallen leaves underneath them crackle.

He glanced back over his shoulder. Krysty caught his eye. She flashed him her gorgeous smile and a thumbs-up.

Mebbe we'll get out of this with all our parts, he thought. At least we still got them all attached so far.

"So, YOU CHILLED that by yourself?" Meg asked.

She stood in the yard by the kitchen door at the back of her sprawling, two-story gaudy, her hands on her broad hips. The expression on her blunt face was far from welcoming. But so far as Jak could tell, that's the way it always looked.

He nodded.

"Use that fancy handblaster of yours?"

He shook his head. "Knife."

"He's tellin' truth, Chief," Cho said, pointing a sausage-sized finger at the dangling carcass.

The kitchen boss stood next to the gaudy owner, wearing an apron over jeans and a T-shirt. She had jet-black hair tied back in a bun so tight it looked as if the skin was fixing to split along the line of her high, wide cheekbones. She had Asian eyes and a pale-brown complexion. She was built along similar lines to her employer, but where Meg's face and form suggested a barrel, the chief cook put Jak more in mind of an adobe brick.

Her assistants had strung the doe up by the neck from a scaffold that stood outside the back door for just such a purpose. They huddled behind their leader's ample cover, a couple of local kids who looked at Jak as if he were a starving Bengal tiger.

There was one, at least, stalking the Wild. He'd seen the unmistakable prints. They had escaped from zoos, along with a lot of other exotic animals, back during the Big Nuke. Like some of them, tigers had done well for themselves in the brave new world, even pulling through skydark....

The tiger was probably as content to steer clear of humans as Jak was content to steer clear of it. There was plenty of game for both. The big striped bastard probably didn't give two shits if it ate taint meat.

Neither did the other things that had left tracks, as large as the tiger's or larger, that Jak couldn't identify.

"Where'd you take it?" Meg asked.

"Couple miles west."

He judged she didn't need to know it had been right in the northern fringes of the Wild, this side of the Red Wall, the giant escarpment that put a sudden end to the north-western edge of the mutie thicket. He might have been a hunter and a fighter, not a businessman, but he hadn't stayed alive this long without knowing how to drive a halfway-decent trade.

She scowled. "Mutie?"

He shook his head.

"Nope," Cho said. "I can tell by looking. Looks plenty healthy. Second year doe, I reckon. Hang it a few days, we can sell the meat for plenty.

Meg sighed and gave her cook a disgusted look. "Way to help me drive a hard bargain."

Cho shrugged. "Not my department, boss."

Meg grunted. She turned back to Jak. After a brief haggle they settled on a price both thought was fair. Or anyway, mutually unfair, which was all a body could really ask for.

"One question, kid," she said.

He didn't bridle at being called "kid" the way he normally would. He was pleased enough she'd accepted his explanation that he was an albino, not a mutie, so he wasn't going to quibble.

"You planning on staying?" she asked.

He nodded.

"All right. Before you drink in my saloon, much less sleep in one of my beds, you're gonna get cleaned up. I got standards."

He frowned. She sighed again.

"All right. I'll throw in a bath free of charge—not like water's hard to come by hereabouts. And I'll get your clothes washed half price. Even throw in some loaner clothes to wear while your duds're drying, which shouldn't take long, the way this wind keeps blowing in from the west. Like it comes clean out of the desert, it's so dry."

Jak thought about it a moment, then he grinned and nodded. He immediately began to strip down.

"One more thing," Meg said. "You do that over there *behind* the shed. Any of my customers pop a squint at your skinny white hide and underparts, they're liable to reckon they're already far gone into the deetees and don't need to buy any of my rotgut!"

Chapter Sixteen

His eyes snapped open.

By what had to be late-afternoon light, to go by color and angle, the first thing they saw was a Malpais face like a lava flow beneath a green turban. A pair of eyes, black and shiny as polished obsidian buttons, twinkled just visible in the middle of its many deep folds.

"Bad news," the face said in a cracked and guttural voice. "He's still alive."

"Takes more than a few mutie bug bites to chill me, you crusty old fuck," Cutter Dan said.

He almost regretted the words as soon as he'd said them. Old Pete had proved himself mighty useful on this trip out, and there was that old touchy Indian pride thing. But though being knocked out had mebbe weakened his judgment—momentarily—it didn't soften his vanadium-steel core a whit. Cutter Dan was a man who looked forward, not back.

He felt a pang from the left side of his face. Well, mostly, he mentally amended.

Old Pete didn't take offense. At least, he didn't show it, which Cutter Dan knew well was not the same thing. But the old man laughed, which was at least a good sign.

"Spirits saving you for a more fitting fate," Old Pete said. "Mebbe hanging from your own gallows, huh?"

Cutter Dan tried to keep his frown from showing too much. He forced a smile.

"Mebbe," he said.

He sat up, batting away the hands that pushed forward to help him. His head freewheeled briefly. He rode it out.

The sec boss looked around. "Where are we?" he demanded. "We didn't backtrack, did we?"

"We didn't want to leave you for the centipedes," Scovul stated, sounding worried and contrite.

"Not that the thought didn't cross our minds," added Edwards, who sounded neither.

"Ace," Cutter Dan said. "You're still with us."

He got to his feet. They were in a cleared space about twenty feet wide. The grass underfoot was beaten down, he saw by the late-afternoon light. But not as if by the random trampling boots of the dozen plus men he saw around him. More as if it had been flattened in a corkscrew pattern, working from the center out.

Triple strange things out in the Wild. The old adage rang through his brain. He didn't want to know what caused that.

But late afternoon?

"How long was I out?" he demanded.

"Three, mebbe four hours," Scovul said.

"Nuke shit. So, the slowcoaches caught up?"

"Yep," Yonas told him. "We brung up the packs, as well."

"Score one for us. Everybody fit to fight?"

Scovul exchanged nervous looks with Yonas. "Not exactly," the man with the eye patch said. "We had two chills back at the farmhouse. McCawber and Jones. Also, Sammels and Rico were wounded."

"Wounded."

"Walking wounded," Scovul said. "More or less. We sent them back to Second Chance with Bennett and Brown for escorts, see about getting some replacements sent out."

"Santee's gonna love that," Yonas said.

Cutter Dan grunted. "Well, he's not here. And when we bring back the fugitives for him, all will be forgiven. So, I take it the pursuit was not continued?"

"Not, uh, in your absence," Scovul said. "Sir."

"And Rico and Sammels may have been hit by friendly fire."

"We seriously got to work on fire discipline," Cutter Dan said, shaking his head. "Later. For now, let's go hunt up a stream, set up a perimeter and get ready to bed down for the night."

"We're not going after them now?" Yonas asked.

"After they got a three-hour head start? Mebbe four?" The sec boss shook his head. "We've run enough for one day. Reckon they have, too. We still got Mort and Old Pete with us, right?"

"Yo," Mort called.

"And me, sir," said the timid voice of the woodcutter.

"Great. So, we can pick up their trail again in the morning. We will run these criminal scum to earth, gentlemen." He smiled. "Matter of fact, I do believe I have a plan to do it."

"ANOTHER," JAK SAID, pushing the empty beer mug across the bar.

"Don't you think mebbe you should throttle back a spell?" Meg asked. "Mebbe pace yourself."

"What? Bartender got conscience?"

She shrugged. "Let's just say we look to be establishing a mutually profitable relationship. I can use a reliable meat hunter. Last one got et by the tiger. And I can sell the hides to a tanner in Second Chance, split the proceeds. Plus you're rapidly becoming a valued, or anyway valuable, customer. So, easy does it, okay?"

Jak frowned. His brain was wrapped in a pleasant fog. His body seemed filled with warmth. But something in her words penetrated.

"Do business Second Chance?" he said belligerently. "Santee?"

"Hey, we do what we got to in order to survive, like everybody else. The Judge is a bastard. If he weren't quite so far away, he probably woulda tried to swallow us up by now with that blood-drinker sec-man army of his. And if that happens, nobody's gonna be safe up here. But radblast it, one of the things holding him back is that he needs us as bad as we need him."

"Crazy man," Jak said firmly.

"Won't argue with you there. But he's a shrewd old nuke head, even if his soul is blacker'n a stickie's. It's mebbe a fine line, between the crazy and the shrewd, but so far he's managed to walk it pretty good."

"Regret," he said. "Will regret."

"Yeah. No doubt. I regret a lot of things in this life, and hope to live to regret a power more. Though if Santee has his way, I admit, I'm likely to end my days kicking my heels at the end of a rope sooner rather than late."

Remembering an earlier subject that was near and dear to his heart, Jak tapped his mug on the knife-gouged, cigarette-burned bar.

"More."

"Your funeral," she said, shaking her head. She took the mug and filled it with a ladle from a keg.

"Do yourself a favor, though," she said, pushing it back at him. "Take it and go get soused at your usual table."

"Why? Not good enough drink bar?"

"Ace by me," she said levelly. "Double worse than you drink at this bar, eight days out of ten, easy. But you're making yourself conspicuous, sitting right here. Not everybody comes in here is a reasonable person. Not everybody who come in that way leaves in the same condition. And I had you sized up as a man who preferred not to draw much attention to himself."

Jak grunted. He started to raise the mug to his lips, then a cagy feeling stole over him. Instead he picked it up with both hands and, cradling its welcome coolness carefully to his chest, tottered back toward his habitual place in the dark—but not darkest—corner of the barroom.

He had a weird prickling sensation, as if someone was watching him. He looked around furtively.

But he didn't see anyone or anything that appeared threatening, just the girl he'd helped out, whatever her name was. Molly, Charly, some shit like that. She was kneeling on the floor with her coal scoop and a whiskbroom, cleaning up the usual slops. But she also seemed to be looking at him in a disapproving way.

At the table he hoisted the mug in salute to her. Beer slopped over his hand. He cursed softly and put the beer down on the table in a hurry. Then he sat in the chair with his back to the angle of the walls and settled down to drink in peace and seclusion.

And screw Carli, or whatever her name was, and anybody else who didn't like it.

VERY CAREFULLY, JAK stepped down the stoop of the Last Resort's back exit.

This one was at the other end of the yard from the kitchen and the rack where Cho's little helpers had expertly skinned and cleaned and butchered the doe responsible for the amount of jack now burning a hole in the pocket of Jak's old jeans, despite the considerable amount he'd already drunk up.

The reason was his current destination: the five-hole shitter out back.

It didn't smell bad. Even with a load of Meg's potent house brew aboard, sloshing in his belly and taking the edge off his senses, he would've been far more aware of that than a normal ville rat or Deathlands wayfarer. But Meg kept the cesspit limed and the shitter and its surroundings policed up as scrupulously as she did the interior of her gaudy.

People didn't get sick in the bayous where Jak had grown up. Not much, anyway. Things had been different, triple different, in the old days—back before the days of blood and fire, and then the long, cold night blew it all to dreck. He remembered Doc and Mildred telling him all about it: people got sick all the time back then.

But then the whitecoats and the generals blew up the world. Epidemics, natural and man-made, had chilled billions—more than the bombs and the quakes and the riots and the starvation. More than the skydark, even.

Those who could get sick and died had got sick and died. It had all been just that simple.

But even this day there were exceptions. Sometimes those man-made plagues busted loose again, by accident or some evil madman's design—there were *reasons* whitecoats were disliked and distrusted more than muties.

And, more to the point, the ancient rule hadn't changed: *don't shit where you eat.*

Doc and Mildred moaned and complained aplenty about the woeful state of personal hygiene in the modern era. And most folk were not careful about keeping clean.

But if you got too careless, with your shit or with your food—and in particular if they got too jumbled up with each other—food poisoning or infection would still chill you, sure as a bullet but often as slow and painful as a gutshot.

At least, that's what Jak's friends told him. Ryan and the companions—Mildred, Doc. His pal Ricky. Krysty, who was just so damn painfully beautiful he couldn't let himself think about it too much right now. J.B. Even Ryan. They had been all right. They had been family. It was too bad that hadn't worked out after all that time.

But now he was free, he thought. Running like a wolf. That was better, right?

As all of that played in his mind, Jak was tottering across the bare, tramped-down dirt toward the plank shack with the crescent moon cut out of the door. And the beer continued to surge and gurgle from one side of his stomach to the other.

That was what brought him out into this warm, dry west wind. Now he felt a pressing need to return some of that beer to nature, which he reckoned was the cycle of life, right there. *Right there.* It was the way he was meant to live, right? Natural?

"Going somewhere, mutie?"

Suddenly a gigantic shadow loomed up, blocking his path to the john like a wall of darkness.

"Remember me?" the voice asked.

Jak almost did. He'd heard that voice before. Somewhere, somewhen. He took another tentative step forward.

The hulking shadow stepped forward, too. A gleam of light from a second-story window splashed across the side of an unappealing face, revealing features with pores you could stick a fingertip in, a bloodshot boar-hog eye, a nasty snaggle-toothed sneer and a curly brown neck beard.

Alarm thrilled through Jak's body. And his sluggish brain. He might have lost his edge, somehow. But his survival instinct was too tight-strung not to feel plucked and be vibrating at a high frequency by the situation he'd some-how fallen into.

He looked around, ready to bolt to safety.

But Neckbeard had brought friends. At least three, all much bigger than Jak, not that that was hard.

The man right behind him looked familiar, too. With the light, such as it was, behind him Jak couldn't make out his features. But he was shorter than the first man, and Jak had seen the way he held himself and the way he moved before.

That was the sort of detail Jak had learned to spot, when he was Jak the hunter, the White Wolf.

"Yeah, you know us. And we know you now, don't we, Ferd?"

"True as toasted toads, Jeff," the first man said. "True as toasted toads."

"What the nuke does that even mean?" growled one of the shadow hulks who hemmed Jak in from left and right. He couldn't make out their features, either. But he could sure smell them. They were at the other end of the rail from Meg and her gaudy in the cleanliness department.

"It means we heard all about how you did the dirty on us the other night, when we was fixing to play with that little mutie gal," Ferd said.

"Yeah," Jeff added. "How you snuck around and tricked us into whaling on each other. Us bros. Typical mutie taint shit, sneakin' and trickin' like that. You taints sure stick together. You must have your own mutie code, like us wag-dudes have our bro code. High five, Ferd!"

"High five, Jeff. And the bro code says now we have to make you pay. We're gonna stomp you good, and bust all your filthy mutie bones. Then, before we dump your busted mutie ass in the shit pool, mebbe we'll let you watch us have some fun with your nasty taint girlfriend."

Belatedly Jak made a move for the knuckleduster hilt of his trench knife. He knew now that he'd drunk himself this deep into rad dust. Under any other circumstances he'd already have unzipped Jeff's belt-hanging paunch, dropped his intestines in greasy purple ropes down his stained canvas pants onto the tops of his horseshit-crusted boots.

Instead, his hand seemed to move, not like a striking sidewinder, but as if he were trying to punch somebody underwater.

But the fist that filled his vision first with a black moon, and then bright exploding red and white stars, moved like nuking lightning.

Chapter Seventeen

"Why are we stopping?" Mildred asked.

Squatting in the clearing in the thorn vines, Krysty glanced at her friend. The low, smokeless fire made of dead undergrowth burned with pale yellow and blue flames. They cast a faint unhealthy light across Mildred's pensive, round face.

"I mean, shouldn't we just be pushing on? We know those dogs are hot on our trail now. And there's a limit to how many mutie rabbits even Ryan can pull out of a hat to save us, next time they catch up with us."

As was so often the case, Krysty had no idea what her friend was talking about, though she'd used the hats and rabbits thing before. But she clearly caught her drift.

"How're your legs, Mildred?" asked Ryan, who was pacing along the firelight's fringe, by the thorny fence that mostly hemmed in the open space. "Looked a mite shaky by the time we stopped."

Mildred dropped her face and scowled ferociously at the fire.

The thicket rustled in a brisk evening breeze. Krysty sensed it was warm and dry, though the thicket mostly screened them from it here. She smelled the drying vegetation—abundant, but with some off scent, some taint that spoke of its mostly unnatural origin.

The spiky vegetation rustled with lots of other noises, too, and reverberated with unearthly cries and sometimes blood-freezing screams. Everybody tried their best to ignore those noises, but she also noticed they seemed to be keeping their eyes' focus soft, to give them the maximum chance of reacting in time if something jumped out of the vines at them. As J.B. and Ryan had taught.

"We need rest," Ryan said. "That's pretty much the story, there."

Ricky looked up. "Mebbe they gave up after those giant centipedes swarmed them," he suggested brightly.

J.B. chuckled. He sat cross-legged next to Mildred, but he had his back turned to the fire, outward from the circle of companionship. He was tinkering up something involving loose black powder and some sheets of heavy, rough hemp paper, modern made, that he'd turned up somewhere the last few weeks.

"Not a chance," he declared, never looking up. "They probably didn't even lose a chill, any more than we did."

"But those Second Chance sec men aren't in any better shape than we are," Ryan said. "Bet on that. We're loaded down pretty heavy, but we do this every day. Not run, but carry the same loads and sometimes worse, mile after mile. They don't. And while they obviously ran light on the chase, they need their own supplies to catch up to them now, before they keep after us. They'll rest the night. They've got no choice. We don't either, not really. So we rest, too. Best we can."

As if to point out the truth behind that last statement, a terrible noise broke out from somewhere to the east of them. There was snarling, squealing and crashing, and the sound of heavy bodies slamming into the ground. Something big was out there fighting something else big.

Though Krysty couldn't see anything directly, no sign of the huge bodies involved in the life-or-death struggle, it was making the thicket shake violently on that side of the clearing. The unseen monsters could be no more than a handful of yards away.

"Shouldn't we, like, go somewhere else?" Ricky asked.

"Naw," J.B. said. "We're here, they're there. That's the way we want it, right? And we got no idea what else is out there."

"Except more bad things?" Ricky said.

"Exactly."

Ryan smiled a hard, mean smile. "There's another reason to sit tight until it gets light."

But he stopped and stood, watching the vibrating vines, his Scout in his hands, as if his single eye could bore a hole through the intervening growth and the night like a sapphire laser, to illuminate what awful menaces were threatening the companions' safety. Krysty actually started to get a little nervous at his unusual fixation; usually he kept his head and his eye in constant motion, always checking the whole of their surroundings for danger.

Then she noticed J.B. had lifted his head from his work and was calmly turning it left and right. *He* was scanning for other danger while his best friend and leader concentrated on the most obvious threat.

He noticed Krysty's attention, gave her a slight smile and tip of his hat. Then he went back to looking everywhere for signs of other, less obvious danger.

Even I forget what an incredible team those two make, she thought. What a team we all make. Which meant the Jak-shaped hole inside her suddenly felt bigger and emptier than ever....

The fight ended suddenly with a deafening, high-pitched yipping receding to the northeast, accompanied by the sound of splintering thigh-thick vines. Krysty's keen ears detected a second set of crashes and thuds as the other monster pursued its equally monstrous foe.

As the noises dwindled and became lost in the general background, which had pretty much died away during the ruckus but now promptly came back, Ryan looked at his friends with a thoughtful frown.

"I should at least do a little recce through the vines around us," he said. "See what other bad news waiting to happen we might have right around us."

"No," everybody said at once.

"We can't afford to lose you, Ryan," J.B. said. "That's the fact, plain and simple."

"I could take somebody along," he protested. "Mildred or Ricky."

"*I'm* not going out in those damned thorns in the pitch black!" Mildred said.

J.B. slapped her thigh. "She's right. Now is not the best time to be dividing our forces. I agree with you, it's lightning-strike odds the marshals will try to make a move on us tonight, and nowhere near enough chance to risk trying to move on. But, same token, where's the gain of stumbling around though the thicket? It's like Ricky said, we *know* there's bad things out there. We don't need to be givin' them a crack at picking us off easy—one at a time or two."

"Might it be wise not to overlook our proximity to the tribe of those curious feathered-reptile muties?" Doc asked mildly. His glasses made his eyes look huge. "They are certainly not operating under the same constraints our merely human pursuers are. Do we want to increase our chances of bringing ourselves to their notice, by additional movement?"

Still Ryan looked mulish. Krysty sighed and got to her feet.

She walked to him and laid a hand on his arm. "They're right, lover," she said. "Step back from the trigger of the blaster—and your pride. We know you're brave and able.

That's because we know you're what's kept us alive these many years, more than anything else.

"But the rest of us? We're no slouches, either. We've all proved ourselves. And we all say it's a bad idea."

She had come *that* close to saying "stupe." While she seldom held back from speaking her mind to the man she loved with all her heart and soul—to say nothing of her body—she reckoned now was the time for tact.

His face was as hard as flint when it turned to her.

"What if I decided to go ahead and go anyway?"

She laughed, genuinely, openly. Because if she wasn't honest with Ryan, they truly weren't life partners.

"Then you'd do what you wanted to do," she said. "Of course. And we'd back you to the hilt. Of course. Nothing that hasn't happened before. We remember all too well the times we said to go one way, and you insisted that we go the other, and you were right and we were wrong, and you saved us all."

But she couldn't resist adding, "This just isn't one of them."

For a moment his face stayed stone. Then it didn't so much soften as move into the crooked, knowing smile she knew and loved.

"Well—happens you're right about that, too," he said. "Trader used to quote an old book that says 'pride goeth before a fall.' Pride's an even more stupid thing to get iced over than jack is."

She drew a deep breath and sighed it out, enjoying the way his eye followed the rise and fall of her breasts inside her shirt. Too bad they were too tired to carry that further—and needed too badly to conserve and build up every scrap of energy for whatever fresh hell the next day would bring.

His grin widened.

"Now that we've got that behind us, what are we going to do tomorrow?" Mildred asked.

"Keep heading north. Same as we did after we ran the sec men into the centipedes. We heard tell Second Chance is smack dab in the middle of the Wild, more or less. We've got no idea exactly where, but we still do know the Wild ends someplace. We've been from one end of the continent to the other, from the north to the south. And up till we landed in it, the only thing we knew about this mess was that it was there."

He glared around the low fire. "Or am I going to hear backtalk over that, too?"

The others stared at him fearfully, Krysty included. It was J.B. who chuckled first.

Ryan cracked a smile. The others joined in the relieved laughter. Maybe too long and too loud. But some things, Krysty knew, a body had to do. Whatever the risks.

"All right, everyone," Ryan said firmly, cutting off the hilarity when he reckoned it had gone on long enough. "Time to turn in. J.B., I'll let you have first watch—just so you and all the rest of you nervous Nellies don't try to sleep with one eye open worrying I'll go for a walkabout on my own.

"If you got to take a piss, do it in the vines. You got to squat, dig a hole and cover it up triple quick. And aim your ass outward!"

Chapter Eighteen

The second hard hit Jak felt was the planet, slamming into his shoulders.

And the third was when Earth collided with the back of his skull, half a heartbeat later.

He just lay there for a moment, trying to breathe and blink away the bloated green balloons of afterimage that floated behind his eyelids. His whole face ached. He wanted to puke. He lacked even the energy to do that.

And he had sobered up enough to know with cold-steel certainty that his night was about to get a whole lot worse. For the entire rest of his life.

His attackers were whooping it up around him. A lucid fragment of his mind recalled with dismay that it had been an especially rowdy night inside the Last Resort. Then the siren song of Jak's full bladder became too loud to ignore. One of the locals named Bat-Ear Harv was having a birthday. He was a gaudy regular, and he and a group of his buddies were raising the roof.

Jak's assailants could blow him to pieces with a wag-chiller rocket without much chance of alerting anybody inside.

A boot toe pushed Jak's upturned face one way, then the other. At this range the smell of horseshit was overpowered by the stink of dirty foot. It smelled like cheese that had rotted runny.

"What's it feel like, mutie?" Ferd's voice came from

some unscalable height. "Knowing we're about to bust every bone in that crime-agin-nature body of yours?"

It was unscalable by Jak in his present, sadly reduced condition, he thought bitterly. Under most circumstances he would have scaled it already, like a monkey on jolt, and be on the fucker's shoulders laughing as he cut his throat through that ugly-ass neck beard. But he could no more have stirred from the hard, cold ground of Meg's back lot than he could've flown to the moon by flapping his arms.

The boot raised to hang poised, a foot above Jak's face. He raged in silent frustration. He could not move. The feeling of helplessness was as black as any he'd ever known.

Something caught the edge of his peripheral vision. He cut his eyes that way, left.

He glimpsed a scurry of shadowy motion that seemed to be behind one of the larger, still unidentified shadows standing over him. Then, out of the night, a two-by-four came whistling to crack itself over the back of the wagman's head with a noise like a gunshot.

At least, Jak thought it was the board breaking.

His boot still in midair, Ferd looked to his right. The end of the board promptly stabbed him in the middle of his face. Jak heard his nose break. This time, the end of the board split clean off, as Ferd staggered back, wailing like a lost dog and clutching his ruined, blood-spewing snout.

Behind Jak's head, he heard Jeff curse. The shorter man's boots crunched on the dirt as he turned to face the sudden, mysterious threat.

The ability to move was slowly returning to Jak. He managed to crane his head back to see Jeff lunge forward, swinging his right fist in a wild haymaker.

Jak was in time to see the fresh board end, jagged and splintery, jab him hard in the throat.

Jeff went down choking, clutching his neck and kicking.

The last coldheart, the other wag-man whose face Jak still hadn't seen, started to step over Jak's body from the albino's right toward the unseen attacker. Jak grabbed a leg, hugged it close to this chest with both arms and rolled to his left. His weight buckled the knee and sent the man pitching forward.

His face hit a rapidly rising knee. It snapped back. Then it was snapped hard sideways by a baseball-bat swing of the board. Though they whizzed by fast, Jak noticed the hands that gripped it. Even in the gloom he could tell, from just that flash, they were small, dark and shiny.

Ferd came roaring back like an angry bear. "You little mutie bitch!" he yelled through the blood that still dripped over his mouth. "I will fuck you up!"

He lunged for her, swiping with his arms. Jak heard a musical laugh.

"Missed me!" he heard the kitchen girl sing out.

Ferd charged after her. Jak saw a skinny, tiny form flit by him. She skipped past Jak's toes, laughing taunts.

Focused on the hot-beyond-nuke-red Ferd, she failed to notice the first man she'd clubbed climbing to his feet.

"Fucking...mutie slut," he said, his words slurred as if he'd drunk a quart of Towse lightning. "Chill...your taint ass, then ream it."

He was shaking his head like a lung-shot buffalo bull as he stood. Apparently the two-by-four hadn't caved in the back of his skull. Or had, and whatever it had caved in he didn't use enough to matter. But it had gotten good and scrambled by the blow.

As the girl deftly sidestepped another screaming charge from Ferd, the man drew a handblaster, cocked it, and aimed it. It was a big 1911-style semiauto, a .45, more than likely. He swung the remade blaster around at the full extension of his right arm, trying to draw bead on the laughing girl.

Jak knew that the way the two were throwing themselves this way and that in the dark, the wag-man had as much chance of hitting Ferd as the kitchen girl. Better, as big as Ferd was.

But Jak was not willing to take the chance. He still felt like what he'd heard J.B. call "hammered dogshit." His head was spinning one way and his stomach the other, and it felt as if his body and limbs were sausage bags of spoiled milk.

The wag-man with the blaster sure seemed to count Jak out. He took a two-hand grip on the 1911 as he tried to track his target on her zigzagging course, which seemed to be bringing her closer to the shitter. His feet shuffled as he turned to try bring the weapon to bear.

He turned away from Jak. The albino's numb fingers found the hilt of his trench knife. They slipped inside and pulled it free with the blade pointing downward from his fist.

"Gotcha now, bitch!" the man yelled.

Jak rolled over and sank the knife into the back of the man's right knee. He thought he felt it punch through the cartilage and wedge apart the rounded tips of the shin and thigh bones.

The blade only stopped when it hit the kneecap from the back.

The blaster went off, almost straight up toward the stars. Joyous rage returned Jak's strength to him. The wag-man dropped, howling, to that buckled knee. His shrieks rose an octave as Jak tore the blade free.

The wag-man shrieked even louder as his ruined knee hit the ground, hard. He threw himself onto his left side, dropping the blaster to clutch at his leg.

Jak threw himself on top of him. As much by feel as sight he crawled up him. Then, sitting astride the man's upturned right shoulder, he raised the trench knife two-handed, as high as he could reach above his head.

He intended to stab it into the wag-man's eye, but the bastard was whipping his head side to side, oblivious to the fact Jak was sitting on top of him and to everything but his own personal world of hurt.

Instead the clipped tip of the blade took him in the right temple. It punched right on through the bone and the brain beneath.

As light as Jak was, as weak as he'd felt mere seconds before, the knife punched clean out the far side of the wag-man's head and pinned it to the dirt.

Letting go of the hilt, Jak rolled off the twitching chill. He landed hard on his right, with his head toward the shitter.

A bellow from Ferd made Jak pull his head back to look. He watched as the bearded wag-man put his head down and charged the tiny girl.

She stood waiting, empty-handed, until he was almost on top of her. Then she jumped to the side.

Ferd smashed head-on into the shitter door. He split it right down the middle and powered on through. From the additional crashing and splintering Jak heard, he judged the big man had busted up the crapper platform inside, too.

He rolled onto his stomach and tried to stand up. He managed to get up onto hands and knees. From inside the shitter Jak heard protracted groaning and banging, and more wood splintering.

Then the noise stopped. A moment later, out strolled the kitchen girl, smoothing back her short hair from her face, which wore a satisfied expression.

"What happen?" he asked.

"I jumped on his back till the boards gave way beneath him," she said. "You might say that he's in really deep shit, now."

He wanted to challenge that outrageous assertion, but then he bent over and started to puke his guts out.

And his consciousness too, apparently, since he blacked out in the middle of it all.

LUKEWARM WATER SPLASHING his face brought Jak back to the land of the living.

He wasn't happy about the fact. His head and body both felt as if they'd been turned inside out. His everything hurt.

He sat up, coughing and sputtering. His brain seemed to freewheel briefly inside his skull. Somehow he didn't topple over.

He forced his eyes open. The yard behind the Last Resort was full of people, and the yellow light of lanterns.

Meg stood a few feet from him, bent toward him with hands on her tree-trunk thighs and a look of something that resembled concern on her big blunt face.

"You'll live, boy, I reckon," she said, straightening. "Though you might not be double glad of the fact for a spell yet. You look like you been drug through a knothole backward, and smell worse. Tony! Elián! Bring beaucoups more water. We've got to sluice him off enough to get him someplace to scrub up proper."

Jak looked around the yard. The faces looking back were only lamp-lit blurs. He felt his stomach starting to rebel again and was glad there was nothing left inside it to throw up

"What…about…Jeff and Ferd?" he croaked.

Meg put her hands on her wide hips and scowled.

"Never you mind about them. We'll take care of them

from here. We know how to deal with that kind of wag-trash."

"And girl?"

"I'm fine," a voice said brightly from his other side. "You are so welcome for my saving your life."

He turned and blinked at her. She stood just a couple feet away. For some reason he noticed she was prettier than he'd thought before.

Maybe it was the way she was grinning at him.

"And thank you for saving mine."

She learned forward and kissed his forehead, which he knew was drenched with sweat and probably things much less pleasant.

"Ew, Chally!" he heard a young male voice call out.

Then the world started turning super-fast around him and he fell right out of it. Again.

"Wh-where...am?"

"I take it that's how you ask, 'where am I?' in that goofy-ass truncated dialect of English you speak. Where are you from, anyway? Mars?"

Jak turned his head toward the voice. He could feel that his head was on a pillow; softness underlay his body. He took that for a good thing.

It wasn't the dirt of the yard, and none of it was hitting him in the eyes. Bonus.

Speaking of eyes, it occurred to him at last to open his. He saw that he was in the room he'd rented for the night on the second story of the Last Resort. He was on the bed, by the relative position of the door and the table with the single oil-burning lantern on it.

By its light, Chally was hanging his damp clothes on a rope she'd strung from wall to wall with carved-vine-wood pins.

"No," he said. "Louisiana."

"Well, that's close. You must've made a favorable impression on Meg, for her to spring to clean you and your clothes twice in one day."

"Any water? Mouth awful."

Chally walked to a small table and grabbed a mug, which she passed to him.

Jak accepted it gratefully, took a drink, rolled the water around in his mouth, then leaned over and spit into a small waste can. Then he took a long drink, handed over the mug and leaned back.

He tapped his chest with a finger.

"Jak."

"So they say," she said.

She was wearing a dark T-shirt and extremely abbreviated canvas shorts. Her legs were long and actually had a bit of shape. As slim as she was, she wasn't a total stick figure.

For some unknown reason, the fact began to interest him.

"What 'bout...coldhearts?"

"You don't want to know," she said. "Upshot was, Bo paid a wag-man—a local wag-man, none of their trash—to haul them into the Wild and dump them."

"Right," Jak said. "Not want know."

"Meg takes her hospitality triple seriously," Chally said. She finished pinning up the last of his clothes. It was his jacket. She'd wisely chosen to hang it by the bottom, with the sleeves trailing on the floor, to avpoid touching the glass and metal fragments sewn all over it. Splashes of puke clung to the jacket, so Chally sluiced it with a few buckets of water to get the garment clean.

She turned to him.

"Meg says that in days like ours, a person has greater

need for firm principles than ever. Whatever those principles may be. She's right."

"What...principles?" Jak asked.

Somehow she caught his drift. "Look out for myself," she said. "And look out for those who treat me right."

She drew her T-shirt up over her head. Her skin was bare beneath. Her breasts were tiny, the nipples little cones that were actually lighter-colored than the rest.

He felt his eyes widen.

She was surprisingly worth seeing. She was a skinny young woman, no mistake. Her hips were barely wider than her waist. But her bush was a mysterious and inviting tangle as dark as her gleaming thighs, and her eyes were wide in a breathtakingly beautiful face.

He would have said the last thing he was ready for was sex. But his cock said otherwise as she swayed toward him by the lamplight.

Chapter Nineteen

Ryan heard just the merest scuff of sound from his right. Long before his conscious brain identified as the scrape of leaves on fabric, he dropped to the game trail and yelled, "Ambush! Down!"

Blasterfire boomed from the thorn vines, so close that the muzzle flare stabbed like a yellow spike right to where Ryan's right side had been an eyeblink earlier.

He drew his SIG. He saw a stain-streaked pants leg and a boot on the ground on the other side of the vine-course, not six feet away. He fired two shots at it.

The tan cloth jerked. A dark spot appeared, an inch above the boot, spreading fast. The sec man screamed, then fell out of Ryan's line of sight.

"Don't shoot, nuke your shriveled balls!" he heard Cutter Dan roar from ahead and to the right. "Take them alive!"

A couple of shots popped out from the vines Ryan had passed anyway, as the last-to-know types got the message. That was followed by brush thrashing and shouts as Second Chance sec men jumped out of the vines to grapple with the companions on the trail.

Ryan quickly transferred his SIG to his left hand and drew his panga as two sec men clambered onto the main vine and jumped out onto the trail. He shot the farther one in the balls before he landed. The marshal hit and curled around himself into a tight, mewling ball of agony.

"Bastard!" the other sec man shouted. He tried to piston Ryan in the face with the buttstock of a longblaster. Ryan kicked him back. He jackknifed clean onto his feet with a spasm of effort.

Recovering his balance, the sec man brought up his weapon as if to shoot. Ryan kicked for the barrel, knocking it skyward. He swung his panga furiously overhand and chopped through the man's left arm just above the wrist.

Holding his carbine muzzle up with one hand, the blond sec man stared at the blood gushing in rhythmic spurts from the stump of his other as if completely unable to figure out what was happening.

Heavy arms grabbed Ryan from behind and pinned his arms to his sides. Breath blew hot down the back of his neck as the unseen marshal hoisted him off the ground with a grunt of effort.

WALKING RIGHT BEHIND Ryan in single file, Krysty was diving for the ground even before the one-eyed man called out his warning.

As she hit, blaster shots erupted from the vines to her right. They missed, aiming high at a target that was no longer there.

Then a body flew from the vine tangle to land heavily on top of her backpack, forcing the air from her lungs.

The extra weight came off momentarily. A hand grabbed the straps on her pack and rolled her onto her back. Then a sec man dropped astride her chest. Leaning forward, he grabbed her elbows and pinned them to the ground.

He grinned at her through his gray-shot brown beard. His face was very close to hers.

"Now that I've got you," he said, his breath smelling of booze and rot, "what am I gonna do with you?"

Savagely she bit him on the nose. Skin tore as he yanked himself free and reared back. Blood sprayed her face.

Krysty bowed her back, thrusting their combined weight off the game trail with all the strength of her legs, butt and lower back. As her assailant teetered, stunned and off balance, she swung up her legs and clamped them around his neck. She dropped her legs hard, yanking him backward and rolling to the side to throw him off. He landed on his face.

As he tried dazedly to get up, she drew her snub-nosed handblaster and, holding it in her fist, slammed the butt onto the back of his neck. He went flat and lay moaning and twitching.

Behind her Mildred was struggling, caught by the arms from both sides. Krysty rolled to a sitting position and shot one man in the leg. As he went down, the other cocked his fist to punch Mildred.

Doc loomed up behind him. He stabbed the sec man in the face with his rapier. The man screamed shrilly and fell into a thorn vine, clutching his face.

As he flailed and wailed, Krysty jumped to her feet.

As THE MAN who had Ryan in a bear hug from behind raised him off the ground, the one-eyed man saw Krysty and Mildred wrestling with sec men. Evidently Ryan had barely walked into the kill zone before some random movement had attracted his attention and scotched the plan. Doc, Ricky and J.B. seemed to be clear of enemies, but didn't dare shoot for fear of hitting the women.

The sec man began to squeeze Ryan's chest. He had one black-furred hand locked on the other wrist. It was quite the reach, given Ryan's backpack and the depth of his chest, but the sec man managed.

His unwelcome embrace was like iron. Ryan's ribs

creaked to the strain. His vision began to get fuzzy around the edges as the sec man's arms tightened like a python constricting a baby. He couldn't breathe.

Time to do something about that.

Ryan's arms were immovably pinned. His own backpack prevented him doing a reverse head butt into the sec man's face. He began to struggle furiously and try to pull his arms free.

When he reckoned everything was lined up nicely, and the man who held him had his full attention focused on his straining upper body, Ryan snapped up his right heel with all his strength.

His calculations were correct. The back of his boot hammered into the sec man's nuts.

The man vented a wheezing gasp, and his right hand slackened its grip on Ryan's left wrist. He snapped up both his arms. The marshal's weakened grasp gave way. The arms burst free of the deadly embrace, and Ryan's boots thudded to the ground.

He turned right, firing his elbow back, catching the sec man full in the face as he bent over to grab for his crotch.

Ryan saw that, like him, the man wore a black eye patch. It did not fill him with feelings of camaraderie. He back-kicked the man in the gut.

The mule kick knocked the sec man sprawling into the skein of vines. He hollered as the long, sharp thorns pierced his back and butt.

He got control of himself and shouted, "They're killing us back here, boss!"

"Right," Ryan heard Cutter Dan rap out from farther down the narrow, winding path. "Time to take the gloves off. Shoot to wound the coldheart bastards!"

Sec men spilled onto the path ahead, leveling blasters right at Ryan.

"Fireblast!" he yelled.

"Gren out," J.B. called from behind.

Gren? Ryan thought, as he started to turn to dive into the vines and take his own chances with the thorns. We don't have any—

"Gren!" the secmen screamed as an object arched out of the sky, trailing dirty gray smoke, and struck the ground right at their feet. They turned and started jostling and flailing at one another in their frenzy to escape.

The tiny smoke trail blossomed suddenly to a giant cloud. It obscured the trail, hiding the frantic sec men from Ryan's view. He smelled sulfur.

"Naw," said J.B. from right behind him. "Just a smokie."

Ryan shot him a quick grin.

"Right," he said. "Remember we passed a place where the trail forked left, mebbe a quarter mile back? Lead the way there. We'll go that way!"

J.B. nodded. He turned and ran past the others, who were holding down warily on the injured and moaning sec men who'd attacked them.

Ryan glanced back. An intrepid sec man leaped out of the smoke, his dark-blond hair flying, holding a Remington 870 pump shotgun in his hands.

Ryan shot him through the chest, and the marshal fell back through the smoke screen.

Then the one-eyed man turned back to his friends. "Go!" he shouted to them, gesturing furiously with the panga.

A few shots followed the companions, but they were fired blind through the dense smoke of J.B.'s bomb. None came close.

It took the Second Chance sec men a while to get sorted out and give chase. The fate of the bold dude with the pump riot gun did not encourage any of his buddies to leap right out in his footsteps. Not even Cutter Dan.

Ryan already knew the sec boss was a hard case, and brave, but not *stupe* brave. Much like Ryan himself.

It didn't encourage him.

Between his pounding boot heels and his pounding heart, the one-eyed man couldn't hear when the pursuit started again. When he hoped he was far enough away to risk a look back around his backpack, the trail between the long strands of intertwined thorn vine had meandered into the line of sight so he couldn't see far enough to tell if Dan and his men were chasing him.

But he knew they were.

Mildred's feet were winging out to the sides as she ran by the time they reached the fork in the game trail. That was a sure sign she was starting to become fatigued, but the Armorer had already jogged up the path, and she followed him with the same dogged determination that had done so much to keep her alive since she was wakened from her cold sleep in Minnesota.

When Ryan, still bringing up the rear, was a hundred yards up the new trail he called softly to Krysty, "Pass the word to J. B. to slow down."

"I can take it, Ryan," Mildred gasped.

"Nuke shit," Ryan said. "Do as you're told."

The procession slowed to a walking pace. Belying the bravado of her earlier words Mildred at once began to stagger like a miner on a three-day bender. Krysty hastily moved up to help support her.

Ryan heard voices murmur ahead of him, then Krysty looked back.

"J.B. wants you to come up and take a look at something."

"You just keep going," he said. "I'll stay where I am."

"He says it's urgent," Krysty said. "Don't worry, lover. I'll hear the sec men if they start to catch up."

He frowned, but nodded. Quickening his pace he moved past the two women.

The trail was opening into another clearing. J.B. stood at the far side, frowning down at something. It looked almost as if somebody had tried to build a fire out of thinner vines and thorn branches and given up without lighting it. Except it had a hollowed-out front.

"It's a shrine," Ricky said. "Look, there's feather bundles and little clay figures in it. And a larger one that looks—"

He stopped and turned an ashen face back to Ryan. "It looks like one of the dinosaur toys my uncle made for me."

A hoarse shout of alarm from Doc made Ryan spin as rapidly as his own fatigue—greater than he'd been letting on to himself—and the weight of his pack would allow.

He saw Krysty standing stock still, her right arm still around Mildred's back. Her own face was several shades lighter than its usual gorgeous ivory.

She was staring down at a spear with its tip buried in her left thigh.

FREE Merchandise is 'in the Cards' for you!

Dear Reader,

We're giving away FREE MERCHANDISE!

Seriously, we'd like to reward you for reading this novel by giving you **FREE MERCHANDISE** worth over \$20. And no purchase is necessary!

You see the Jack of Hearts sticker above? Paste that sticker in the box on the Free Merchandise Voucher inside. Return the Voucher promptly...and we'll send you valuable Free Merchandise!

Thanks again for reading one of our novels—and enjoy your Free Merchandise with our compliments!

Pam Powers

Pam Powers

P.S. Look inside to see what Free Merchandise is **"in the cards"** for you!

▲ Detach card and mail today. No stamp needed. ▲

© 2013 HARLEQUIN ENTERPRISES LIMITED. ® and ™ are trademarks owned and used by the trademark owner and/or its licensee. Printed in the U.S.A.

FREE MERCHANDISE VOUCHER

> 2 FREE
> BOOKS
> and
> 2 FREE
> GIFTS

Please send my Free Merchandise, consisting of
2 Free Books and **2 Free Mystery Gifts**.
I understand that I am under no obligation to buy
anything, as explained on the back of this card.

166/366 ADL GECK

Please Print

FIRST NAME

LAST NAME

ADDRESS

APT.#   CITY

STATE/PROV.   ZIP/POSTAL CODE

NO PURCHASE NECESSARY!

GE_314_FM13

Chapter Twenty

"Krysty!" Ryan shouted. He lunged toward her, shoulder-ing a startled Doc out of the way.

He was already too late.

It was as if boobies had been set off in the vines to both sides of the clearing, blasting out bodies instead of shrap-nel, long, sinuous, feathery bodies with long tails and long snouts full of razor teeth. Spears and clubs were clutched in taloned hands. In the blink of Ryan's eye they filled the space between him and the redheaded beauty.

He heard his other friends shout in warning and alarm. He only had thoughts for Krysty, the love of his life, who was wounded and who needed him. The rest would have to fend for themselves right now.

Dino-muties turned toward him and jabbed the air with spears. They opened their long jaws. Inside, their mouths were bright red and full of sawlike teeth. They hissed as if they were angry catamounts.

Ryan's survival instincts overrode his concern for Krysty. The muties were being a little too blatant with their threats, meaning they really wanted him to look at them.

Meaning...

He snapped his head left. A mutie was bounding at him with big steps of its powerful hind legs. It thrust a spear at him.

Ryan stepped back with his right foot and pivoted clockwise. His left hand batted the spear just behind the end, steering it safely by his side.

The dino-mutie was either going too fast to stop, or just intended to get close and finish Ryan with its claws; it kept coming. The one-eyed man swung his left elbow back into the creature's face.

The mutie ran right into it. A tick later Ryan realized he might have been sticking his arm into the razor-toothed maw—better than his head, but non-optimal. Instead, it was coming so fast the point of his elbow took it right on the side of the head.

Ryan heard bones break with a crackle like a big man stepping on a stack of dry twigs. The dino-mutie squawked, fell on its tail, then dropped onto its side kicking feebly. It seemed to be in its death throes.

Light bones, Ryan thought.

From behind him he heard the boom of the stub-barreled shotgun mounted on Doc's LeMat revolver.

"I have your back, Ryan!" the old man shouted. "J.B. and Ricky are coming!"

Ryan drew his panga as he looked rapidly left and right. There was no reaching the women; the muties had him blocked. Doc's handblaster cracked again, firing conventional bullets this time. The thunder of J.B.'s shotgun joined in.

And still the muties kept pouring from the Wild, jaws snapping, yellow eyes rolling with fury and hate.

THE BUCKSHOT CHARGE from Doc's short-barreled shotgun, slung beneath the longer barrel of his LeMat revolver, crumpled the mutie in midleap and dropped it like a wing-shot mourning dove. It landed near his right boot.

He whipped his head left, knowing what he'd see, more

of the feathered fiends springing forth from the vines with jaws agape and murder in their yellow eyes.

He fired four .44 rounds from the revolver's outsized cylinder. Blood sprayed. The monsters shied away.

Doc knew they'd rally and come on. Or those behind them would leap pass them to the attack. Seasoned fighter as he had become, since he'd been freed from his thralldom to the horrific Jordan Teague by Ryan and his friends, Doc was already rotating his upper body back to his right.

Another feathered lizard was jabbing a spear at his back. Doc sidestepped and shot it through the head.

Turning back and forth with an alacrity that belied his apparent age, Doc blasted the rest of the .44 bullets into the attacking horde. Again they moved back.

Again they squalled in collective fury and surged forward.

But Doc was ready for them. He had hurriedly holstered the LeMat, seized his swordstick and whipped out the slim, lethal blade.

A mutie leaped for him, swinging a section of stout vine branch that had been fashioned into a crude club. It still had six-inch thorns jutting from it.

Doc deflected it past him with the sword's sheath. As he did he pivoted left, stabbing the mutie through the neck.

As it fell, strangling on its own blood, Doc ripped the steel blade out of its feathered throat. Two more muties closed in, poking spears at him. He parried both and feinted at the nearer creature's eyes.

Then he wheeled to slash a mutie attacking from behind and cracked another smartly alongside its yellow crest with the swordstick sheath. He began to turn in place, fending and counterattacking, not fast enough to dizzy himself, but fast enough to keep from making his back a target.

The fact that it was padded and protected by his own full backpack helped.

The muties formed a circle around Doc. They darted their heads like serpents at him, hissing and screeching. They poked at him with spears, but none was bold enough to press the attack.

For the moment. "All right, you feathered devils!" he yelled. "Come at me and be damned to you!"

And then, to his horror the old man saw Krysty go down.

KRYSTY WAS NOT the sort to freeze.

Not from fear. Not from horror. Least of all from surprise.

But that was what she did when the dino-mutie's spear arced out of nowhere and hit her in the thigh.

Freezing was the most lethal of the three things that usually happened to a person when danger dropped and adrenaline dumped. Flight and even fight could chill a person, too—because if control was lost when the adrenaline blasted through a person's veins like the potent drug it was, if a person lost his or her presence of mind, power and speed were gained but judgment and skill were lost. A person was just as likely to trip into something running or run face first into a tree; in combat, a person could flail his or her arms powerfully, but with little focus the blows were laughably easy to dodge and were weak even when they connected.

But freezing stuck a person square in the kill zone. Dead to rights in the sights of an enemy who already had all the advantage he was likely to need.

Krysty froze, but only for an instant. Then her survival instinct, her hard-earned skills and most of all her will, with its strength and determination, kicked in.

Even as the bushes blossomed with the white-rimmed scarlet flowers of gaping mutie mouths, she yanked the spear out. Blood squirted, the same color as the mouth lining of the attacking creatures. But it wasn't a serious leak. She knew from the location it hadn't hit her femoral artery.

Of course, if it had, all her problems would be over within a few minutes, regardless of what the muties did. Forever.

She heard Mildred's blaster bark from her right as she wheeled, spear in hand, to face the dino-creatures attacking from her left. By habit the two women put themselves back to back.

A mutie darted toward her. It was pure luck that they were far enough into the clearing that the nearest thorn vine tangle was at least a dozen feet away. It made it impossible for the muties to strike from cover. Apparently instinct or bloodlust prevented them from simply showering their prey with spears from the tangle. They wanted to feel blood on their claws and jaws, and taste it spurting hot on their tongue.

The lead attacker had a slate-blue back that was almost pretty. When it wasn't reared up, it was surprisingly small, no higher than Krysty's waist and seemingly not much thicker around than its spear.

It thrust at her with the weapon. Angrily, she knocked it aside with the spear she'd just plucked from her leg. She kicked the mutie under the chin with her right boot. Its head snapped back and it collapsed as if shot in the head.

But her own wounded leg buckled. She fell heavily on her buttocks.

"Krysty!" Mildred called from behind her. She sensed her friend trying to turn to aid her.

"No!" she shouted. "Eyes forward!"

She saw Mildred's arm whip back. Yellow flame

flashed from the muzzle of her blaster, pale against a sky screened with high, thin clouds. Muzzle blast slapped Krysty in the face. A mutie shrieked in response and collapsed next to the fallen redhead.

Krysty rolled her green eyes up to see another mutie snapping at the back of Mildred's neck from the other direction. Krysty swung the spear in her left hand. The blow was clumsy; by luck more than aim the tip raked the creature across the tongue. It uttered a strangled squawk and snapped its jaws shut.

Mildred spun her face back counterclockwise. "What the fuck?" she yelped as she found herself staring into the yellow eyes of a furry little dinosaur-shaped predator with blood leaking from its shut mouth.

Krysty watched just long enough to see her friend swing her right arm back around, still outstretched, with her blaster clutched in her fist. The weapon slammed into the side of the mutie's head and knocked it sprawling.

By sheer combat instinct Krysty was already gripping her spear near the end of the haft with both hands and swinging it in a high arc like an ax. It knocked down another spear being thrust at her by a charging mutie.

She heaved it back up. The creature's momentum impaled its throat on the sharp steel tip. Blood sprayed over Krysty's arms and face.

She yanked the spear out. Planting the butt against the ground inside her left armpit, she began to lever herself upright. The ground seemed like a safe place to stay; she couldn't fall any farther. Her left leg was obviously weakened by the wound, and she was losing blood. That would weaken her overall and slow her down.

But she knew the haven offered by staying on the nice, warm ground was false. The muties weren't showing any signs of letting up their assault, and neither were their numbers decreasing. Her group's sole chance of surviving lay in somehow fighting its way out of the death ground, which meant first that Krysty had to be mobile, and second that she and Mildred had to help the others by fighting their way to join up with them.

Using the spear as a crutch, her powerful right leg and what strength remained in the left—more than she thought—Krysty levered herself upright. She swayed, a bit light-headed from shock and the blood she'd already lost. Shots cracked from behind her and from her companions.

She didn't feel any pain yet, just numbness. She knew the pain would come—if she lived long enough for the adrenaline to begin wearing off.

But for now she found her leg would support her as she raised the spear to block another attack, then buttstroked the mutie across the left forearm, breaking the bones.

All she could do now was fight as long as she could. And hope and pray to Gaia that was enough.

RYAN DREW THE SIG with his left hand and fired into a mutie's chest. It fell back among its comrades.

Another darted in from the left, stabbing with a knife. It thought it was attacking from Ryan's blind spot, but it failed to account for the way he constantly kept his head turning, right and left. The Deathlands warrior turned to blast the mutie, then used his knife to knock aside a spear flashing toward his face from the front.

Another mutie sprang from the right. Ryan had no time to react.

A deafening roar filled the clearing. The mutie's body crumpled, erupting feathers and blood.

"Coming up on you, Ryan," he heard J.B. call.

A moment later the Armorer and Ricky had joined Ryan. They arranged themselves at the points of an outward-facing triangle, J.B. at Ryan's right shoulder, Ricky at his left.

"Ace," Ryan said. "Save ammo as much as you can."

"Teach an old fox to hunt rabbits," J.B. said good-humoredly.

For a moment the muties fell back from the trio. They continued to screech, shake spears and clubs, and snap their toothy jaws at the embattled humans.

"Doc," Ryan called, "join up. Then we can fight our way to the women as a group."

He could see that Krysty was back on her feet, towering above the feathered mutie bodies swarming through the thirty yards separating them from Doc. His heart had nearly stopped when he'd seen her go down. But from the way the muties who pounced on her went flying back, trailing blood pennons and despairing squawks, he realized she'd put too much weight on the wounded leg, using it to support her weight for a kick.

The muties melted back like mercury before a finger as they and Doc moved toward each other. Great, Ryan thought. They didn't dare shoot to clear the way for fear of hitting each other. The same with Krysty and Mildred.

"Why aren't the dinos running?" Ricky asked in tones as puzzled as desperate. "We've chilled and hurt so many of them!"

"Indeed," Doc called, "they have incurred sufficient losses to dishearten most tribal groups and send them running. Arrgh!"

The last was a sort of strangled battle cry, uttered as he flourished his sword and his its sheath crazily at the mutie mob swirling between him and his three friends. The dinos parted abruptly. Doc straightened his lapels with his thumbs and took his place with his friends, between J.B. and Ricky.

"Enough to rout most disciplined army types, too," J.B. said.

"Something's got them hot past nuke red," Ryan said. "Reckon they got more grievance than just hating on us for invading their domain."

"That structure J.B. and I were looking at," Ricky said. "It looked like a shrine. Mebbe this is holy ground to them?"

"That seems eminently possible," Doc said. "Very little stirs rancor as much as religious wrath."

It was possible, Ryan thought. Ricky was the only one in the group who still actively believed in any religion—if you left out Krysty and her veneration of Gaia, the Earth Mother, and that wasn't religion so much as a sort of working relationship.

"The 'why' doesn't find us any more bullets for our blasters," Ryan muttered. "What we need now's a way to get out of this with all our parts intact."

"A little help here, boys," Mildred called. "They're starting to get frisky again."

The muties surrounding Ryan's group were also pressing closer. Cries from the Wild around them suggested more dino muties were flocking to the scene.

"We're coming," Ryan yelled back to the two women standing back to back. Both of them carried spears. "Just hold out."

Then to his immediate companions, he said, "Hold off shooting as long as you can. Once we form up we can try blasting through the kill zone."

He started forward, taking small steps. The nearest muties, who had begun racing around them in both directions, probably to make themselves less obvious targets, stopped and shrieked menacingly at them. They prodded at the air with their spears.

"Why don't they just stand off and throw those spears at us?" Ricky asked.

"They like the taste of hot blood on their tongues too much, I reckon," Ryan said.

"They are pack predators," Doc added. "Far more humanlike than stickies. But far more primitive than we—far closer to the truly feral."

"Not closer than all of us," Ryan said with a grit-toothed smile. "They want to fight up close? On my call, charge the bastards!"

As if they understood him—a bit too late it struck him that they might—the muties lunged forward instantly to the attack. At once they were pressed to furiously defend themselves. Ryan used his SIG to parry with and struck with his panga, crushing lightweight bones and sending out great red sheets of blood. Doc used his sword and its sheath in lethal combination. J.B. had his shotgun gripped by the barrel; it was a full-on riot and combat scattergun, built for this kind of rough trade. Ricky had plucked out a spear that was stuck in J.B.'s backpack and was using it mostly as a quarterstaff.

To Ryan's sick horror he saw the muties surge toward the two women as well. He could see reinforcements springing from the thicket now, dozens of them, crests erect, screaming their war cries, feathered warriors, fresh and vying to be in at the kill.

And then a storm of blasterfire erupted from back along the trail.

Chapter Twenty-One

The blue-gray ranks of feathered warriors faltered as bullets sleeted into them from some source still unseen by Ryan and his companions.

"Krysty! Mildred!" Ryan shouted. "Now's your chance to join us! Run!"

The muties nearest the four men kept on attacking, even more savagely than before. Ryan launched himself among them, smashing with the butt of his handblaster, swinging his panga in whistling, death-dealing arcs.

But as he did, he heard a triumphant shouting voice coming up the trail. The blasterfire continued to rake laggard muties away from either side of the two women.

At Ryan's shouted command Mildred and Krysty turned toward the men and began to race forward.

Krysty's left leg, weakened by the wound and unchecked blood loss, gave way beneath her. She folded to the ground with a faint cry of despair.

"Krysty!" Ryan shouted, louder this time. He tried to lunge ahead, into the phalanx of mutie spears still waiting for him.

He felt a hand like an iron claw grip his right biceps. It halted him dead in midlunge. He swung his head to snarl an order to let him go or die and found himself looking into J.B.'s steady gaze. The Armorer characteristically didn't even say anything. He just shook his head once.

The suicidal frenzy driving Ryan suddenly vanished. He actually sagged at the knees. Briefly.

Then he straightened and looked back.

Krysty, obviously more weakened by the bleeding than he'd thought, waved a feeble hand at him.

There was nothing wrong with Mildred's voice, despite the fatigue evident even a hundred feet away in the gray cast of her features.

"Go on!" she yelled, waving her arm frantically. "You can't help us!"

A man wearing the red-white-and-blue armband of a Second Chance marshal bounded into view. He had a large-frame revolver in his fist, though he wasn't Cutter Dan. He was tall but ganglier, with a shock of dark-brown hair over a long face.

Ryan snapped a shot his way. He had to aim high so as not to risk hitting Mildred, but the man dived into the vines anyway.

The marshal began to curse furiously at the thorns puncturing his flesh.

His heart feeling like lead in his chest, Ryan turned his back on the woman he loved and his loyal companion.

"This way," he told the other three males, gesturing past the vine-branch shrine to where an opening in the briars revealed the game trail's continuation north. "Power it out of here, *now*."

Instead Ricky tried to hurl himself back toward Mildred and Krysty. "No!" he raved. "We can't abandon them! The sec men will shoot them!"

Already following his own command and running like hell, Ryan risked a glance back. Doc and J.B. had the kid by his arms and were holding him back.

"Son," he heard J.B. say. "The one thing we know for

stone certain is that those coldhearts won't shoot them. They wouldn't risk cheating Santee of his fun."

Whether it was the Armorer's calm authority, or the sense of his words, Ricky gave up his futile, harebrained struggles and turned to run with the rest of them.

The last fan-tipped tails of the mutie horde were vanishing into the scrub. As always the long, slender lizard-like bodies could move through the thorny vine snarl like eels through seaweed. Sec men came boiling out of the mouth of the trail from the south to surround the women. A couple tossed blaster shots after the fleeing quartet.

The last thing Ryan heard from them before he vanished with his comrades into the cover of the Wild, and a trail that fortuitously bent quickly to the right, was the buffalo-bull voice of Cutter Dan bellowing, "Cease-fire, you dickheads!"

"Son of a gaudy slut," said Edwards, emerging from the vines where he'd pitched himself for cover from Ryan's blaster shot. "Why'd you make us stop shooting, C.D.?"

"You wasn't shooting no-how, Edwards," Belusky said. "All you was doing was flailing around and cussing up a storm."

"Well, *yeah,*" Edwards said aggrievedly, holding up forearms bared by rolled-up shirtsleeves. They were each twined with thin trails of blood from numerous small punctures.

"Shut it," Cutter Dan ordered. He slowed from an easy lope as he came into the clearing. He held his burly Smith & Wesson Magnum revolver in his hand.

His men had secured the women already, tying their hands behind their backs, briskly and with no funny business. For their part, the two women, hellcats though they undoubtedly were, didn't put up much of a fight. They did glare green and brown murder at Cutter Dan, though.

"They ain't so much," Edwards said dismissively. "After what they put us through I'da thought they woulda fought us tooth and claw."

"Don't lie, Edwards," Scovul told him. "You don't think."

"They're smart enough to know it won't do them any good at this point," Cutter Dan said. He smirked at their angry faces. The black woman was on her knees, the red-head lying on her side on the ground. "Also smart enough to know we got strict orders to bring them back alive, and we don't want to disappoint the Judge on a matter like this, do we?"

"Don't forget the part where we want to stay in good shape to drink your blood later," the black one said. "After Ryan Cawdor rips your heart out!"

Cutter Dan laughed. He was riding a natural high of triumph. He could afford to be magnanimous with the captives just now.

He knew the fate that awaited them. So did they.

Then he noticed the red pool spreading beneath the red-haired witch. "Speaking of blood, somebody best jump on getting a tourniquet on that leg pronto. Or be the one to explain to Judge Santee why he let one of his prize gallows ornaments bleed out in the middle of the nuking Wild.

"And don't get any bright ideas about copping a feel. Either woman, any time. Or I will personally chop off the offending hand and toss it into the vines for the deathbirds to cook for dinner."

"Deathbirds" was what the human residents of the Wild mostly called the cantankerous, weird half-bird, half-lizard, mutie tribe that dominated the western end of the giant thicket. Nobody actually knew if they ate human flesh or not, though they certainly had a taste for ripping at it with their teeth when they were trying to take you down. But everybody just naturally assumed they did.

"Aww, boss," whined one of the sec men Santee had grudgingly dispatched to replace the men chilled and wounded at the debacle at the abandoned farmhouse. "Ain't you gonna let us have any fun?"

"Put a sock in it, Evrard," Yonas ordered. "These two are strictly off limits. Or did you think the chief marshal was joking, you disgusting maggot puke?"

Cutter Dan grinned indulgently. "Thanks, Yonas. But you can ease back off the trigger of the blaster. We'll run into some more caravan rats on the trail soon. Then you can get your jollies on."

He walked over to where the women were surrounded by sec men. The marshals were all facing outward now, gripping their weapons. The muties had flown off like frightened birds when they found themselves unexpectedly caught between two fields of fire, but Cutter Dan's men weren't fooled. They knew the creatures were still out there, watching like the hawks they vaguely resembled, looking for the slightest sign of inattention and weakness.

"You all did an impressive job on the deathbirds," Dan said, surveying the broken and shot-up bodies heaped throughout the big clearing.

"Just wait and see what we do to your thugs and you, you stoneheart scum sucker," the kneeling woman spat out, "after our friends come for us."

The smile dropped away from Cutter Dan's face to be replaced a heartbeat later by another, far less pleasant smile.

"Talkative one, aren't you," he said to Mildred. "For that, I'll see if I can put a word in with the Judge to make sure you get to see all your friends swing before you feel the noose shut the words off in your own bitch throat."

He turned away; he'd let the woman get past his composure.

Cutter Dan blamed her for that.

But he'd already told her how he meant to make her pay. So rather than wasting any more breath of his own on the subject, he started pointing at his men.

"You, you and you—yes, you, Evrard—get the women up and heading back for Second Chance. Scovul, you take charge of the detail."

One of the men was Evrard, but he was the only one in the crew from among the men Cutter Dan had spotted looking eager when the man bitched about not being allowed to make free with the female captives. Scovul would be able to handle him during the trip.

"Yes, sir," his lieutenant said, but he looked dubious.

Cutter Dan put a hand on his shoulder. "Don't worry, friend," he said. "You just drop them off, give a quick report to the Judge, and you'll be back in no time."

Scovul nodded.

"You mean for us to carry this red-haired one the whole way?" Edwards asked, as the women were dragged to their feet. Krysty's head lolled, and the woman's arms hung as if she were barely conscious.

She was sandbagging now, Cutter Dan reckoned.

"She's powerful large," Edwards said. "Meaning no offense, ma'am. For you are beautifully proportioned."

"I should make you tote her yourself," Scovul said, "for being such a pussy."

"They say you are what you eat, Lieutenant!"

"Then you're shit, Edwards," Belusky said.

"Hey, now. Be nice. It's a hero wounded in the line of duty you're talking to here, bro."

"A stupe who got holes poked in his ass diving out of the line of fire, more," the sec man said dismissively.

"You know what?" Cutter Dan said. He ticked off one of the men he'd first detailed to the escort mission with his finger. "You stick with us, Millz. And you—"

He pointed to the largest of his marshals, a six-eight giant built like a buffalo and with certain facial similarities behind a mighty walrus mustache.

"You take his place. You can help carry the redhead if you have to."

"Got it, boss," the huge man said.

"Ace, Zerblonski. Anyway, all you need to do is get her to the Martonville road, commandeer a wag. Then you can all ride back to Second Chance in style. Do it, Scovul."

"Sir!"

"Don't we need to press on right away?" asked Yonas, now Cutter Dan's second in command. "The others are getting away."

"Remember where they're headed," he told the one-eyed marshal. "They won't get far. We can take our sweet time from here. Catch our breath, keep an eye out for the muties. Anyway, you don't seriously think those boys'll run off and leave these beauties behind, do you?"

Yonas shrugged. "Never can tell what's in a coldheart's mind, boss. Cowards, all of 'em, anyway."

Cutter Dan laughed. "Then you haven't heard the stories about Ryan Cawdor I have. He's many things, few of them good. But no one who ever faced him ever called him *coward.*"

"I heard tell few who ever faced him lived to tell the tale," Edwards said.

Cutter Dan showed the beanpole marshal his brightest, widest smile.

"Well, we're just about to change that, then, aren't we?"

SOMETHING FLICKERED FAST into Ricky's left-hand peripheral vision. He barely had time to blink his eye and flinch.

Sheer reflex made him turn his face to the right, away from the unknown object. That meant that the mutie spear, thrown from concealment in the vines, only grazed his left cheek before streaking by to bury itself in the dirt on the right-hand side of the path.

Ricky yipped and swung his Webley handblaster that way. He saw nothing.

"Move," said J.B., who brought up the rear of the four-man party. Ricky obeyed.

He hadn't realized he'd even slowed his pace, much less become rooted to the spot.

The youth dabbed at his cheek with his left hand. His fingers came away spotted with blood. It was dull, almost rust brown in the twilight.

Doc glanced back around his pack. "Keep pressure on it," he advised. "That should give it a chance to clot and stop."

Ricky nodded and pressed his fingers hard into his cheek. He ignored the brief sting.

It had been, best as he could calculate, three hours since they'd gotten chased from the clearing of the shrine. The sun had already passed out of sight behind the tangled briars to their left. The warm wind had started up again, leaching the water from their bodies so that Ricky had to drink frequently from his canteen despite his determination to shepherd his dwindling stock of water.

After the first two hundred yards, Ryan had had them slow, first to a trot, then to a determined walk. It was clear the sec men weren't giving chase.

"Cutter Dan knows we're not going far without Mildred and Krysty," Ryan had said.

"The man's too clever by half, as my English friends would say," Doc said, adding sadly, "*Would* have said."

"Nothing worse than a clever sec boss," J.B. stated. "Not even a stickie with a can of gas and a light."

That was when a mutie jumped out of the thicket and slashed at the Armorer with a clawed hand. J.B. leaped nimbly back. The swipe only laid open the tip of his nose.

"Dark night," he grunted, then crushed the creature's narrow skull with an overhand swing of his M-4000's stock.

Since that moment they had been shadowed relentlessly by the muties Ricky couldn't help thinking of as dinosaurs, even if they were covered in feathers. Most of the time they didn't attack. They just stayed a constant presence, evidenced by chirps and whistles as they communicated with each other, the odd rustle or shaking of the thorns and glimpses of sinuous bodies sliding along the vines or racing along the ground.

When they did attack, they attacked solo, almost always from the left, now. The spear thrown at Ricky had been an anomaly. The creatures continued to show a marked preference for getting up close and personal with their foes.

Ricky took his fingers off his cheek and checked them for fresh blood. There wasn't much.

"Why aren't they pressing us harder? The way they swarmed us back at the clearing I thought they were determined to finish us off."

"They mostly wanted us to leave, then," J.B. said. "Now they're blaster shy. We chilled a lot of them. Hurt a bunch more. If we're off their special patch of Wild, they're not as bold."

"Is it possible that what are attacking us are young, unfledged warriors," Doc asked, "seeking individual glory, or perhaps to win full membership in the tribe?"

"Possible," Ryan said.

Ricky was surprised Ryan would comment. As keen a mind as he knew their leader to have, Ricky was often surprised and not infrequently exasperated that Ryan showed so little interest in knowledge for its own sake.

But when their survival was at stake, Ryan was triple curious. Ricky realized that this whole time Ryan had been driving his mind hard, trying to figure out why the muties kept attacking them, both in order to try to predict some of their moves in advance and to figure out how to make them stop.

It was better, Ricky realized, than thinking about the fate of his friend Mildred and his life-mate, Krysty. Though once he'd cooled down from his initial panic, Ricky had also seen that Ryan was right, as usual. For now, the captured women were safer than the men were.

"Which begs the question," Doc said. "Why do they continue to harry us at all?"

"Keep us heading the right direction," Ryan said grimly.

"And they only chuck crap at us when we slow down," J.B. said pointedly to Ricky's back.

"Sorry!" Ricky's cheeks flushed.

Fortunately for him, the game trail had been steadily widening for the last half hour or so. The reason wasn't hard to work out. Other trails kept joining it from the sides.

"We need to start scouting for a place to camp for the night," J.B. called to Ryan.

"See anything promising?"

"Nope."

"I think mebbe we're getting near the edge of this mess," Ryan said. "Sooner or later we've got to run out of thicket. The fact so many trails are running together suggests we found a fast way out."

"Good," Ricky said. "It's getting dark."

With a crashing of brush, a mutie burst from the vines, raced several paces across the path, and sprang at Ryan. He flung up his left arm. The creature fastened its teeth on his forearm and kicked its legs off the ground to slash it Ryan's flank with its double-large killing claws.

"Fireblast!" Ryan exclaimed. Then he hacked the mutie's head off with a stroke of his panga.

The body fell kicking. The jaws continued to hold on to Ryan's arm. Was it Ricky's imagination, or did the yellow eyes continue to roll in the severed reptilian head?

Ryan stuck the knife tip in between the jaws and levered them open. The mutie head fell snapping to the trail.

"You fit to fight, Ryan?" J.B. called, not sounding particularly concerned.

Ryan held up his left arm and examined it with his lone eye. "Amazingly, yes," he said. "Thing's teeth didn't even get through the coat. Got a nuke of a bite on it, though."

He had never broken stride the whole time, which reminded Ricky that the distance between him and Doc was increasing again. He stirred his legs to close it up quickly, lest one of their shadowers chuck something else at him.

The teen hoped with all his heart that they were getting close to the edge of the Wild. His legs were about to give out, and he was starting to breathe with a bit of a wheeze.

Ryan disappeared around a bend in the path. Ricky pushed himself even harder to catch up to Doc so he could see.

"Not so close," J.B. called reprovingly. "You don't want the muties to be able to take you both out by throwing a double-long stick."

Ricky slackened his pace slightly. Then he came to the bend and almost stumbled.

Not forty yards away the Wild stopped. He could see the land open up to either side.

His heart soared. They were free of the terrible mutie-haunted tangle, and presumably free of their dogged mutie pursuers.

Then he saw that Ryan had stopped dead, still twenty yards shy of the thicket's end. He was staring upward. Even past the bulky backpack Ricky could see his shoulders slumped as if in discouragement.

Then Ricky's eyes resolved what at first they had not been able to make out due to the deepening evening shadows—and the way they'd focused laser tight in his almost desperate relief that they were nearly out of the woods.

Out of the woods—or the vines, anyway—sure. But not away free.

Not by a mile.

Or, to be more exact, not by the sheer hundred-foot cliff that rose before them like a wall beyond the thicket's edge.

Chapter Twenty-Two

"You sure this is safe?" Ricky asked. He walked behind Doc, who followed Ryan. J.B. brought up the rear.

Ryan snorted. "Of course it isn't safe."

"How many times I got to tell you, kid," J.B. said, in a tone that told Ryan the Armorer was shaking his head, "that there's no such thing as 'safe' in the Deathlands?"

"Well," Ricky said, "I meant, comparatively."

"Enough!" Ryan said.

By the last light of the day they made their way along the base of the steep red cliffs that formed an impassable barrier just beyond the northern extremity of the Wild. Dirt had apparently fallen from the cliff, forming low, irregular foothills. Over the years they had acquired coats of grass and other ground cover. Brush grew on and among them, densely in places.

There were also jumbles of big rocks piled up against the base of the cliffs, here and there. And for some reason the lower part of the red clay wall was pierced irregularly by caves, some mere crawl spaces, some as big as the room of a predark house and high enough for even Ryan or Doc to stand upright in.

"This is a classic dip-slip formation," Doc said, as if lecturing a class at Oxford, back in his day. "I surmise the bedrock underlying this clay fractured and was upthrust during the colossal earthquakes following the Third World War."

"That's ace, Doc," Ryan said quietly. "Now just stow it for later. We don't know what might be waiting for us up ahead."

"I quite understand, my dear Ryan."

Ryan glanced back in irritation. Doc looked sheepish and drew a finger across his lips in a zipping gesture. Ryan shook his head and faced forward again.

He progressed at a cautious walk, his SIG in his right hand. There was abundant concealment and cover both here along the foot of the cliffs, Which was a good thing, since they couldn't climb the wall anyplace they'd come across yet, and the only alternatives were to walk around exposed or go back to the shelter of the Wild, both of which were definite no-gos as far as Ryan was concerned. And none of the other three had so much as suggested either.

He stepped over a tiny stream where water trickled from somewhere above in the cliff, hidden now by the rapidly congealing darkness. That was even better luck. They'd refilled their canteens, which were almost down to water vapor from all the fighting and running they'd had to do.

Of course that kind of luck couldn't last. They lived in the Deathlands, after all. A person was spared one day only to be chilled the next.

Ryan spotted two men. One squatted with his back to the cliff, the other stood with his longblaster slung, looking off across the hundred yards or so separating the red clay wall from the scarcely less forbidding wall of thorn vines, as if danger was likely to come from that way.

Then again, Ryan reckoned, maybe it was. It wasn't like the Wild's end was some kind of magic fence to keep the muties and other unfriendly wildlife in. And these were unmistakably Second Chance sec men, so they presumably knew the Wild and its ways better than Ryan did for all his enforced familiarity.

The thoughts flickered lightning fast through his mind as he snap shot the squatting man. The marshal *oofed* in surprise then fell over.

The other man turned toward Ryan. His black eyes were wild in his bearded face as he tried to unsling his bolt-action longblaster. He got tangled up.

Ryan didn't care. He gave him a double tap, two shots through the sternum, barely the width of his little finger apart.

The first man started hollering, whether to raise the alarm or just plain in pain. He fumbled out a Beretta handblaster. Ryan shot him again. The sec man stopped making noise.

J.B. rushed past him with Ricky hard on his heels. "Cover me!" the Armorer said.

Ryan was taken by surprise, but he took advantage of the chance to drop the SIG's partially depleted magazine and insert a full one. Doc stepped up with a swirl of his long black coattails, his LeMat pointed at the brush beyond the clear space where the sec-man sentries had been.

Quickly, efficiently, J.B. and Ricky stripped the two marshals of their weapons and magazines.

While they were still looting the pair, Ryan heard crashing from the brush beyond. Hoarse voices shouted in confusion and alarm.

Without hesitation, or even looking up from his work, J.B. raised his Uzi on its long sling in his right hand and triggered a 3-round burst. Two more followed, one slightly left of the first one, one to the right.

Now men yelped in alarm. The noise stopped advancing and turned to a thrashing that sounded a lot like diving for cover any which way.

"Go," J.B. said to Ricky when they were done. He looked back at Ryan and Doc.

"You too. Find a place to hole up. If the sec men get too frisky I'll teach them better. I'll catch up with you."

"Right," Ryan said.

Ricky dithered. "But J.B.—"

Ryan took two long steps forward, grabbed him by a strap on the back of his backpack and started towing him bodily back the way they had come. After a brief moment's resistance the kid smartened up. He turned to run as fast as he could back along the cliff base.

"That cave we passed, mebbe a quarter mile back," Ryan said. "Right after we started out."

"Indeed," Doc said. He matched Ryan stride for stride with his long legs, barely breathing hard. "It offered an excellent stronghold from which to stand off the ruffians."

It did. It was one of the larger caves they'd looked into, wider than the entryway, which suggested to Ryan, anyway, that humans might have scooped it out. Doc assured them the geology, much less the time scale, was all wrong for a cave formation.

Better still, there was a roughly semicircular empty space in front of the entrance, with lots of nice rocks and clumps of scrub to screen the cave mouth.

From behind Ryan came the snarl of J.B.'s machine pistol. The one-eyed man kept running and never looked back.

"You have got to be shitting me."

Mildred's words seemed to affect her listeners like a bat to the foreheads. Eyes went wide; jaws went slack.

Her hands, like Krysty's, were tied in front of her by rough hemp rope. Securely, worse luck. Chafed wrists was the only outcome of her attempt to loosen the bonds and wriggle free. So she contented herself with sweeping the office with a gaze, which wasn't hard. It was a cramped, dusty, musty, cluttered little thing. That was part of what honestly surprised her.

"Language!" the fat, sweating man who stood behind the Judge finally managed to sputter. "Prisoners should show due respect for the power and majesty of this court."

"Respect?" Mildred echoed contemptuously.

She thought about spitting on the floor. By the looks of it, she wouldn't be the first. And some of them had been tobacco chewers, if the stains were any indication. But her daddy raised her to be better behaved than that. Or anyway, better behaved than these people.

"You claim you're restoring the United States of America," she said, "from a crappy, grimy little armpit of an office like this? With a greasy, quivering blubber-butt for a bailiff, and a clump of sec goons who smell like they haven't changed their pants in six weeks?"

"Mayor," the fat guy said. "I'm the mayor of Second Chance. I serve as honorary bailiff to His Honor—"

"Who's the biggest joke of all!" she flared, right at the Judge's thin, haggard, saggy face where he sat behind the desk drumming spider-leg fingers on the one clear spot among the papers. "Some old dude in a black bathrobe who claims to be a judge? *Please*. A delusional schizophrenic with paranoid visions of grandeur is more like it.

"I have *seen* the United States of America, gentlemen. I lived in it. I was raised in it. And let me tell you—the butt-pocket dictatorship you got here in the thicket is not the United States!"

For a moment she thought she had gone too far. Her origin in the twentieth century was usually kept a deep, dark secret, for her companions' safety as well as hers. While most of the hatred and rancor that persisted from the ruination of the world in the Big Nuke—which was fair enough, she thought, inasmuch as the bad effects also persisted—was concentrated on the whitecoats, politicians and generals who had produced the disaster, and the mutants who were one of its unfortunate legacies, there was plenty of ill will for plain old twentieth century folks as well. People these days reckoned they shared the blame for blowing up the world and screwing things up so royally.

They weren't wrong about that, either, Mildred thought.

But the fat mayor just smirked, and muttered to himself, "She says *we're* crazy." The Judge just gave a thin smile and drummed his fingers in pistol-shot ripples.

"Powerful talk," he said, in a stone-dry yet somehow fervent voice. "You might well give a thought to the position you find yourselves in, ladies."

"Position?" Krysty repeated.

Mildred glanced at the redhead, who stood at her side, similarly bound. She was beginning to be afraid she'd overplayed her hand—and by extension, her friend's.

But Krysty's strong yet finely structured face was set into a perfect mask of haughty disdain in the feeble light of the one lonely lantern that stank as if it ran on oil squeezed from the asses of syphilitic stickies. She tossed back her fire-red hair. Her flawless emerald eyes fixed Judge Santee with gigawatts of laser death stare.

"The *position* we are in is of helpless captives who are condemned in advance to the gallows," Krysty said. "Just like all the 'accused' who fall victim to the insanity you proclaim to be justice. If you fear so much to hear the truth from the likes of us, who are totally in your power, then you are nothing but the lowliest of cowards!"

Her words rang despite the muffling effects of the shelves of jumbled, crack-backed books. They were so sharp and strident that Mildred imagined she saw the air thicken with dust and mild their impact raised.

They almost raised her ire too. Powerless? she thought angrily. Speak for yourself, sister. I always have power, however small. Even if it's just to spit in the executioner's face as he fits the noose around my neck!

Then she reconsidered as she figured out what Krysty was doing. Defying the slimy bastards, sure. But also reassuring them that she and Mildred were helpless captives, good little victims who would give their captors no problem at all, which would give them the scope to unleash a world of hurt. With or without the help of their menfolk.

They'd done it all before, by themselves, when they had to.

These thoughts were still shooting through Mildred's mind when one of the sec men who had escorted them—Evrard, his name was, a long drink of water with jet-black hair and pale skin—stepped up and slapped Krysty's face.

Her head barely moved, though it was a full-palm blow whose impact cracked like a whip. She didn't even blink, but her eyes flared even more furiously than before above the red handprint glowing to life on her alabaster cheek.

"I'll chill you for that," she said quietly with absolute conviction.

Well, there goes the helpless act, Mildred thought. *C'est la* fucking *vie*.

"That was uncalled for, Marshal," Santee said in tones of brittle annoyance. "When you rise to abuse by vermin, you lower yourself to their level. Place yourself on report. Cutter Dan will deal with you himself when he returns from successfully completing his assignment."

As if realizing he'd screwed up big time, the sec man stepped hurriedly back into his place at the bookshelf-lined wall behind Santee. Now he braced to attention even though the Judge couldn't see him.

"Yes, Your Honor!" he snapped. Even in the bad light Mildred thought he'd gone a shade paler. And was perhaps showing a hint of green around the gills.

With another man of Santee's obvious age. Mildred figured the black-haired bastard would've been able to count on Santee forgetting by the time they were all out of the office and it was time to get back to the exacting business of counting his own fingers again. And maybe prying off his shoes to count his blackened, reeking toes as well.

Not Santee, Mildred knew. *He* probably remembered every little sight, real or imagined, from the time he was four.

"Very well," Santee said, sitting back. "Clearly you are aware of the nature and gravity of your crimes. Just as clearly you feel no remorse for them. So we need protract proceedings no further. I sentence you to death by hanging at a time to be determined by me."

Mildred looked at Krysty, who looked at her. The two women grinned.

"*There's* a surprise," Mildred said. "Anyway, we know you won't do anything to us until your bully boys bring our menfolk back. Providing they do, of course."

Judge Santee leaned forward. His smile was as wicked as anything Mildred had ever seen. And she'd seen her share of wickedness, before she was diagnosed with inoperable cancer back in her original first life, and many times over since she'd been thawed from her long, cold sleep.

"Oh, they will, Ms. Wyeth," he said. "They will. Cutter Dan is the best. Of all the coldhearts of the Deathlands, he was the coldest. Set a thief to catch a thief. It is why I recruited him first of all, to be my Chief Marshal, back when I was just setting out on my great work.

"And as for your time of execution—make no comforting assumptions about the time remaining to you, ladies. To use the term promiscuously, justice will be executed at the time justice decrees. Whether sooner or later, you have no way of knowing. So rest easy with the thought that you could be taken forth and placed in the noose at any time!"

He leaned back as if exhausted. Something in his manner suggested to Mildred he was eager for a cigarette in classic post-coital style.

"Now, get them out of my sight. And leave the office door open. The stink of their evil permeates the air!"

Evrard and his partner hustled forward to grab a woman apiece. Other sec men waited outside in the hall to help escort them to jail. There was no point struggling here, any more than there had been back in the clearing when the sec men suddenly came out of nowhere to surround them, especially not with Krysty's injured leg. Mildred had been able to browbeat their captors into freeing her hands so she could properly clean and dress the spear wound on the wag trip to Second Chance. All a show of resistance could be was a show, and it could only end with them being more exhausted and battered, and less fit to plot a way to bust loose and bring these self-righteous assholes' little psycho fairy castle crashing down around their hairy ears.

She didn't take Santee's threat of execution at any sudden random time seriously. He was too big a sadist not to wait to have the whole crew in his power before he started swinging them off the gallows, if for no other reasons than the happy hours he could spend calculating in which order he would make them watch their friends die, so as to inflict the maximum torment on the dwindling number of survivors.

He'll hang Ryan last, of course, she thought. And

Krysty next to last. Of course, it could be the other way around....

She pushed hard against the image that sprang into her mind, of the Judge deliberating here in his chambers, with his pants open and his necrotic old pecker in his hand....

Don't be too unkind, girl, she thought, as hard hands hustled them out the door. He did call you "young lady."

Chapter Twenty-Three

"Mind if I join you?"

The soft words didn't take Jak by surprise. Even well buzzed on a bellyful of Meg's best homebrew beer, his senses were keen enough to hear the kitchen girl approach.

Nor was his brain too fogged to appreciate the fact that she'd been making extra noise as she walked between the outbuildings where the shadows lay even deeper than the night. She was smart enough to want to avoid startling Jak at any cost, and yet she was always ready to let Jak feel her tongue's well-stropped edge whenever he showed any sign of underestimating her. That helped to focus his mind, booze or no.

He shook his head. He had come out here to stand awhile next to a storage shack, listen to the crickets and clear his spirit, even more than his mind. Jak liked the Last Resort well enough, but he just started feeling cramped and uncomfortable if he stayed between walls for too long a spell.

The albino needed to breathe outside air, even if it came in the form of a warm, dry wind carrying the unnatural taint of every vile mutie monster in the Wild, which teemed and oozed and slithered in a profusion he'd barely glimpsed. He just needed to breathe air that hadn't gotten filtered through two dozen sets of not triple-healthy lungs before reaching his. Or his nose.

She came up beside him. Chally, of course. She had on

an olive drab T-shirt that left a hand's breadth of her flat belly bare, shorts with the ends rolled up that emphasized the slim length of her legs. It was a usual work getup for her, but Jak appreciated the sight all the same. She looked good, if you actually bothered to *see* her.

Somehow, when she was working inside the gaudy, she managed not to be seen or heard or noticed. But whenever she came around Jak, she seemed somehow to make a point that he *did* notice her and not just become aware of her presence with his preternaturally sharp senses.

Chally put her back to the wall of the storage shack, resting her shoulders and rump against it. Then she joined him in looking up at the stars. She hadn't given him so much as a glance.

"You've been coming here for days, now," she said to the clear sky. "And I still don't know much about you."

"Not like talk much."

"That's a fact. Those're the most words I've heard you string together at one time since I met you, I'm pretty sure."

She looked at him then.

"So what's the deal, O-white-skinned-man-of-mystery?"

Jak grunted.

He intended that as refusal. She took it that way.

"Oh, well," she said lightly. "I *was* gonna spend my break with you. But I'm done playing around with somebody I don't know thing one about, beyond the not triple reassuring fact he can chill a deer with just a freaking knife. I've had the edge taken off by now. I can do without again for weeks. Months. *Years*. Done it before, and I can do it again. So, if you don't want the sweet thing anymore…."

She pushed off from the crude plank wall and started

walking back to the gaudy. She twitched her narrow hips as she did. It made her butt cheeks do fascinating things in the tan canvas shorts.

"No," he called after her. "Don't go."

The words came out of him like teeth to pliers, but he made himself say them.

She stopped and glanced back at him over her shoulder.

"What's this? You've started to rediscover the miracle of human speech?"

He blinked at her. He wasn't stupe. Nobody could live even as long as he had, the way he had, if he was a simp.

But she made him feel stupe, sometimes. It made him mad. But not double mad. Because he knew she didn't mean to do that, make him feel stupe. Somehow.

She went to stand beside him again. Right where she'd been, not looking at him. Not touching. But close enough he could feel her heat.

He started to talk, then. Haltingly, because that was the only way he knew how. He started by describing how he'd grown up in the Cajun country of the southern coast, on the run and fighting back against the stoneheart Baron Tourment, who'd chilled his family and driven him from his home.

Just naturally that led to him telling about meeting Ryan and the rest. How he was willing to fight Ryan himself, at first, to get to his enemy, and how Ryan and his companions helped him destroy the baron.

He faltered, then.

"That's…it," he said. "Ran with them years."

He felt ice-cold sober now, and hollow inside in a way he couldn't name.

"Bastard words," he said. "See how make feel?

"It's not the words," she said. "It's what you feel that makes you say them."

He looked at her, his eyes widening in alarm. Had he said that out loud? That kind of behavior could get a person chilled when he or she was creepy-crawling around the worst monsters the Deathlands had to offer. Animal, mutie and human.

"And congratulations," she added. "You're starting to communicate like a normal human being."

Jak frowned ferociously. He felt as if he ought to take offense.

He wasn't sure why, though, once he thought about it.

"Not get used," he said.

She laughed. "That's my boy! You have a wicked sense of humor, when you put your mind to it. Or, I reckon, when you *don't*. When you stop blocking it off, just let it run free."

He shrugged. Just because he'd let his tongue run wild for a spell there didn't mean he had to make a habit of it. Or intended to.

Mebbe should cut back on drinking, he thought. Like Meg says. Double funny she'd do that, running gaudy bar.

"So," Chally said, and she was looking at him now. "Seems like the story's just beginning. You started running with this Ryan Cawdor and his bunch. For years, right? And now you don't."

She stopped talking. After a moment he realized she'd asked a question without actually asking one. He nodded.

"It seems you must've been pretty tight with them," she said, "running with the same pack for so long. So, what happened? Why'd you suddenly up and cut loose from them?"

Jak frowned and ground his teeth. He was frustrated. He wanted to share it with her—to let the whole story out. But he couldn't.

It would leave him too open. Too vulnerable. He'd spent

his whole life fighting for all he was worth against that feeling.

Now he felt like he needed a drink. Many, many drinks.

"Too—many—rules," he finally gritted out.

"That's it?"

The albino nodded tautly. His stomach was knotting itself up. Mebbe better eat before drink more, he reminded himself. He sometimes just forgot to eat once he got a few beers in his belly. And he felt it in the morning, too, when he woke up both ravenously hungry and feeling like puking up all the food he hadn't even eaten.

She sighed theatrically and shook her head.

"Oh, well," she said. "I guess a girl's got to be satisfied with what she gets."

She reached up and touched his cheek. He actually shied away from the contact like a frightened horse, but she persisted, moving closer to gently stroke his cheek.

He decided to let her.

"Listen," she said. "I'm proud of you. I know it's not easy for you to talk. Like, *at all*. And you did. You opened up to me. At least some."

She kissed him on the cheek and stepped back, her eyes shining in the starlight.

"Seemed as if you needed to. Triple bad. And I reckon there's more where that came from. But you've done more than enough for one night. And I've got to get back to work."

She stepped back again and promptly skinned out of her T-shirt. The halter she wore beneath came off next. Her nipples stood out from her small, conical breasts, almost quivering with arousal.

She folded the shirt neatly and placed it on top of a nearby barrel. The halter went on top of it. Jak made a noise low in his throat.

"But not right away," she added. Chally opened her shorts and peeled them and her underpants down her skinny but shapely legs. She stepped daintily out of them without letting them touch the ground. She kept her battered sneakers on. The pants joined her other clothes on top of the barrel.

Then she turned, put her hands high up on the wall, bowed her belly forward as though she were stretching like a cat.

"But no reason we can't make the most of the time we've got left," she said. "If you feel like you're up to it...."

He showed her how up for it he was.

Chapter Twenty-Four

The sec man thought he was being prime sneaky, Ryan thought.

His eye focused through the scope of his Scout longblaster, he watched the man creep along behind where the Wild ended as if chopped off by an invisible blade. He was not so successful at the sneaking part.

Ryan lay screened by scrubby brown growth. It had started to get some green during the rains, but they were days gone by. The warm west wind that had blown more or less steadily since then had kept it dried out.

The morning was deceptively pleasant. The air was cool. A light breeze blew from the south; by midafternoon, Ryan knew, the warm wind would begin to blow out of the west again. The sky was brilliant blue brushed with high, thin, purple clouds.

The Wild was even more deceptive: a beautiful green blanket stretching as far as the eye could see, rippling gently to the breeze, streaked and swirled according to the odd linear growth pattern of the mutant thorn vines that made it up. It looked like the scenes of parks or the grounds of English manor houses that Ryan had looked at in predark magazines.

Nothing at all like the hell on Earth it was. Even by the standards of the hell around it.

Ryan, J.B., Doc and Ricky had been holed up here by the red clay wall for two days. They had water—that was the good news. It trickled down out of the cliffs in a number of different locations.

The not-so-good news was the food. There wasn't a lot of game within easy reach. They had some jerky, dried fruit, even a few self-heats. Plus they could live off their own fat for days, even if none of them had much anymore. Not even Ricky, who had started off a pudge and now was as trim as the rest of them from tramping all over the Deathlands.

The bad news? Everything else. They were well and truly trapped here. The dinos, as Ricky called the feathered muties, walled off the way to the west. A recce by Ryan and Doc had discovered that the fugitives weren't the only ones who could hole up in the natural cover at the base of the cliffs. The muties only showed themselves enough to let the humans know they were there. They respected their blasters too much.

But not enough to roll over and let them pass.

The companions already knew Cutter Dan had men guarding the way east along the cliffs, and the thicket had a large number of Second Chance sec men in it, too, like this incautious one who seemed to be trying to creep up to get a shot with his own longblaster at the defenders.

The so-called marshals had made a few tries at them. They'd left at least three of their number lying in the open as chills and hadn't tried any more.

Time was not on the side of Ryan and his friends. If nothing else, hunger would force the four to venture out. Or, more likely, try to bust out and die in a blaze of glory.

Ryan grunted at the thought. It was better than passively waiting for death and better than chilling yourself.

Or Cutter Dan could reach the end of his patience rope, say fuck it, and order a balls-to-the-wall attack. Especially if it was true he was pulling in reinforcements from somewhere. Faced with a massive assault, the trapped men would run out of ammo soon enough.

Worst of all, for all of them—Ryan and J.B. in particular—was the knowledge that their women were being held prisoner by the maniac Judge Santee. The certainty that the bastard would keep them alive and intact until he had captured the four men, or at least until Cutter Dan brought their heads back, wasn't so certain anymore. Obsessed as Santee was with watching people swing and inflicting the maximum psychological pain as a sort of dessert topping, the one thing that could be truly predicted about a lunatic was that he would be...unpredictable.

Sooner or later we're going to have to try to break out, Ryan thought. But put their heads together though they might, they so far hadn't been able to come up with a plan that seemed like anything but throwing their lives away. And the lives of Krysty and Mildred. Even J.B., that master of traps and tricks, kept drawing blanks.

Ryan frowned.

Nuke that kind of thinking, he thought. Something'll come up. It always does. That's one good thing about this fucked-up world: things are always changing in ways nobody can predict.

And if nothing does come up, no opportunities arise, they'd find a way to make them happen. Because that's what they did.

The one-eyed man had the rifle propped on his rolled-up coat. Instead of holding the foregrip as usual, his left hand rested across the buttstock. Now he used it to snug the weapon firmly against his shoulder while he drew a deep breath.

The sec man stopped, hunkered down. He looked left and right, and then, as if sensing he was being watched, which Ryan's own experience had proved again and again was a thing a man could actually do, he turned his face toward the cliffs. And slowly, reluctantly, he raised his head until he was staring right at Ryan.

"Say goodbye," Ryan growled. Then he caught and held his remaining breath and squeezed the trigger.

The longblaster bucked up. Ryan cycled the action and drew it back down. With an expert's touch he returned it to almost the exact position it had been when he fired.

The man's head was still centered in the reticule, but it had snapped back, and a pink cloud was still fanned out behind it. The cloud began to fall out of the air like fine rain as the sec man collapsed bonelessly.

"Can't let you boys get too complacent," Ryan said. He slithered backward out of position, tugging his coat with him. When he was down out of sight from below, he got up to a crouch and duck-walked off to another of the vantage points he and J.B. had scoped out.

Ryan and company couldn't afford to get complacent, either. They weren't the only ones in the Deathlands with scoped longblasters—or the skill to use them.

WITH NOTHING BETTER to do, Krysty and Mildred were sleeping away the early evening wait for the dinner that would be brought by their jailers. Then Krysty was wakened by the clatter of a key turning in the lock in the cell door.

She snapped instantly awake, fast enough that she kept herself from stirring. She continued to lie on her side on the straw mattress, pretending to be asleep.

Mildred happened to be lying on her side facing Krysty. The redhead saw her friend's eyes open just a slit. A slight nod told her Mildred knew she was awake, as well.

It wasn't their evening meal. The jailer usually banged with a truncheon on the bars in the window in the heavy wood door to warn them to stand back before opening it to set down their trays. This was something else.

As the door began to open, Krysty went ahead and swung her legs down to sit up. She didn't see any point in trying to play possum. The action caused a pain to shoot down the outside of her right thigh, which was bandaged beneath her jeans.

The door was flung wide abruptly, accompanied by the harsh call of, "Stand back or get beat down."

A woman was shoved through, struggling furiously, to sprawl on the concrete floor.

Krysty and Mildred jumped to their feet. A fresh mattress was tossed in, to land on top of the new arrival. She lay dazed, with her palms on the concrete and her body slightly raised.

"What's going on?" Krysty demanded.

A pale face sneered from beneath a shock of black hair. It was Evrard. They had already discovered that he had been told to stay in Second Chance rather than return to the hunt for Ryan and the others.

"Got somebody to keep you bitches company," he said. Evrard had at least another pair of burly sec men. Armed with clubs, backing him up. Krysty suspected at least a couple more were out of sight in the corridor. "Don't go getting too attached."

Laughing nastily, he closed and locked the door.

Mildred knelt beside the woman to help her up. "Let me get a look at you," she said.

But the woman shook her off. Or girl—she couldn't have been older than twenty. Krysty watched as she rose. She swayed, slightly. She steadied herself briefly with a hand on the shoulder of Mildred, who stood up with her. She nodded thanks to the healer, then marched to the door.

"You bastards!" she shouted out the little barred window. "Your time is coming! The people of Second Chance have had enough of your cruelty and lies! You can chill me, but you can't chill the truth!"

Mildred looked to Krysty and raised an eyebrow. "What's that mean, exactly?" she more mouthed than said.

Krysty shrugged. "Who knows? But she's certainly on a roll."

"You've trampled our faces in the mud for too long! And we're not going to take it any more! We're going to rise up and pull you down!"

At least a dozen other voices joined in. "Yeah! Pull you down! The day of reckoning is coming, you cold-heart bastards."

"Enough!" bellowed a voice that was way too loud and authoritative to come from Evrard.

"Shut your filthy traitorous yaps or we'll make you pay!" That definitely was Evrard.

"Don't let them silence you!" the woman screamed out the cell-door window.

Then she sprang back so rapidly she lost her balance. She would've fallen and given the back of her skull a nasty crack on the hard floor if Krysty hadn't stepped up and caught her. Krysty let her injured leg fold beneath her, but under control, easing the two down.

As she did, Krysty saw the end of a truncheon jab through the bars where their new cell-mate's face had been.

"Let her go!" the other prisoners were clamoring. "Let us go! Nuke Santee and his bullshit justice!"

"I said *enough!*" the bull-voiced man roared. The other prisoners were shocked into silence.

Before they could get started again, Evrard said, "Shut your filthy holes. And keep 'em shut or we'll drag a few of you taints out and string you up."

After a moment's shocked silence, a young man's voice said, "You wouldn't dare! Santee's asleep by now. Everybody knows he goes to bed at sunset. He'd make you swing for hanging anybody without him getting to watch, and you don't dare wake him up!"

The sec men laughed hoarsely.

"That shows what you know, gallows-bait," Evrard said. "You don't know the Judge, and that's a stone fact. He'd get up off his deathbed to watch a hanging at midnight in midwinter!"

That seemed to end the discussion. The newcomer collapsed onto the floor.

Mildred knelt by her again. "She's been roughed up pretty bad," she said, examining the woman, who now seemed stunned but was responding. "Something big must have gone down. From how we were treated, I'd say Santee doesn't like getting his play-toys smudged or bent. He wants them looking nice and neat when they're twisting in the wind."

"That may not be helping, Mildred."

"Sorry." Mildred helped the woman onto her mattress and got her laid down on her back. "My bedside manner always sucked. There're reasons I didn't go into practice but stuck to research, instead." Krysty wasn't sure it was a joke.

Using water from the big bucket they'd been provided and rags that were still clean, Krysty and Mildred got the blood wiped from under the woman's nose and got her generally refreshed. She sat up, smoothed her short, black hair away from her face, smiled at them, and nodded.

"Thanks," she said. "I'm Sharleez Down. My father was Sam Down. Used to work as boss millwright for that rich bastard Gein. Until Santee had him hanged for daring to try and beg for better treatment for the people of Second

Chance. Whom Santee and his cronies treat like animals. We'd be better off if we were actual slaves. They'd value us at least a little, then."

She was a good-looking young woman, Krysty thought. Brown skin, dark eyes. Medium height. Strong build without much extra. She was a bit too strong featured to be called pretty, but perhaps the passion that knotted her brow and turned her lips to near-white compression lines had something to do with that.

And also the black eyes and puffiness from having been beaten. At least she'd stopped bleeding.

"I'm Krysty Wroth," she said. "This is Mildred Wyeth. She's a skilled healer. You're in good hands."

"Thank you," Sharleez said. "Kindness to strangers isn't something you find everywhere these days."

"You just have to know where to look," Mildred said archly.

The young woman laughed, briefly but heartily. She had spirit, Krysty thought.

She looked around with her brows furrowed in puzzlement.

"When Santee told his goons to take me off to the cells I was expecting something, well…"

"Dirtier?" Mildred said.

"Yeah. Among other things. More bugs in the bedding. Less, well, *comfortable* bedding. That sort of thing."

"It's one of the nicest cells we've ever been in," Krysty said. "We get decent food and enough of it, and plenty of water for all kinds of needs."

Sharleez looked at her strangely.

"You two spend a lot of time in jail cells? I mean, you don't look the type."

Mildred chuckled. "Looks can be deceiving, girl. We've

been in some of the worst. And to tell the truth, plenty of gaudy-house rooms that were way worse than this."

Sharleez shook her head. "But why? Santee's such a harsh, cold man. No, not cold. Cruel. So why would he treat his condemned prisoners so well?"

"That," Mildred said. "We're his condemned prisoners."

"You've seen Santee's public executions," Krysty said.

Sharleez dropped her eyes. "Yes, I have. They try to make everyone attend. It's impossible to avoid all the time. And *all* his executions are public. My—my father's was an exception. There was no advance notice. It was a spur of the moment thing, apparently."

Krysty and Mildred sat in silence for a moment.

"Santee loves to put on a show," Mildred said. "He doesn't want to hang unsightly victims as part of his twisted morality play. You've noticed, haven't you?"

Sharleez frowned, then nodded. "I guess I have, yeah. I just haven't thought about…what that really meant. I just didn't want to think about Santee and his goons doing anything…nice."

Mildred snorted a laugh. "Nothing 'nice' about it, girl. He does it for him, not us."

"What brought you here?" Krysty asked. "Speaking out against your father's murder?"

"No," Sharleez said. "Although it would have. Because I was finding it harder and harder to hold my tongue in public. Even though I knew it was vital to our cause."

"Your cause?" Mildred asked.

"Freeing Second Chance from Santee's tyranny. I've been working secretly for that for months."

"I'm surprised you're not in worse shape, then," Krysty said.

"Oh, this?" Sharleez touched her face, then winced. "That happened when they were arresting us. I tried to make them shoot me, actually, but they used the other end of a longblaster on me, instead."

"They didn't interrogate you?" Mildred asked.

"Oh, sure. But they don't do physical stuff. That's not Santee's style—or even that bastard Cutter Dan's. They go in for intimidation, threats, psychological torture." She shrugged. "And the Judge doesn't want to damage his show pieces, just like you said."

"Who betrayed you?" Krysty asked.

Sharleez uttered a bitter laugh like a fox bark. "That obvious, huh? Rad-scum named Kreg Modeen. Thought he was the best. He was the worst, instead. He led the sec men right to us this afternoon. They chilled Andi and Jeth. Took me and two others prisoner."

She shook her head. "Wish I knew what they paid him."

"Mebbe the lives of his loved ones," Krysty said.

"Mebbe," Sharleez agreed. "But it doesn't let him off for what he's done. Not just to us. To Second Chance."

"What do you mean?" Krysty asked.

"See, that's the double shame of it. Triple. We were getting *so* close to being able to move. Lots of people in this ville are ready to act, whatever the risks. And they chopped the head off, all nice and neat. One cut."

"I'm surprised Santee didn't make an exception in his no-torture rule, then," Mildred said. "Get at all the juicy details. Make sure of nipping this rebellion in the bud."

"You don't understand how utterly arrogant the man is. He believes his own line of rad-waste. And he believes in the 'moral lessons' his murderous so-called justice teaches. The power to cow the people into submission."

She shrugged.

"And you know what? He's probably right. When they hang the three of us tomorrow morning, it'll probably put the whole resistance down. For months, mebbe years.

"So, you know, it's funny in a sad way that bastard said not to get too attached to me. It's not like you'll have time to."

Chapter Twenty-Five

Krysty looked at Mildred. "That settles it," she said. "It has to be tonight, then."

Mildred could hardly believe her ears. She tipped her head sideways toward the new arrival and rolled her eyes in her direction.

"Should we be discussing this sort of thing—you know?"

"Why not?" Krysty asked.

"Well, how much do we really know about our new friend here? Can we trust her? Why should we?"

"Why wouldn't we? We're condemned. She's condemned. We're all kind of in the same boat, here."

"But what if she reckons she can, like, trade information for freedom?"

"I'm right here, you know," Sharleez said stiffly.

"No offense, hon," Mildred said, "but we don't want to make the same mistake you did, that landed you here in our plush accommodations with us."

"What information could she or anybody else possibly hope to gain?" Krysty asked. "We already told them we have no idea where Jak went after we broke him free of the gallows. And the last we knew of the whereabouts of Ryan and the rest was when the marshals caught us. What would Santee plant an informer on us for? He probably knows more about where our menfolk are than we do."

Mildred sighed. "Just can't be too careful," she said, then realized that was just as lame as it sounded.

She realized Sharleez Down was staring from one to the other with saucer eyes.

"You're *them*," she breathed.

"By definition," Mildred said. "For appropriate values of 'them.'"

"The ones who broke their friend the albino kid free from the gallows!"

"Don't let him hear you call him 'kid,'" Mildred muttered. "He's a grown-ass man."

"The ones who defied Judge Santee and all his sec men, and lived to get away! The only ones ever. And put a scar on the face of his sec boss, Cutter Dan Sevier! You're— wait! Don't tell me! It was you two in the wag, all swaddled up like mourners? The ones who threw the smoke bombs!"

"Guilty," Mildred said. "In fairness to Judge Stick-It-Up-His-Ass, he doesn't only hang innocent people."

Suddenly Sharleez put her face in her hands and began to cry. She moaned and sobbed disconsolately. Her whole body shook.

Mildred and Krysty stared at her in astonishment. The physician would have been worried about the sudden outburst attracting the guards' attention. Except it probably wasn't exactly an unusual event here on Death Row.

"What?" she asked. "What did we do that's so much worse than you being sentenced to—that is, here."

Sharleez struggled visibly and eventually fought her emotions under control.

"Not you," she said, panting as if she'd run a mile with a mutie panther on her tail. "Me. Us. With you joining us the resistance's morale would shoot through the roof! You'd inspire everyone! But here, my friends and I are going to die tomorrow. And you will, too, whenever they catch your friends. So here you are, turning up when everything's hopeless—"

She spiraled promptly back into tears.

Krysty laid a strong, gentle hand on her shoulder.

"Listen to me, Sharleez," she said, pitching her voice low so it wouldn't carry. "You and your friends aren't going to die tomorrow. At least, not at the ends of nooses, and we aren't either."

Sharleez looked up, her face red, her eyes even puffier than the butt of the longblaster had left them.

"Are you crazy? We're locked in a cell with bars on the windows and an immovable door. We're not getting out of here ever again. Until they come to take us to the gallows."

"About that," Mildred said. "Not exactly."

Sharleez was so intrigued, or maybe shocked, that she snapped right out of her crying jag.

"What are you talking about?"

"Are you sure, though, Krysty?" Mildred asked, suddenly concerned. "You're still weak. Still healing."

"Well, I have healed," Krysty said. "Some. The rest has done us both a lot of good. And anyway, what am I saving myself for?

"Wait!" Sharleez said in alarm. "Don't throw your lives away over me! You just met me." She laughed. It had a savage edge to it—near crazy. "Listen to me talking like a simp. We're all doomed."

"Things just aren't that simple," Mildred said.

"And nobody's talking about sacrificing themselves," Krysty added. "Though there are costs involved."

"What about the boys, though?" Mildred asked.

Krysty laughed. "We can't just hang around helplessly waiting to be rescued, like screaming female hostages in some old Hollywood vid. Ryan and the rest will do what they can, when they can. They've got their own problems."

She grinned suddenly at Mildred.

"Anyway, it's not like this is the first time we've released ourselves on our own recognizance, is it? Anyway, much as I hate to admit it, I'm getting double bored."

"Me, too," Mildred said.

"So, it's decided?"

Mildred thought for a moment.

"Yeah. You heal fast. If you feel fit to fight, let's do it."

"Do what?" Sharleez said, almost imploringly.

Krysty looked at her. "I need to ask you to do something," she said, "that I really hate to ask."

"What?" Sharleez asked. "I'll do anything."

"Trust us."

"HEY, EVER'BODY! HEAR the latest news?"

Heads turned in the late-afternoon gloom inside the Last Resort's bar as the voice came booming in the door. Jak had just sat down at the bar proper.

It was Bobb, the ville drunk, a red-faced perpetually cheerful mess of a man, about the same height and general build as Meg but with lots more by way of gut spilling over his belt buckle. He had strands of hair so soaked in accumulated grease and grime their color was impossible to tell dangling from beneath an almost equally befouled trucker's cap.

Somehow he was always the first to know the latest gossip, whether from inside Esperance or from the Wild and surrounding Deathlands. Jak knew that despite his massive indifference to the subjects—along with most other human interactions—because whenever Bobb found out something juicy, he immediately trucked down to the Last Resort to tell everybody about it in his foghorn voice.

"You're going to tell us regardless, I expect," said Meg dourly, without looking up from where she was wiping down the bar with a rag. "So at least park your carcass and pay for a brew first."

He trundled in and sat a few stools down from Jak. He gave the albino a companionable smirk and nod. Whatever else you could say about him, he was a friendly drunk. And if he knew Jak was an albino instead of a mutie, it clearly made no difference to him either way.

Bobb's arrival meant there were now two patrons seated at the actual bar, although the gaudy had its usual late-afternoon crowd already, fifteen or twenty customers seated at the tables or benches along the walls. That included a trio of obvious coldhearts fresh in out of the Deathlands.

Jak kept those three always within the edges of his peripheral vision. Unlike the jovial local boozehound, they did seem to have some problems with Jak to judge by the hard looks they kept shooting his way.

There had been a lot of traffic coming in from the Deathlands to the north the last day or so, he'd overheard Elián telling Anthony. They mostly looked like hardcases.

The giant Osage bouncer, Bo, unspeaking and unsmiling as always, straightened from behind the bar with a bottle of brown fluid the hand-scrawled label called "whiski" in one ham hand. He was lending a hand tending bar, with the evening rush coming on. His still relatively clean apron made his scalp lock, the broad red stripe above his forehead and the matching red wedges painted beneath his piercing black eyes, look all the more unnerving.

"Of course," Bobb said, favoring the crowd with a big, broad smile, "I could tell my highly pressing and important news a lot more freely if I wet my whistle first."

Someone in the crowd had to have signaled they'd take the hint and buy for him, because Meg laid down her rag and started drawing a mug from a wood cask on a shelf. Jak didn't see. He was dividing his attention between the coldhearts and Bobb. Jak was not the sort to assume that, just because the drunkard looked completely harmless, he actually was.

Something about the man or his manner had Jak's nerves all standing on end, for sure.

Bo sensed it too. He stood like a statue, glaring out over the gaudy crowd with unfocused eyes. He made no move to offer the bottle to Jak, who had other things on his mind right now, anyway.

Bobb drained half the mug at a gulp.

"Ahh," he said, wiping foam from his beard, which was in about the same state as the hair hanging from beneath his cap. Or maybe worse, by way of food stains. "That hit the spot. So where was I? Oh, right. The big news.

"Well, I can tell you this. It's big. Remember those coldhearts who busted one of their gang off the Second Chance gallows mebbe a week ago, right from under Santee's pointy nose?"

That brought a general rumble of assent that made Jak's blood run cold and his skin creep even more than it had started to. He wondered how many here knew he was the one who escaped the gallows, as he tried desperately to keep his face and body language from showing how exactly he felt like a jack-lit deer, right now.

But nobody seemed to be paying Jak any attention. Their focus was Bobb.

"Well, the word has come down the pike that Cutter Dan and his men have the fugitives trapped. Right up against the base of the Red Wall. They been standing off the marshals so far, but he's put the word out that a big bonus would be paid for recruits reporting directly to him. And he's started hiring mercies off the Deathlands too."

The crowd went still. Dead still.

No stiller than Jak. It was as if the blood running

through his veins, already chilled by Bobb's opening words, had all pooled into his stomach and then congealed in a big, nauseating, icy clot.

"He's started to get 'em, too. Smart word says it's only a matter of a day or too before Cutter Dan goes in to smoke 'em out regardless. So anybody interested in earnin' a little extra jack best hustle their butts west down under the Wall, sign up while there's still openings."

He drained the rest of his mug and thumped it down on the bar with a sigh of satisfaction.

"Not as if they's anybody here'd piss on them Second Chance pukes if they was on fire, o' course."

That brought a chorus of surprisingly muted assent from the crowd. All except for the three coldhearts. As one they stood up and without a word headed for the exit.

"Don't hurry back, Dyson," Meg called. "You go sign up to play bullyboy for that blood drinker Santee, you won't be welcome here any more."

Their leader, a tall, shaved-headed man dressed in black leather, with the butt of a sawed-off double-barreled shotgun sticking up behind his left shoulder, stopped at the swing doors and turned back, a sneer on his long, scarred face.

"When we come back here as marshals," he said, "which we will, you won't have a choice about letting us in."

"Leave," Meg said firmly. "While you can still walk to do it."

He and his companions did. The rest of the bar uttered a collective sigh of relief and turned back to their drinking with even more serious interest than before.

"Still want this?"

It took a moment for the words, which sounded like an

iron cannonball rolling around in a rain barrel, to penetrate the roaring silence that seemed to surround Jak.

Bo was looking at him. Though the tanned-leather features were as impassive as ever beneath their paint, he was obviously pained. If anything, he liked talking even less than Jak did.

It came to Jak he'd been doing a power of it, the last few days. That seemed distant now, and receding fast.

He nodded convulsively. Bo twisted off the top and shoved the bottle across the bar to him.

Jak grabbed it with both hands like a drowning man thrown a driftwood log. He started to raise it to his lips.

Then he stopped. He held the bottle up before his eyes and just looked at it for a long moment. His heartbeat boomed in his ears like a giant tribal drum.

Slowly he upended the bottle and watched as the amber contents gurgled out and down onto the sawdust-covered floor.

The whole bar erupted in outraged babble. "Why, nuke your eyeballs, Whitey," a voice cried—whose he neither knew nor cared. "That's a crime against good whiskey!"

"Easy," Meg said, in a voice like her own heavy hand slapped down hard against her bar. "He paid for that whiskey. It's his privilege what to do with it."

Looking neither left nor right, Jak hopped down from the stool and stalked toward the hall where his rented room lay.

Chapter Twenty-Six

It was right around midnight, Mildred judged, when Krysty stirred on her pallet and sat up.

"Right," she said, stretching like a cat. "It's time."

Mildred sat up on her own straw mattress. She'd been pretending to sleep since the jailers had collected their dinner trays a couple of hours before. She was too keyed up to really sleep.

Sharleez sat against one wall with her knees drawn up. She was staring at Krysty like an old alley cat spying an eight-legged mutie rat the size of a Shetland pony. Mildred had seen those. Not a pretty sight.

But what seemed to be alarming the young Second Chance firebrand was the way Krysty's long red locks writhed around her shoulders like scarlet serpents. Krysty had really been asleep, if Mildred was any judge, but now that she was awake and ready to roll, she was feeling a few nerves of her own.

Mildred couldn't blame her any more than she could blame Sharleez, who had obviously just decided to assume her new cellmates were complete loonies and probably needed to be watched closely. But then, Mildred knew what Krysty was capable of.

And what it would cost her.

The redhead stood, rolled her hips and windmilled her arms to get the last kinks out. The straw-stuffed mattresses weren't *that* luxurious. Then she stalked to the cell door as noiselessly as a big cat and looked out the grille.

"No one in view," she said softly, turning back. "You ready, Mildred?"

The physician stood and stretched, too, bracing her hands on her hips and leaning her upper body back. She winced at the cracks and pops she heard. They sounded like a brisk little firefight a block away; she was half surprised it didn't bring the jailer right down on their necks.

But then, they probably got used to ignoring a wide variety of loud and unsettling noises.

"Yeah," she said, drawing out the word. "I'm sick of this joint. They forgot to leave a mint on my pillow when they turned the sheet down. Again."

Then she grinned. She'd thought Sharleez's dark eyes couldn't get any wider.

Turned out she was wrong.

The local woman stood. She looked apprehensive, then she shrugged. "You want me to attract the guard's attention or anything?"

Krysty shook her head. She seemed somehow businesslike and distracted, as if her attention was firmly focused but on something far away, which Mildred, at least, couldn't see.

"No need," she said, more briskly than usual. "Just stand there in that corner. Yes, by the front wall. Away from the door."

Sharleez looked puzzled, but obeyed. "And?" she asked.

"Stay there," Krysty said, "until we tell you to move."

Meanwhile Mildred had picked up her mattress and stood holding it in both hands just to the side of the door, as if preparing to step through.

"Remember what Krysty told you earlier," she said to Sharleez, "that she hated saying?"

"Uh, 'trust me'?"

"Yeah. Well, I hate saying it, too. So consider it in full effect until further notice."

Sharleez made a helpless little waggle of her hands and rolled her eyes.

Mildred nodded to Krysty. The redhead put her face up by the barred window in the stout cell door.

"Who's out there?" she asked. "Who's on guard?"

Mildred thought she heard a half-stifled noise of surprise, then an even less-stifled yawn.

"Who's that?" It was Evrard's voice.

Krysty smiled.

"It's one of you bitches in the Very Important Prisoner cell, isn't it?"

Krysty smiled wider.

"It sure is. Me. Krysty. The red-haired one. You're the tall, intriguing, handsome one with the dark hair, aren't you?"

Sharleez opened her mouth and made vomit-inducing gestures with her forefinger. Mildred wagged her own finger at the young woman and tried to look stern. Also not to crack up.

She realized that was, in part, a nervous reaction.

Nervous about what, girlfriend? she chided herself. We've done this sort of thing a dozen times.

But she knew that something could go wrong. Something could *always* go wrong.

"That's me," the sec man said, sounding as if he had taken a break to puff up his chest.

"Well, come over here," Krysty purred. "I got something to show you."

"What for?"

"I reckon if I treat you nice, mebbe you'll treat me nice."

"What good's that gonna do? You're still under sentence of death."

That surprised Mildred. She would have thought the black-haired marshal and his issues with women would have been well past the point of thinking with the big head.

Reminds me never to underestimate anybody, she told herself. Even jerks like Evrard.

"Well," Krysty said, drawing out the syllable. "Prisoners have been known to escape before."

"Not from—" He stopped.

Krysty was showing all her teeth now, but her expression no longer looked much like a smile.

"Sure, honey," he said. Mildred could hear his steps approaching the door. "If you treat me good enough, we might be able to work out something."

Krysty closed her eyes. She tipped her head slightly back and began to quietly chant a prayer to the Earth Mother. Nostrils flaring she drew a deep breath.

Her rib cage seemed to expand. The sec man's face appeared, framed in the little window. His black eyes opened wide as he saw the way Krysty's inhalation had pushed her generous breasts even more prominently to the fore.

"That's a good start," he said. "Show me what you got."

"Sure," Krysty said in an oddly deep tone. She reached up both hands, grabbed the bottom of the little window and heaved.

With a splintering crash, the whole door popped inward out of its frame.

Mildred crouched, ready to spring forward and toss the mattress over Evrard's head. But there was no need. The door buckled vertically right down the middle. The two halves were still stuck partially together, and Krysty thrust them back through the opening to slam the sec man in the face and drop him to the floor on his buttocks.

Krysty stepped through, pulling the broken halves the rest of the way apart and tossing them aside. Mildred followed right on her heels.

The marshal's nose was broken. His blood was shockingly bright against his blue-white skin, even in the low lamplight of the jail corridor. He was fumbling to get a handblaster out of his holster.

Krysty put both hands on top of his head and picked him up off the concrete floor as if he were a doll. He tried to scream. His face went red as she put on pressure. All he was able to do was emit a desperate squeal through his nose.

He kicked frantically, but without the focus to do more than bruise the redhead's shins. His hand came up with a Beretta M9, the military model. Mildred recognized that; she had learned a lot about various handblasters from J.B., though she had known a lot before she had met him.

She also knew that to do about this one. Dropping the mattress, she stepped forward, grabbed the pale, hairy wrist with one hand and the blaster muzzle with the other. Before he could manage to click off the annoyingly-placed safety, she torqued the weapon sharply toward her.

When a person did that, he or she could perform the move in such a way as to give the blaster-holder the option of just letting go and sparing himself having his finger broken by the trigger guard. Mildred listened to the bone snap with grim satisfaction.

A big brass ring of keys hung from Evrard's belt by a D-shaped carabiner with a straight gate. She snapped it free, then hurriedly plucked two reload mags from carriers on the belt.

She stepped back. *Well* back.

Evrard was flailing both hands helplessly at the arms like iron bars that held him by his head. His busted forefinger flapped ridiculously. His kicks were getting weaker, as if he couldn't breathe. He'd quit the thin keening sound and was making weird little grunts.

Then the muscles stood out on Krysty's forearms. The veins popped out. The sec man's face went white, and his eyes bulged out of their sockets.

His head burst like a watermelon dropped off a roof onto a sidewalk. With similarly messy explosion. Mildred was glad her intuition had led her to step back as far as she had.

"Sharleez," she called, softly and tautly, as the body fell to floor with the final firings of random neurons. "Come outside now."

She prayed the young woman had the sense and the presence of mind to do it, and also the fortitude not to hurl when she saw the mess Krysty had made of herself, the walls and floor, and not least, the Second Chance marshal.

When Sharleez stepped out of the cell a moment later, Mildred was holding the key ring stretched out toward her in her left hand and the Beretta stretched out in the right toward the door at the end of the corridor. The sec men had a squad room with half a dozen bunks toward the front of the jail. Mildred did not want any unpleasant surprises.

Sharleez had her lips clamped shut just as firmly when she looked up from the twitching chill on the floor to Mildred. But she was already reaching for the keys.

"Find your friends," Mildred commanded tersely. "Open the cell. Let them out. No questions."

Sharleez asked none. She took the keys, clutching them carefully in both hands, as if afraid they might suddenly try to wiggle free like a captive salamander, and stepped across the corridor to the door. She did try to avoid as much of the spilled blood and dough-colored brains as she could.

Mildred glanced at Krysty. Her friend still stood with eyes squeezed tightly shut. Her hands were clenched into fists.

Sharleez started sorting through the keys. Her hands were shaking so badly she kept losing her place and having to start over. Mildred tried not to roll her eyes.

The clock was ticking here. Krysty in this state was like a flare. She could burn like this for only a very short time, then she would abruptly burn out.

"This is real," Sharleez said, to the jingle of the keys on the ring and the impotent clunking when she finally got one stuck in the lock only to find it didn't do the deed. "This is happening. Not just some condemned-person fantasy run out of control. We're starting an avalanche here. We'll have to make our move in a day. Mebbe two. And what will we do without weapons?"

"You got weapons," Mildred said. It struck her as more productive than snapping at the young woman. "You just have to be aware of them."

"Against sec man blasters? We can't have blasters. The marshals can do spot checks anytime, with the penalties for refusing to let them on your premises the same as being caught with one!"

"Yeah, and let me guess what that penalty is. There are plenty of ways we can fight without blasters, and plenty of ways to get blasters. And now, we really do need to move this along...."

She was amazed that the guards in the front of the jail hadn't responded yet. Apparently they were used to random noises, even loud ones, coming from the cells at night. It couldn't possibly last, though.

"Got it!" Sharleez said. Mildred's knees almost gave way in relief as she heard the key turn and the lock open.

Sharleez yanked the door open so hard she almost fell

over backward. A man came out quickly, then stopped. He turned and threw up in the cell.

"Gross!" Mildred heard a woman exclaim from behind.

"Enough!" she snapped. She wondered why she had been bothering keeping her voice down; Krysty had made enough noise ripping that damn door down to wake the equestrian statue of Ulysses S. Grant a block away. "These all your friends?"

A woman was holding the shoulder of the stooped over puking man. Another man quickly slipped past them into the corridor.

"Those two in there," Sharleez said. "I know this one, too, but he's not one of us."

"What about us?" a voice called from another cell-door window. Others took up the cry in an increasingly desperate clamor.

Mildred had no idea why the sec men *still* hadn't checked on the commotion. She now suspected they just thought the prisoners had found some annoying new way to make noise and hoped Evrard could handle it so they wouldn't have to interrupt their sleep or their card games or whatever to come help out.

"Give him the keys," Mildred told Sharleez.

To the extra man, she said, "Open the other cells and let the prisoners out."

"Why should I?"

"Because a woman with a blaster told you to, dumb ass!"

"Do it, Ed," Sharleez said, pressing the ring decisively into one of his hands before he could bolt. "Or I swear on my father's grave I will hunt you down and make you sorry."

Ed took the keys and, still juggling the heavy ring, went as fast as he could to the next door down. Apparently he was even more terrified of Sharleez's vengeance than he was of a crazy black woman who'd just threatened to shoot him. Well, they already knew the young woman was a spitfire. It was time to see if they saw her as a leader.

Mildred looked at Krysty. She was still as rigid as an over-inflated tire and looked as likely to explode at any moment.

"Quickly," the redhead gritted.

Usually when she embodied the power of Gaia the Earth Mother Krysty did not talk. Mildred wasn't sure whether this was a good sign or not.

"Get your friends back in our cell," Mildred told Sharleez, "and stand the hell out of the way."

"But how will we get out?" the newly freed woman asked. She was a slight young woman with long, straight blond hair. She was helping to the steady the man, who had a bush of curly dark hair atop his head. He still wasn't too steady on his pins. "The front's swarming with armed sec men!"

"No problem," Mildred said. "If you do what I say *now.*"

Sharleez grabbed her female co-conspirator's wrist, and the blonde grabbed the arm of the woozy dude. Sharleez towed them back into the cell like a Mississippi tugboat with a couple of barges.

Krysty followed. She was walking stiff-legged now, like Frankenstein's monster in the movies. She was holding out against the exhaustion, the inevitable crash and burn that followed the burst of power and energy she expended after calling upon Gaia.

When the Gaia power ebbed, it took with it all of Krysty's strength, and even her consciousness. It left her completely helpless for a period of hours, sometimes as much as a day or more.

Hold out, Krysty, Mildred pleaded silently.

The door at the end of the hall was yanked open. "What

in the name of Satan's wide-open asshole is all this nukin'
noise ab—"

A short, stocky sec man with a dirty-blond neck beard
stopped midstep and midword as his eyes took in the utter
bloody chaos in the hall. They quickly focused on the hole
in the muzzle of the blaster Mildred had taken off his pal.

She shot him dead between the eyes. He dropped right
in the door. She heard startled exclamations from outside
and cranked off half a dozen more quick shots. It was a
waste of ammo, sure, but she wanted the sec men to flinch
and stayed flinched for a spell.

They wouldn't for long, regardless. But maybe long
enough.

"Mildred?" she heard Sharleez's voice tentatively say
as she bolted for the door. "Krysty? What—oh, my God!"

Mildred came around the door in time to see Krysty
grip the outer window and pull a four-foot-wide section
right out of the cinder-block wall.

She dropped the fragmenting section, which was taller
than she was, onto the ground in a cloud of its own dust
and lesser debris. Then she collapsed into the same cloud
as if she'd been shot through the brain.

"Krysty!" Sharleez screamed. She hadn't struck Mildred as the screamer type, but given the circumstances,
Mildred was willing to make allowances.

She risked a quick glance back down the hall. A white
face was poking around the jamb of the open door. Mildred
snapped a shot that way, but she deliberately aimed high
so as not to hit any of the yipping, frantic prisoners whom
Ed had dutifully released into the corridor and freedom.

"Good luck hanging on to it," Mildred murmured on
their behalf.

She strode toward the hole in the wall. Outside the street
was black. Judge Santee, or his favored plutocrats, appar-

ently didn't believe in wasting fuel on things like street lighting. Unless, presumably, there was a good old after-dark hanging-bee going on.

"Right," she said crisply to the three liberated resistance members, as if by adopting a businesslike, reasonable tone she could make them accept what they'd all just witnessed as reasonable. Or, at least, not freak right out.

Mildred bent over the now-unconscious Krysty. She was sprawled prone on the rubble, showing no more life or muscle tone than an empty burlap sack.

"Let's each grab an arm, and then Sharleez you guide us to the nearest safe place you can. *Now.*"

After a moment's hesitation, the three obeyed.

Chapter Twenty-Seven

Jak heard the door open.

Then he heard a soft footfall inside his small, neat room. Something was set down right beside the door.

He didn't look up or stir at all from where he lay facedown on the scratchy wool blanket covering his bed. He knew who it was. He had heard her coming down the hall.

"You're going," Chally said. It wasn't a question.

He sighed and pushed himself up. Then, turning, he swung his legs over the edge and sat up.

"Why say that?"

"You are, aren't, you?"

Jak looked down at his jeans.

"Why I go?"

"Because your friends are in danger."

"No friends."

"Yes, friends."

She came and sat down on the hardwood floor a few feet away, facing him with her knees drawn up. Her skin shone almost like metal in the light of the oil lamp.

"Listen," she said. "You're a lone wolf by nature, sure. You even told me your enemies called you the White Wolf when you were just a kid—when you've never even told me your real name. You grew up hunting solo because you had to. You had nobody else you could rely on when that baron took your family from you. No one you could trust. Except yourself.

"But a wolf's true nature is as a pack hunter. And you found yours. Found people you could trust. People who trusted you. You got a taste of pack life. Now you'll never feel complete without it."

He glared at her.

"What you know 'bout it?"

She shrugged. "Only what you've told me. And what I know about the world, from books and also from listening to people who've seen a lot more of it than I have."

Jak looked away. He was so angry right now he was honestly afraid of what he would do to her if he looked at her.

And that wasn't what he did. He didn't pretend to be a good man—scarcely thought of it, even less than Ryan and the others did. A person did what he had to to survive.

But a man didn't raise a hand against a friend unless survival hung on it. And maybe not then.

"You found friends," she said, and his shoulders hunched up. It was as if she could read his mind. He didn't like the feeling. "Real friends. You stayed by their sides for years, and they stayed by you. I don't know what happened out there, after they busted you off crazy man Santee's gallows. Yeah, we all figured that out really quick. Those of us here in the Last Resort, anyway. And, like Meg says, we got no use for the Judge and his stonehearts.

"Anyway. Something happened out there in the Wild. You split from them, but it wasn't big enough to break you apart forever."

He turned a glare on her, but she failed to wither beneath it.

"How know?" he asked, his voice barely more than a whisper.

"Because when you heard what was happening to them, you poured out the whiskey you paid for, the good stuff that Meg imports all the way from the Cumberland range, and you came straight here to lie down like you'd taken sick and haven't touched a drop to drink since you got here. So that means the news hit you hard. Way too hard for people you'd kicked the habit of caring about."

He looked down at his hands, flexed the fingers.

"Mebbe," he said, in what passed for a more normal tone with him.

She sighed heavily.

"Listen, Mr. White Wolf. One way or another, we're done now. It's over between us."

Jak frowned at her. Not because he was mad anymore. He didn't know what he felt, other than confused.

It was her turn not to look him in the eye. It struck him how rare that was, in the time they'd spent together. Usually her gaze was right up in his, challenging, teasing.

"I'm starting to feel afraid," she said. "Afraid I'll never feel complete without you. And that can't happen."

She looked back at him, her eyes shining with tears she refused to shed.

"I won't need you. I won't let myself need anybody. That's not a way to live. Not in this awful world we live in. But I reckon—not in any world, ever. Because if I need you, and feel I can't live without you, then I am weak and you are strong. And you can only feel contempt for me in my weakness, somewhere deep down in your soul."

She shook her head. "And I can only feel contempt for myself, which would come out as resentment against you, double sure. I've seen it happen, plenty of times. So either you've got to leave me, or I've got to leave you."

She stood up fast.

"If you stay here, you won't be the man I'm falling for, anyway. You'll just be another sopping-bar-rag loser who's afraid to live the life he was intended to!"

His eyes met hers.

"Yeah," he said. This time his voice was firm.

Chally sighed again. A shudder passed through her body. She shook her head once, quickly.

"Right. I knew that." She smoothed her short hair back away from her face. "We both knew that. I just needed to run my mouth until you decided to face the fact."

He stood up and started for the door. She stopped him with a hand to his chest, inside the open front of his dangerously sharp jacket.

"Not so fast, cowboy. I brought a few things for you."

"Things?"

She turned back and stooped to pick up a day pack she had set down by the door when she stepped inside.

He briefly regretted leaving Chally behind, but he had no strong emotional ties to her. She was a nice girl, and had saved his life, but she had just been a pleasant diversion. Jak knew that, even though the young woman had felt more.

Now he burned with the urgency to go. His companions needed his help. And he had to set things right with Ryan.

She straightened, turning, and handed it to him. Jak almost dropped it. It was heavier than it looked.

"Careful, there," she told him. "Don't want to drop that."

"What in?" he asked.

"Just a few things Meg and I threw together. Some pronghorn pemmican we made, to keep you going for a spell without having to take the time and energy to forage for food. Plus a few little things Meg picked up over the years. Things we're triple sure you'll find a use for. Or your friends will."

He opened the pack just a little and glanced inside. His eyebrows rose.

"Why?" he asked her.

"Well, for starters, Meg's taken something of a shine to you. I have too, mebbe a little.

"More to the point, you're going to go help your friends. That means you're going to hurt Cutter Dan and his stone-heart sec men. And that hurts Judge Santee. Did we mention we don't much care for them up here? You hurt them hard enough, they'll have to forget all about trying to strong-arm us and take us over. At least for a year or two."

She smiled.

"And I think you're just the man to hurt them that hard. You and your friends."

A slow grin spread across his face. He nodded, then slung the small pack over his back.

Chally stepped away from him. She tipped her head to one side and looked coyly at him from the corners of her big, dark eyes.

"You want—" she ran the back of a finger down between her breasts "—me one more time?"

He shook his head.

"Okay," she said, and stepped out of his way.

He went to the door and opened it.

"At least just tell me your name."

He looked at her.

"Jak," he said, and walked out the door.

"SHARLEEZ IS RIGHT," Alyssa, the blonde young woman, said to the circle of skeptical faces. "We have to act quickly. The Judge and his men will leave us no choice."

They were gathered in a well-preserved old house. It was one of the better ones in the generally sorry ville, with hardwood floors and a pitched roof that was patched enough to keep the rain out. It had clearly been lived in recently, and just as clearly was untenanted now. Mildred felt mild curiosity as to why. But she knew enough about life—and more to the point, death—in the Deathlands to really want to know.

Mildred, Alyssa, Krysty and Sharleez sat facing ten current and prospective resistance members. Some sat in wooden chairs or rusty folding metal ones. Others stood.

Most of them had dubious expressions on their faces.

"If the Judge's men move," asked an earnest man, who looked young despite the way his neat, dark hair was receding from his forehead, "what can we do about it? They hold the whip hand."

"Maybe not," Mildred said.

"Mebbe so," called a voice from the foyer. "In fact, we definitely do."

A tall man with a neat red beard and a red, white and blue armband on the sleeve of his blue, yellow and white plaid flannel shirt strode authoritatively into the room. Though he wore twin handblasters on his hips, he wasn't holding one.

The four Second Chance marshals who suddenly appeared to flank him in pairs sure were. Two held semiauto longblasters, two pump shotguns.

They had the plotters dead to rights.

Chapter Twenty-Eight

Mildred had jumped to her feet, as had Alyssa, Sharleez and several others. The new members of the circle had terrified looks on their faces.

"Look what we have here," another voice said from behind the squad leader. A sixth man stepped in beside him. He was a short, trim dude with round glasses and a sandy goatee. He also had a supercilious smirk and was shaking in his head in mock consternation.

"Some people never learn," he said. "Sharleez, Sharleez. Haven't you got it through your thick skull that justice always wins? Or at least, Judge Santee does."

"Kreg. You bastard," Sharleez almost spit.

"Round 'em up, boys," the squad leader ordered. "This'll keep the Judge happy for days, having this many assholes to swing off. And it'll bust the neck of this discontent bullshit for good and all."

The longblaster-armed quartet began to spread out around the room. The conspirators put up their hands. A couple wept openly.

"Sharleez, what have you done to us?" asked the man who'd been talking about the whip hand and who held it.

"That one," Red Beard said suddenly, pointing to Mildred. "With the beaded braids. She's one of the coldheart gang that masterminded the jailbreak."

He smirked at her.

"You won't be cheating the Judge's justice a third time,"

he said. "You're going from here right straight to the scaffold."

Mildred gave him her best defiant glare. It was all she could do under the circumstances. A sec man with a Mini-14 maneuvered to come up behind her chair.

"Yes, Sharleez, what have you done?" Kreg Modeen asked, shaking his head again. "Looks like you've gone and brought death and destruction on your little traitor pals."

"Looks to me as if you're the one doing that," the firebrand snarled.

He chuckled. "I knew you were naive, Sharleez," he said. "But I honestly never thought you'd be so triple stupe as not to warn the rest of your little wannabe-revolutionary friends to take care of me. Or at least avoid me. And look what happened. They led me right here. They actually *invited* me to this little seditious sit-down, can you imagine that?"

Sharleez smiled at him sweetly as a scattergun-armed sec man approached to restrain her.

"But I did warn them about, you, Kreg," she said.

He frowned uncomprehendingly.

"Nuke shit!" yelled the squad leader. "It's a trap!"

"No shit, Sherlock," Mildred said, and back-kicked the chair into the shins of the sec man behind her.

A trapdoor opened in the ceiling. Krysty dropped from the attic above. Her full 150 pounds of muscle and fury landed astride the shoulders of the red-bearded marshal and crumpled him to the floorboards.

Mildred stooped as she spun, grabbing up the hickory ax handle she'd stashed under her chair. The sec man behind her had doubled over at the sudden pain in his shins, the barrel of his blaster pointed at the floor.

Mildred wound up a baseball swing and smashed him

across the face with her ax handle. He staggered back, dropping the blaster.

She moved quickly to snatch it up. The sec man was still on his feet, clutching his bleeding face with one hand and moaning. Mildred hit him again one-handed, breaking his hand and dropping him. Then she let the club fall and turned to cover the room with the Ruger.

Krysty had her powerful thighs clamped tight on the sec squad leader's head. She rolled sideways forcefully. Mildred winced as she heard his neck snap.

She'd seen Krysty do that move before. It always got to her, actually made her neckbones ache in sympathy, though sympathy was the last thing a coldheart sec man piece of drek like that deserved.

Other people had appeared behind the other sec men, one from an ancient empty wardrobe, more from other doors into the room. Mildred saw a shotgun-armed sec man turn in time to catch the business end of an ax—this time complete with head—square in the side of his face. He went down with a scream and almost instantly began to strangle on his own blood.

Two of the would-be resistance types Sharleez, Alyssa and Mildred had been giving their pitch to had jumped the other shotgunner and were grappling with him. They'd already twisted the weapon so his finger wasn't on the trigger and the barrel was pointed toward the ceiling. Their moves could use work, the physician thought briefly, but they had good instincts.

The other rifleman was already down. Niles, the bushy-haired guy with the weak stomach they'd busted out with Alyssa, gave Mildred a thumbs-up with the hand that wasn't holding a bloody baseball bat.

Kreg Modeen stood staring in utter paralyzed shock...

until Sharleez stepped up to him and kicked him in the balls.

He doubled over. Krysty reared up behind him, her sentient hair waving around her head. She trapped his arms from behind in a double arm lock and yanked him upright.

He was groaning and dribbling thin oatmeal-like puke down his goatee. His glasses had been knocked askew.

Then he shrieked at a glass-shattering pitch as Sharleez, smiling horribly, stepped up and slit his throat. It was the swift dispatch of a traitor.

Mildred heard a scuffling behind her. Her heart jumped in her throat, and she looked hastily around.

Damn! she thought. Forgot to make sure the dude I clubbed was out for the count.

He was trying to push himself up out of the pool of blood that had flooded out of his head. The floor looked as if a bucket of blood had tipped over. With his other hand he was trying to get something out from behind his back, doubtless a weapon of some sort.

"Coldheart bastards," he gasped. "Set us...up."

"That's right, bunky boy. Ax?"

Ted, the sturdy Asian man who had finished the job he had started on the shotgun sec man, was standing across the room holding his ax and looking bemused beneath all the blood spatter. When Mildred held up her hand, he snapped out of it and tossed the ax to her.

She caught it with her left hand, ignoring the gore and clumps that clotted its head as some of it dropped onto her hand. She laid the longblaster at her feet and turned back to the wounded sec man.

His hand was coming from behind his back, fast. But Mildred was already in motion. She just had time to register that he'd pulled out a nasty little black Beretta hidie when her overhand chop split his skull clear to his maxillary bones.

Her stomach turned over when she heard a wet, heavy plop behind her. Once a person had heard someone's intestines fall onto a hardwood floor, the sound was never mistaken for anything else.

She wrenched the ax free. No need for a follow-up shot this time. She didn't need to be a medical professional—and at least semipro killer—to know he didn't need another. She stooped to scoop up the little handblaster that lay by his lifeless fingers.

Nice piece, she thought, turning it over in her hand. It was a Beretta Bobcat, Model 21, with a tip-up barrel. A classic. Too nicely made for a shit caliber like .25 ACP, she thought, which she quickly confirmed it was.

She stuck it in a pocket and picked the Ruger back up. Only then did she turn.

Mildred saw blood flood down the front of Kreg Modeen's shirt and his intestines were coiled on the floor. Sharleez had slit the man's throat, but it wasn't enough; she had also decided to eviscerate him.

Krysty dropped him to the floor, then she staggered back against a wall, and slid down to sit shaking her head wearily.

"All good?" Mildred asked.

"Sec men are all chills," Niles reported. This time the blood and even the guts didn't seem to faze him at all.

"Coming in," a voice called from the back of the house. A young woman appeared from the door to the kitchen.

"No one's watching the place from outside," she reported.

"Arrogant bastards," Mildred said.

"I told you," Sharleez replied. She was standing looking down at Modeen's corpse with an unreadable expression on her face.

Mildred guessed there was history there, a story Sharleez wasn't telling. But Mildred and Krysty would never find out, and it didn't matter now.

"Anybody hurt?" she asked the room.

"I don't think so," Alyssa said. She had picked herself up from diving to the floor and crawling under her chair when the balloon went up, which as far as Mildred was concerned was a perfectly serviceable response and spoke well of her. Nobody was sizing her up as the rough-and-tumble type.

That was why she was part of the bait of the trap, rather than the jaws.

Aside from her, Sharleez, Krysty, Niles and naturally Mildred, no one else who'd been at the confab had a clue about what was going down. A couple of people huddled on the floor, moaning and weeping. Another guy stood by the wall shaking his head and muttering, "So much blood...." over and over again.

But there were the two, a young man and a young woman, who had successfully disarmed the other scattergun sec man and gotten him to the floor. Somebody had cut his throat for him, too, Mildred noted dispassionately. The paunchy, balding, meek-looking middle-aged man who had brained the other rifleman with a heavy wooden chair then beat him to death, now sat backward in it over his victim, slumped in physical and probably emotional exhaustion.

Well, Sharleez, Krysty and I have got ourselves at least a few more front-line fighters, she thought. Along with the ones who helped spring the ambush. That's a start, anyway.

"Strip the bodies of anything valuable," Sharleez commanded. She sounded as brisk and businesslike as if she'd gone to grad school for this sort of thing. She was currently kneeling to clean her Bowie knife, using the shirt of the sec-squad leader whose neck Krysty had broken. "There're a couple handcarts in the alley out back. Niles and Ted will show you where. Load the sec men into them and cover 'em with the old blankets out there. We'll wheel them into the Wild and dump them for the coyotes and the mutie centipedes."

She didn't specify who was to do what, other than the bushy-haired kid and the Asian-looking man who were to show them where to take the bodies. But several of them immediately got busy tossing the fallen sec men. Amazingly, one of the women who'd collapsed stopped crying her guts out, got up off the floor and got to rifling the pockets of the man Ted had axed like a pro.

"What about that one?" asked the older man over the back of his chair. He nodded his balding head at Kreg Modeen's eviscerated husk.

Sharleez stood up and sneered. "Leave him. Mebbe when they find this place they'll think all the blood came from him. If not..." She shrugged.

Ice cold, Mildred thought, not altogether approvingly. Well, looks as if the long-suffering citizens have got themselves a true coup leader. Whether that's good for the ville in the long run or not is...not our problem.

She walked over to Krysty, who was still sitting by the wall, looking dazed.

"How you doing, hon?" she asked. "Fit to fight?"

Krysty looked up at her and smiled weakly. "No," she said, taking hold of the forearm Mildred stretched to help her up. She did most of the work to stand, which was a good thing, since Mildred could never have lifted her with just one arm. "But it looks like I'll live."

Mildred lifted her friend's arm over one shoulder to help prop her up. Then she smiled around the slaughterhouse the meeting room had so abruptly turned into.

"And that, boys and girls," she announced, "is how you get blasters when you don't have them."

"They're not gonna fall for that trick again," Ted called from the direction of the back door.

"They won't have to," Sharleez said. "Now, let's get out of here before someone comes looking for their lost little lambs and sees us."

Chapter Twenty-Nine

Ryan snapped awake to a short, low whistle that might have been a birdcall.

It wasn't. He already knew that. He opened his eye to see J.B. hunkered down a few feet away, just enough to one side of the cave mouth to avoid being silhouetted against the mauve sunset light.

The one-eyed man sat up scratching his head. The others had insisted he take a break and catch some sleep. He'd resisted, even though he was the one always harping about how missing sleep when you didn't have to was as good as loading bullets in your enemies' blasters. Trader taught him that.

And the others had been right. Even two hours did him a lot of good.

If all that was left was to go out fighting—and it looked that way—he wanted to give it his all and make sure he took as many of the bastards with him as possible on the last train west.

"What'd I miss?"

"Nothing much," J.B. said. "A bunch of movement down there in the weeds. No doubt about it. Cutter Dan's pulling in a load of reinforcements from somewhere."

J.B. paused to glance out. Just smart habit, checking surroundings, especially entries and exits. All that was visible was the purple sky and a few puffy orange and pink clouds.

"Ricky dropped a couple scouts sneaking around. Clean head shots, both times. They're scoping out the most-protected lines of attack."

Ryan grunted a brief laugh. "Didn't find them, then."

"Not those two."

Ryan picked up his Scout and stood. "Time to go spell the kid, I reckon. Doc, wake up."

The old man stretched and yawned where he lay on his coat on the hard-packed clay floor. "Morning already? How time flies when I lie beside you, Emily, my love."

Ryan shook his head. His jaw clenched slightly as he looked away. Sometimes Doc wandered away through the swirling, chaotic mists of his memory, reliving the nightmare of his captivity in the hands of a sadistic baron, or the equally heartless whitecoats of Operation Chronos or, as now, the lost, loving family the whitecoats had ripped him away from....

It didn't matter, Ryan told himself. The old man was just waking up. And when the bullets started to crack past their ears, he always snapped back to the here and now right sharp.

If he didn't, well, it probably didn't matter much in the long run.

Ryan stepped out into the twilight. The west wind blew fairly strong, warm and dry. It smelled of the lush growth of the Wild. It carried a strange tang that served to remind him that the pretty, swirly green blanket down there was anything but inviting and anything but natural. As if a reminder were needed.

Suddenly bullets were striking dust and chips off the rocks at the front of the little ledge in front of the cave. They howled as they ricocheted past Ryan's ears.

Even though the angle was plainly wrong for any to hit

him, Ryan flung himself face-first in the dirt. J.B. joined him, as Doc did a moment later.

Ryan crawled forward to where Ricky lay with his back against a red rock, clutching his DeLisle to his chest like a teddy bear.

The burst stopped. Ryan risked a quick look over cover.

He saw what he expected to see: nothing. Just the slope below, dotted with rocks and brush and carved with little channels by the water leaking perpetually out of the base of the Wall, and a ways off the blank edge of the Wild, itself as sharp as a wall.

"They got themselves some serious ordnance," Ryan said.

"Sounds like an automatic rifle," J.B. replied. "Not a machine gun. Or even a BAR."

He frowned as he thought about it. "I'm thinking G3 by the sound. Dark night, I hate those German longblasters. Got a way sharper recoil than a 7.62 mm has any right to have. Only nastier piece I ever shot in that class was a Remington 742 semiauto carbine. And that bastard was a full-on .30-06."

Ryan scratched his cheek. The hair on his cheeks was starting to move past the stubble stage into outright beard territory. He'd had other things on his mind than shaving the last day or two.

"They're sending us a message," he said.

"So what is it a preface to?" asked Doc, who'd crawled up alongside the others.

"Glad you could join us," J.B. said with a grin.

"Cawdor!" The voice boomed out from below, and echoed along the cliff face. "I know you hear me. Answer!"

"Cutter Dan," J.B. said. "Shoulda seen that coming."

"I hear you," Ryan yelled back. He did not poke his head up. He was not that stupe. "You ready to surrender?"

"You mean you're offering?"

Ryan barked a laugh. "I mean you. We got you and your blood drinkers right where we want you."

A moment passed, then Cutter Dan laughed. He had a pretty fair volume on that, too.

"Keep telling yourself that. You got until sunup. You can decide to do the right thing, save yourselves a mess of pain and worrying and messy dying, and just give yourselves up to face justice. If you don't, I got a hundred men surrounding you now, all of 'em armed for bear and hungering for a share of the bounty on your varmint hides!"

"KRYSTY."

The red-haired woman stirred. She was awake now, but her body was reluctant to leave the bed in the steeple of what had been a predark church. Not because it was so comfortable, but because she was still so exhausted, even after sleeping most of the previous day.

She sat up reluctantly. "What is it?" she asked, brushing the hair back off her face and looking out the window. The dark gray sky was clear. The sound of crickets came in through the open window.

That reassured her, in a way. The former church, and current resistance safe house, lay outside the main part of Second Chance. Much of the ville did, which accounted for its housing a larger population than Krysty had expected from the generally sorry straggle of buildings they'd seen when they freed Jak.

"Got trouble," Mildred said. She stood silhouetted in the doorway.

"Nobody's about to attack us, though, right?" she said.

"I'd let you know. But we need to get you back down-stairs fast."

"What's the rush?" Krysty asked, standing slowly and stretching.

"To talk Sharleez and the other resistance types down off the ledge."

Mildred wouldn't explain as she led Krysty down the stairs by candlelight. "So what'd I miss sleeping all day?" she asked.

"Just what you thought," Mildred said. "Nothing. But Sharleez and her core group have been sending out feelers all day, trying to find out how much actual support they can muster when the shit hits the fan. That and arguing strategy. Watch the step, there, it's loose."

Krysty hesitated just before they reached the landing and the stair switched back. "Thanks."

"One good thing is, we're not getting too much of the usual 'can't we just get along' crap. Especially since that trick of yours last night got pulled off so brilliantly. Now that they helped chilled five sec men—and one lousy snitch—all without getting anybody on our side more than mildly dinged, most of the people we were finding such a hard sell have turned into aspiring blood drinkers. Now they know the marshals can be beaten."

"We got lucky," Krysty said.

"Yeah. You know that they say it's best to be lucky *and* good. And we're going to need to be both, starting right about now."

"Why, Mildred? Why won't you just tell me?"

They'd reached the bottom of the stairs. Mildred led them out into the center part of the church, where a few pews that hadn't been salvaged for lumber actually re-mained. Krysty thought she'd read they called that part the nave.

"Because I thought it'd be easier to just let them," she said. "That way you don't have to listen to it twice. And believe me, they're going to want to tell you *all about* it themselves."

A clump of people stood talking in low but clearly excited voices in the middle of the open space. It was dark except for the light streaming in the windows and the open door.

A man's voice rose above the barely suppressed clamor. "But clearly, it's all over now!" he exclaimed. "We're beaten. This ends it. The whole thing!"

"For crap's sake, Quent!" a woman hissed in exasperation. "Keep your voice down, will you?"

"What difference does it make, Candace?" Quent said, still too loud. "If there are any sec men close enough to hear me, that means they're already surrounding us!"

He stopped and looked around. By the pallor on his face, already drained of color by the faint light, and the size of his eyes, Krysty judged he had succeeded in spooking himself.

"What's going on?" she asked calmly.

Everybody turned to look at her.

"Thank goodness you're here," Sharleez said. She hurried over to the two women.

"We need to be either figuring out the best way to make a deal," Quent said, his voice rising more shrill and strident than before, "or running away as fast as we can! It's *over,* people!"

Mildred stepped up to him. He was half a head taller, but she stood almost touching him and tipped her head back.

"Shut it," she said in a low, deadly voice. "Or I'll put my fist in it."

Despite Quent's height advantage, Mildred looked solid

enough—and angry enough—to snap him like a twig.
Evidently Quent thought so, too. He shut his mouth and
hunched his head down between his shoulders like a turtle
regretting that it had forgotten to wear its shell.

Krysty nodded. "Just tell me, simply and quietly, what
happened, please."

She really didn't have any standing with these people,
except as mysterious possible liberator. And maybe *that
red-headed witch,* according to the people whom she'd
helped break out of jail the night before last. She trusted
those stories had been written off as overwrought exag-
gerations.

That didn't leave her with much to back up her authority. But Sharleez, by far the dominant personality Krysty
had seen in the group, stood with her. So she reckoned
calm, confident command was the tone most likely to do
some good.

Several people started talking at once. Sharleez held
up her hand. The voices cut off.

Quent frowned behind his glasses and shifted his
weight from foot to foot. Mildred gave him her most furious glare. He shuffled right to the back of the pack and
tried hard to look inconspicuous.

"It's Santee," Sharleez said. "Of course. He's made his
response. He had his marshals round up twenty citizens
of the ville at random. He's holding them hostage."

"He says he's going to hang them!" a woman whose
voice Krysty didn't recognize said. Her voice started to
rise. Her eyes got bigger and she stopped talking.

"He says we have until dawn tomorrow to turn ourselves in," Sharleez said. "Then he'll hang four of them.
If we haven't surrendered, half an hour later he'll hang
four more. And so on."

"What happens if he runs out of hostages?" Mildred asked. "I never got that part."

Sharleez's brow knotted like a fist. She was clearly having trouble holding her rage in check. But she was, which Krysty felt was promising.

"Then he'll have his sec men round up more," she said through clenched teeth.

Krysty looked around the six or seven others gathered inside the former church. She saw lots of glints of starlight on eyeballs and postures of defeat or near terror.

"And who exactly does he demand give themselves up?" she asked.

"You and Mildred," Sharleez said. "Alyssa, Niles. Me. But also a bunch of unspecified people Cutter Dan's deputy marshal, Suazo, calls 'ringleaders.'"

"It wasn't *exactly* Suazo," said a young woman who stood to one side diffidently. Obviously she didn't feel included in this group. There seemed to be class divisions within the resistance, too.

As usual.

"He mostly stood there all puffed up and trying to look important, while the proclamation was delivered by that fat bastard, Mayor Toogood."

"This is Norah," Sharleez said. "She's the one who brought the word, just now. She was there."

"I saw a fat guy who sat through the commotion last time we were here. Is that him?" Mildred asked.

"Uh-huh."

"He's the mayor? What's he doing playing ring announcer for Judge Santee's favorite spectator sport?"

"He likes keeping himself in the public eye," one of the men said. His voice was deeper than Quent's, as well as calmer. "Just plain likes attention."

"And he's ambitious," Sharleez said. "He's the least

well-off of the four—uh, make that three, now—rich folk who run Second Chance along with Santee. So I guess he's trying to court popularity."

"While telling the ville folks all about why the Judge is about to hang their friends and loved ones," Mildred said. "That ought to go over well."

"So, to start with," Krysty said, "you've got an open-ended threat. Looks to me as if the Judge has granted himself unlimited license to just go on hanging innocent townspeople until he decides every malcontent in Second Chance has turned herself or himself in."

The others looked at her as if they hadn't even thought of that. For people living under such a heavy-handed, brutal regime, the ville's citizens were not good at the whole conspiracy thing.

That was not her and Mildred's problem. Krysty felt bad that they were using the ville folk, but it didn't mean either of them would stop.

They might help the oppressed citizens win at least a shot at a better future or bring them unqualified disaster. Either way, as long as they and the other companion got out of it alive, they'd all sooner or later just shake the dust of the place from their heels, and never look back.

It wasn't pleasant; it was survival. It always was about survival.

"Please," Quent said, overcome by emotion. He did keep his voice down this time. "You have to understand. We can't do this. Santee has won. It's checkmate, game over."

"Really?" Mildred said. "You planning on turning yourself in, Quent?"

"Well, let us say I am not the most prominent figure in our underground freedom movement."

"Not for lack of you telling everybody how you ought to be in charge all the time," Candace stated.

"Please," Sharleez said. The commotion the group was starting to generate again died just like that.

The young woman was speaking to Krysty. "What *can* we do? I got into this to save the people of Second Chance from Santee's butchery, not to speed up how fast he hangs them."

"We have two choices," Krysty said. "One, we can all give ourselves up like good little boys and girls, and spend the rest of our short, unhappy lives wondering who's going to the gallows next."

That produced a leaden silence from the entire group, including Quent.

"And, of course, trusting Santee to keep his word."

She let that sink in. But only for a moment. "Or we can realize that we have nothing to lose."

"What do you mean?" Quent asked, getting loud again. He *oofed* as someone elbowed him in the ribs.

"She means that we're as good as dead already," Sharleez said in a flat, hard voice. "Isn't that right?"

"Yes," Krysty agreed. "So, given that fact, it couldn't be clearer what we need to do."

"Don't leave us hanging," the deeper-voiced man said. "To use an unfortunate term. What do we do?"

She smiled brightly around at them all.

"Attack."

"WHAT TIME IS IT?"

Yawning, rubbing sleep from his eyes with his left hand, Ricky lumbered out of the red-clay cave. His right hand held his DeLisle. He might be the youngest of the group, but he was still going to show that he belonged with these people.

That meant being ready for action at any time. No matter what the circumstances.

A low fire of dry brush crackled in the center of the ledge before the cave. It was positioned where nobody could see its glow from below. The only higher vantage was at the top of the cliffs, and if Ryan and J.B. weren't concerned about anybody spotting it from up there, neither was Ricky.

The two men sat on either side of it. At the fringes of the wan, yellow light the campfire cast, Ricky could see Doc's long legs sticking back from where he lay keeping watch at the edge. The soles of his boots were nearly worn through, and his right heel was in bad need of repair.

Ricky saw the white-haired head raise up.

"Judging by the position of the Big Dipper," he said, "and the time of year, I surmise it is approximately two in the morning."

J.B. looked at him and grinned. He had his M-4000 taken apart and was cleaning it.

"You got a place to be, boy?" he asked.

Ricky walked over and hunkered down by the fire. He shook his head.

"So, what's the plan?" Ricky asked, trying to sound chipper.

"Plan?" J.B. repeated.

Ryan just shook his head. He had his knees drawn up and sat staring between them at the fire.

"They got us locked up triple good here," J.B. said. "Try as we might, we haven't figured a way out of this one yet."

He shrugged and began putting the blaster back together.

"So, are we going to try to break out?" Ricky asked.

"Got a prime defensive position here," J.B. said. "We figure we can chill more of the bastards by lying up under cover and making them come to us. Of course, if you're too impatient to get on with dying and all, you can just hop on down and charge them, single-handed, like." He shook his head. "Not likely to make a whole lot of difference, one way or another."

Ricky sighed and hung his head. For a fact, he was almost tempted to follow the Armorer's advice. The prospect of living sweating out the hours left until dawn, second by grinding second, terrified him far more than getting shot to pieces by Cutter Dan and his horde.

"So, you reckon he'll really wait for daylight?" he asked.

Ryan snorted. "No chance in hell," he said. "He's giving us a chance to get nervous and call the whole thing off, 'cause that'll be the cheapest solution for him. But once he decides we're not coming down the hill with our hands up, he'll rush us, hope to catch us sleeping."

"So—"

And suddenly, without the least bit of warning, there was a fourth man standing at the little fire.

Ricky brought up his longblaster to shoot.

Chapter Thirty

"What the nuke took you so long?" Ryan asked. He didn't stir from where he was sitting.

Jak opened his mouth and gave that silent wolf laugh of his.

J.B. got up, though. He walked over and solemnly and without a word shook hands with the white-haired young man.

"By the Three Kennedys!" Doc exclaimed. He started to climb up from his lookout position. "Could it be—"

"Pipe down, Doc," Ryan said. "Hold your position until relieved."

"But is it true? The prodigal son returns?"

"Yeah."

Ricky couldn't contain himself. He ran up and caught Jak in a big bear hug. Ryan was pleased he had the presence of mind to grab him low and not slice his hands to shit on all the weird sharp stuff Jak had sewed to his jacket. Jak took it pretty well. He went rigid but didn't freak out and try to knife Ricky or bust free or anything. He even managed to flap his hands feebly against Ricky's sides a couple times.

So, basically, he was triple happy to see Ricky, too.

"How you been keeping yourself, Jak?" J.B. asked, as Ricky pulled back and then, realizing what he'd done, slunk away.

The kid didn't have good impulse control yet, which

didn't stop him from overreacting when he realized he'd acted impulsively again.

"Busy," Jak said.

Ryan noticed he had a gleam in his ruby-red eyes that wasn't just the feeble glow of the fire. And that the pack he wore on his back, though it had a largish satchel strapped to the outside of it, was still appreciably smaller than the full-sized backpack he, like the others, carried his possessions and equipment in.

Now the albino unslung the pack and squatted to lay it on the ground, ceremoniously, at J.B.'s feet.

"Time get busy," he said, pointing a white finger at the Armorer's chest. "Brought present."

"You did, did you?' Reflexively J.B. glanced at Ryan.

"Go on," Ryan urged. "Open it."

J.B. leaned forward, opened the day pack a fraction and peeked inside. Suddenly his face lit up. He nodded slowly.

"Yeah," he said. He raised his head and looked at Ryan. "Reckon we can put this stuff to good use, at that."

"How long till dawn?" Cutter Dan asked.

He paced restlessly across the mostly level ground of his camp a quarter mile east of the area where their targets had holed up. He wanted to have a base that was safely out of sight and earshot of the fugitives, not merely out of blaster range. It gave him more scope to act without tipping his hand.

A handful of his lieutenants sat around several low campfires drinking coffee from metal mugs. Others came and went from the caves and tents that he and the thirty-odd men under his command slept in. He paid them little attention. He was constantly scanning the night with his eyes and other senses, constantly seeking some hint as to what his enemies were doing or information that might give him some advantage.

Cutter Dan was the first to admit he had no idea what that would be. That was one of the reasons he had kept his vigil all night long. He would only know it if he saw it—or heard, or sniffed or felt it.

That, and he wanted to be as alert as possible in case his spies or the seventy or so men he had stationed just inside the Wild reported some breakout attempt or other unusual activity by their quarry. You could never trust a man like Ryan Cawdor to simply stay put and meekly wait to die.

Old Pete had emerged from a tent a few minutes before and now sat wrapped in a blanket, drinking coffee. His nephew, Mort, squatted silently nearby.

"'Bout an hour," the wrinklie Indian said without looking up. "Hair more, mebbe."

Cutter Dan didn't bother asking him how he knew. He simply accepted it. The old Choctaw had proved steady and reliable throughout this whole manhunt. Anyway, that was what he had hired an Indian for in the first place, to know shit like that.

The chief marshal nodded decisively.

"Ace on the line," he said, turning to the nearest fire. "Scovul."

His lieutenant, who had returned from Second Chance, looked through the steam rising from the mug of coffee he'd just drawn from the big pot on the fire. "Sir."

"Get the men up. I want 'em ready to move in ten minutes."

"Yes, sir," Scovul said. His black face was stone, but the way he turned the mug upside down and emptied it between his boots where he squatted spoke eloquently of his disgust. Ah, well, when a man took on the duties of a

U.S. Marshal, as defined by Judge Santee and, of course, Cutter Dan, he agreed to take the bad with the good.

"Sir?" Belusky asked in surprise. "But you gave the coldhearts till dawn to surrender."

Cutter Dan smiled benignly. The scar down the left side of his face only tugged a little, at the bottom near the end of his mouth.

"I lied."

THE SKY WAS still black and full of stars as Cutter Dan made his way west along the foot of the red clay wall. The west wind blowing in their faces carried the slightest tang of smoke, confirming what he already knew: that his prey was waiting for him just a couple hundred yards ahead.

From somewhere in the long line behind him he heard somebody curse. At least the stupe bastard muffled it. Cutter Dan had his detachment moving in single file in order to hug the cliff as tightly as possible. He wanted to maximize their cover and minimize their chance of being spotted in case the coldhearts had set a scout out this way. The footing was irregular and treacherous, especially in the dark. But his men would have to suck it up and deal with it.

Cawdor was *not* going to cheat Cutter Dan again.

Down in the thicket, he knew, the greater part of his force waited, quivering with eagerness for the attack like hounds on a leash. He had alerted them to be ready to move on their enemies by having one of his men wave a torch around from their camp by the cliffs. Yonas's men down in the weeds had acknowledged with three flashes of a bull's-eye lantern. All according to plan.

Cutter Dan hadn't lied to Cawdor about the bounty Santee and his rich toadies had offered. He just hadn't bothered mentioning the other part: that Santee was getting tired of waiting and had also sent word relaxing his insistence that the fugitives be taken alive.

Of course, Cutter Dan hadn't shared the contents of that sealed dispatch with his men, either. He wanted their quarry alive and didn't want anybody tempted to take the easy route.

Especially since he'd eked out his force with scarcely vetted volunteers from the Wild villes, farms and encampments beyond Second Chance, not all of them absorbed into Santee's redo of the United States. Yet. And, most of all, because of how many mercies he'd been forced to take on to make sure his prey didn't get away again.

Like the trio who'd come down from Esperance, east past the Wall's end, a day or so ago. And *that* was a cesspit that was due to get cleaned out pronto, just as soon as this nasty business with the coldhearts who'd dared steal a prisoner off the Judge's own gallows, right under the Judge's own nose, was all wrapped up.

They were bounty hunters, the leader claimed—Dyson, his name was. Or, at least, that was the name he gave Cutter Dan, who was in no position to care. He was almost sure he had paper on one or more of those three, most likely on Dyson himself. But Santee had long ago authorized amnesty for those who signed on with his marshals, once Cutter Dan had convinced the old man that they were going to need a lot more warm bodies for his ambitious campaign of conquest than were liable to find in Second Chance alone.

The chief marshal had sent those particular three warm bodies on as an advance party, fifty yards or so ahead of the main column led by Cutter Dan. The only ones out ahead of them were Old Pete and Mort. In case the coldhearts had an ambush laid, Cutter Dan figured the Indians could take care of themselves. They were good at that.

And if Dyson and his stonehearts couldn't, well, like Cutter Dan's favorite uncle used to tell him, "a good scout is a dead scout." Better they get blasted than the sec boss or his actual, sworn-in sec men.

Plus then he wouldn't have to pay them, of course.

He glanced back. Scovul was following close behind, a Marlin lever longblaster in his hands and a look of intense concentration on his dark, mustached face. Behind him came the rest of the platoon, winding its way along the cliff base, looking in the starlight like some kind of giant sinuous multilegged creature—like one of those awful giant centipedes from the Wild, but a thousand times bigger.

Cutter Dan heard a sound from ahead like a night bird call. He stopped and raised a hand to halt the column behind him.

Old Pete rushed toward him, longblaster in hand, jogging at a pretty good clip for such an oldie. He seemed to have a lot less trouble negotiating the uneven ground and random vegetation underfoot than the sec men did.

The oldie halted about ten feet away. "Smell," he said.

"What?"

"Smell," the oldie commanded.

Scowling, Cutter Dan raised his head. He sniffed the air, then he sucked down a deep breath.

He almost busted out coughing. "Smoke," he said. "What the fuck? Are they piling brush on the campfire? Do they think they can get away from us using a smoke-screen? Or are they trying to smoke *us* out?"

Old Pete shook his head. His long, white hair wagged emphatically beneath his turban.

"Not campfire," he declared.

"What is it, then?" Scovul asked.

The Choctaw scout turned and gestured to the west with an open hand.

"The Wild burns."

Chapter Thirty-One

"Nuking night shit!" Cutter Dan exclaimed. "Send up the attack signal! *Now!*"

Scovul reached to his belt and pulled out a flare pistol. Raring back, he fired it up and away from the Wall.

"I go," Old Pete said. "Sister's son needs me." He turned and ran back the way he'd come, faster than before, vaulting the clumps of brush like a pronghorn.

The flare cast a weird pink glare up the face of the Wall and across the Wild as it soared like a red rocket. Instantly, a quarter mile of the mutie thicket's hedgelike northern border flashed alive with strobing blaster flames.

Cutter Dan's plan had been to work his unit into position close to Cawdor's camp. Then he would signal his men down in the Wild to open fire, to get the enemies' heads down and serve as diversion. At which point he'd make his move. He'd *hoped* for a quick, clean capture, or kill if it had to be that way.

Of course, he was too smart to count on that, but it didn't cost anything to hope. Didn't cost *him,* anyway.

But now that plan was blown sky-high. His favorite uncle also used to say that no plan survived first contact with the enemy. Fine. Cutter Dan knew how to improvise with the best of them.

As the crackle of dozens of blasters began to punch at the chief marshal's eardrums, he saw the source of the smell Old Pete had come back to tell him about. It was as if a gray curtain had descended in the west to the Wild itself. It seemed to stretch back into the thicket for hundreds of yards.

"Look, C.D.," a sec man called from behind Scovul. "You can see the flames."

"Holy shit," Scovul breathed.

The curtain hadn't descended, of course. It was rising, and now Cutter Dan saw what it was rising *from:* a ragged orange crescent of flames, arcing far back into the dense mutie growth. Even as he watched, some of the flames leaped up into the air about ten or twenty feet.

"Oh, fuck me," Cutter Dan whispered.

He turned and shouted and waved his arm, although nobody could really see the gesture from more than mebbe thirty feet away. "Follow me! *Charge!*"

He turned and set off running as fast as he dared toward the fugitive encampment.

BEHIND HIS SCOUT longblaster, Ryan waited.

He had left his companions dug in near their cave to await the inevitable attack by the stoneheart bastards who were more interested in collecting their bounty than escaping being burned alive. Doc and J.B. both had longblasters looted from chilled Second Chance marshals. As marksmen, they were plenty good enough to take a toll on any sec men who showed aggressive intentions.

Jak was the one who'd started the fires. He'd come up with some new way to make the sec men's lives miserable, now that he'd done that.

As Ryan knew all too well, if there was one thing the wiry albino was good at—after sneaking and scouting—it was guerilla warfare.

Ryan had his own job to do. He had set up on a red clay buttress wide enough to lie on at an angle, protecting his body from blasterfire, and it had a tuft of some kind of weed on top that added cover. He had his Steyr Scout longblaster propped on his rolled-up coat. With his naked eye he was scanning the trail along the base of the cliffs to where it undulated out of view, a hundred yards east.

They'd noted that spot for future reference while doing the recce a couple days back that led to the discovery that Cutter Dan had blocked their escape that way.

Now, Ryan knew, that blocking force had shifted to a strike team. Even if the chief marshal hadn't chosen to jump his deadline by an hour—and Ryan was double sure he had—the fact that his men stationed in the Wild had opened fire would bring him rushing this way to attack his prey.

Sure enough, two figures came into view. Ryan shifted to his glass, which was set to its lowest magnification.

It wouldn't have made any difference had he stayed with open sights. First one shape then the other flitted through his field of vision and simply vanished in the scrub beside the trail, too fast for even his lightning reflexes to sight in and fire.

In the vague, predawn light seeping up the western sky, he did catch an impression of dark faces and a feather bobbing in a hatband. Indians from a nation in the area. Trackers.

That's one of the ways they've been able to stick on us so tight, Ryan realized. He had taken ir for granted that Cutter Dan would secure the services of guides who knew the Wild, or this stretch of it, by payment or intimidation or whatever combination the sec boss thought was called for. But they wouldn't necessarily have the skills to follow the trail of their elusive targets.

He sighed. Yeah. So they had their own equivalents of Jak Lauren. And we had none.

Ryan didn't slack either his attention or his readiness. He was so alert, and so confident in his sniper skills, that he didn't automatically trigger a shot when another figure appeared around the bend in the cliff face.

It lumbered clumsily by comparison to the fleeting shapes: a big guy, shaved head gleaming pale in the scope, all duded up in dark leather with a longblaster's butt jutting from behind his left shoulder. The man wasn't wearing a marshal armband, so this was one of the mercies Cutter Dan had hired.

He had two other similarly equipped men following. Too close. One good burst from a machine gun or even an automatic longblaster would've taken them all out.

Ryan waited to see if they were the head of the enemy column or just scouts. He reminded himself that there were a pair of much more skillful, lethal foes approaching him rapidly—and unseen. He was acutely conscious of the sniper's most deadly danger—getting lost in the glass, which was particularly acute when you had but one eye. Although, by sheer luck, the eye that was missing was on the side next to the cliff.

What he needed was what a sniper usually had: a spotter who could double as sec when the shooter was focused on his target. But the three companions he'd left behind to hold back sec men from the thicket weren't enough as it was, even helped out by a few dozen rounds of ammunition Jak had scored somewhere during his solo adventures.

The shaved-headed stoneheart and his pals continued down the trail toward Ryan. No one else appeared behind them right away. Scouts, then.

He centered the reticule on the shaved head's brow, pulled in a deep breath, let some out, caught it. Squeezed.

He was aware of the tall man raising his face slightly even as the blaster roared and kicked upward. When it came back down, fresh cartridge duly chambered, he could see the man falling forward. The whole upper half of his head was missing.

The smart thing for someone under fire to do was to dive for cover. But like so many coldhearts, naturally including the breed called sec men, they were mainly bullies, used to preying on the weak. The remaining pair initially froze in place.

The man who'd been walking closer to the leader and behind his right shoulder had dark hair and a beard. Ryan put his second shot right between them. He went down.

The third man had a sort of short landing-strip Mohawk shaved onto the top of his head. He regained his senses and turned to run. Ryan had to snap off his third shot without proper aim.

But his bullet hit home. Lower right back, Ryan reckoned. The mercie rolled down into the brush and set to squalling like a treed catamount.

Three down, Ryan thought with satisfaction. Nothing took the starch out of enemies' peckers like the sound of one of their own shrieking in agony. Occasionally it backfired and turned them berserk; Judge Santee's bullyboys hadn't shown Ryan that kind of mettle.

The one-eyed man eased back from the scope. He turned his head to take in as much of the surroundings to his open right side as he could while keeping alert for more sec men appearing along the cliff-base trail. Those two trackers were out there, and if they weren't actively stalking him right at that second, it was because they were advancing far more slowly than they had been.

They'd be here, sooner or later. And not triple much later.

But that wasn't really what he was waiting for.

"WHAT'S THAT SMELL?" Doogle asked. He was one of the new guys, a fresh marshal recruit out of Sour Springs, southeast of Second Chance.

There was a lull in the shooting to either side of Edwards as men reloaded. They were firing all but blind at a partially obscured cave near the base of the Red Wall that Yonas and their noncoms had tried to point out as the target. Edwards wasn't sure all the sec men were actually firing at the right cave.

Nuke withered, he wasn't sure *he* was.

"Smoke," Edwards said.

He was stuffing .30-30 cartridges into the loading gate of his Winchester lever-action longblaster. The enemy camp was a good two hundred yards away from his position, near the west end of the Second Chance line. It was a questionable shot at that range over iron sights even in broad daylight. At night, the people he was shooting at had about the same chance of being hit by a shooting star as one of his bullets.

Or anybody else's, likely. Edwards was a farm boy, country bred and raised. Not one of these high and mighty ville types. And screw-up though he might have generally been—this whole discipline and regimentation thing turned out to be alien to his nature—he knew blasters, and he knew how to shoot.

But that was part of being disciplined and regimented: you did what you were told. Or triple-bad shit happened to you. And as long as Cutter Dan and his crazy Judge were buying the ammo, Edwards reckoned he might as well burn it up blowing holes in the night.

But that smell bothered him. A lot.

"What's burning?" he asked.

"Those bastard deathbirds are roasting a wild hog for

breakfast," growled Sawtell, the mercie from back east across the Sippi. "Who gives a shit?"

"Nobody's cooking nothin'," Edwards said. "I'd smell a thing like hog for breakfast, for sure. Trust me. Especially after this many days of cold beans and hardtack. With only mutie piss water to drink."

"Less jawing, more blasting," Yonas rapped out, walking up behind them.

"I smell pork cooking," Doogle said. "Makes me hungry."

"What the nuke—"

"Fire!" somebody shouted.

Somebody else shrieked, "Glowing bastard night shit! I'm on fire!"

Edwards snapped his head left. "Blind NORAD," he breathed.

An orange wall of fire jumped up not fifty yards to the west of them. The flames were higher than a tall man's head, and he could see at a glance that the blaze extended well back into the thicket.

A whole bunch of hollering came from the men stationed that way. Some of it was the mindless keening of men in intolerable agony.

"What's burning?" Sawtell yelled. "This shit's all green!"

"Dead growth, you stupe," Edwards said. "The stuff's triple thick in all that tangle, triple dry with this wind."

This *west* wind. Blowing right at them and getting brisker by the second with the dawn. He felt the heat now and smelled the acrid stench of burning hair, along with blazing dry vegetation and the barbecue smell of burning human flesh.

Edwards saw frantic action through the screen vines,

silhouetted against the orange hell-glow. "Oh, rads, it's moving too fast!"

Men flung themselves into the vine course that separated them from the group around Edwards, heedless of the thorns that plunged deep into limbs and bodies and faces. That pain meant nothing compared to the hideous pain of the fire.

Edwards saw a sec man thrashing at the twining briars some twenty yards away. It was Bennett, his eyes as wild as his brown hair and extravagant mustache.

His yells turned to shrill screams as a gust of wind caused the fire to billow into him. Horrified, Edwards saw Bennett's hair became a blazing halo. His mustache caught fire and burned like a wick.

Then the dried-out undergrowth around him and in front of him took light. He bellowed in despair and torment as the flames gushed up to envelop him completely. And then the fire moved onward, leaving him a frantic, wailing shadow in the inferno. Then only screams, joined with the dying screams of his comrades. Then silence.

"Nuke this!" Sawtell yelled. He bolted straight south, into the depths of the Wild.

"Come back, you damn stupe!" Edwards yelled after him. "You'll burn!"

Doogle set off at a run to the east. He got hung up in a course of the briars and began to thrash and wail, alternately cursing and begging for help.

Yonas's handblaster cracked. Doogle grunted and then hung limp, crucified backward on thorns.

"Only one thing to do now, men!" the one-eyed sec leader said, raising his voice to be heard down the line. It had a lot of competition from the roar of the flames and the screaming of its victims, though these were dying out. But the wildfire was moving inexorably onward as if hungry for more.

Yonas had holstered his handblaster and unslung his M16. He swung it downward, held one-handed by the pistol grip.

"Charge!" he bellowed.

Never thought I'd be glad to hear that order, Edwards thought, as he headed out, sprinting toward the still-unseen enemy strongpoint.

GOT SOFT, JAK thought, hunkered down just inside the outer skein of vines. He had actually been breathing hard when he reached the northern edge of the mutie thicket.

Of course, he'd had a triple-hard sprint of a quarter mile, over and through the twining vines, slipping between the thorns as best he could while he set dozens of tiny fires in the abundant dry, dead growth. He used torches he'd prepared with the container of kerosene that had been among Chally's and Meg's parting gifts.

He'd planted tiny seeds of fire that the wind and readily available nutrition caused to sprout to towering flames with shocking quickness always just right behind Jak's heels.

It was a terrible risk, even though he was carefully setting the blazes downwind of him. Nothing could guarantee that a shift in the wind, even a brief one, might not trap him in a pocket of flame and condemn him to the intolerable, howling death he was inflicting on many sec men on the other side of the fire, which had now changed from a wall to a sort of quasi-living wave, surging inexorably east.

It had been stupe easy to infiltrate back through the waiting ranks of Second Chance marshals on the northern edge of the thicket after his quick reunion with Ryan, J.B., Doc and Ricky. He'd gone out the same way, after all. As dark as it was, it wasn't remotely a challenge. He was lithe, fast and savvy. This was his task to accomplish.

Despite the dark, he'd had little trouble just skirting the territory marked out by the strange feathered-lizard muties. Even at night it was easy to spot tribal signs—if you had the eyes for them. Jak did, just as he'd learned his friends had not.

The chorus of inhuman shrieks rising from the far side of the rolling inferno was music to his ears. The bastards were getting just exactly what they had coming, by his reckoning.

Mildred, that big predark softie, claimed Jak was hard-core even by Deathlands standards, and perhaps he was. But when the situation called for his hardcore survival skills, they had kept him alive, as well as the others.

Now Jak was back to doing that again. It just felt right. Felt natural.

The object he pulled out of his jacket pocket was anything but natural. It was just a little metal box, no bigger than the palm of his hand. It had a little antenna and a big red button. Plus a little toggle in the base, inset so he had to whip open one of his butterfly knives and use the tip to switch it from *off* to *on*.

Like all his other senses, Jak's nocturnal vision was much keener than his friends' despite his albinism. More like an animal's than a man's. He was proud of that.

Though he made exceptions for a very few friends— Chally and, he reckoned, Meg, with Ryan and the rest something even more—Jak was not impressed with what he'd seen of humankind. As a rule, he liked animals better.

Now he was able to make out the dark line of sec men threading their cautious way forward along the base of the Red Wall. Even with the ever-constant threat of the fire he was setting to speed his steps, he'd only just made it in time.

But he had, and now was the time for some real fun.

He could easily see the last big knee of red clay between his friends' encampment and that of Cutter Dan's blocking force. The leader of the barely visible procession was just about to reach it.

J.B. and Ricky loved to tinker with machines and other tech stuff. Jak didn't know anything about it, and cared less.

What he did know was that the Armorer was as good at that as Jak was good at sneaking and peeking. Jak's pal Ricky was no slouch, either. Between them, the pair had been scavvying up components and tinkering them into… parts, for weeks. Actually, they were always playing with scavvy in their downtime, when they were repairing or maintaining weapons.

He'd been able to make one particular set of devices from some of the gifts Chally and Meg had provided Jak before he left the Last Resort. Right when they were needed most.

Jak held out the little box with the antenna pointing just to the right of the red clay knee.

"Bastard sec lose," he said, and pressed the big red button.

Chapter Thirty-Two

"Come on!" Yonas shouted, waving his longblaster again. "They can't even shoot us here! It's too dark! We got their asses!"

They'd made it about a third of the way from their base in the Wild to the coldhearts' nest. Though the fire had already swept through the place where Edwards had been lurking, it was still blazing east across the thicket. And from the horrible sounds that continued to peal from that direction, the flames were still consuming sec men and mercies who had been too stupe or laggard to bust out and join the impromptu charge.

A glance left and right had told the lanky marshal that thirty or forty others had made it out, and also that the main fire and the pockets of blaze it had left in its wake were in prime position to silhouette the straggling line of attackers.

Having delivered his inspirational yell, the detachment's boss turned his head forward—and stopped dead in his tracks.

Edwards saw why: the other group of Second Chance marshals, snaking their way along the cliffs under command of Cutter Dan himself, were suddenly swallowed by a series of giant puffs of smoke and red dust that burst straight out toward the Wild and their advancing comrades.

Yonas was standing stock still staring when the left

top of his head just suddenly flipped off. His head jerked back, spraying blood in the still-faint dawn light and spilling chunks of brain as his body collapsed to lie jerking among the weeds.

A series of deafening thunder cracks hit Edwards in the face as a stretch of the cliff a good thirty yards long came crashing down, obliterating the Second Chance column in a red clay avalanche.

THE FIRST BLAST caught Ryan by surprise.

He saw the cloud of smoke, dust and debris blast right out of the cliff like a horizontal volcanic eruption. Then the sound and shock waves hit him.

The sound was brutal—like a blaster shot right by his ear but magnified a thousand times. The wave hit him in the face like an invisible boot, tugging like hurricane winds at his coat.

Then it was by, leaving only the ringing in his ears and a rumbling sound as a whole section of the Red Wall fell.

If Jak had done his job, it was falling right on top of Cutter Dan and his men on their way to attack the companions.

Radios for communication were too hard to maintain, and batteries were too hard to come by, to make it worthwhile for his companions to carry them, except under unusual circumstances. But a radio remote detonator was dead easy. So J.B. habitually carried at least one he had improvised in his pack. With his apprentice, Ricky, who was even better with electronics than his master was, they'd also managed to put together some tiny, simple radio receivers for setting off explosives.

All they'd lacked were the blasting caps and explosives. Then Jak had turned up out of nowhere. And whoever he'd been hanging with since he parted company with his friends, he'd made a good enough impression that they gifted him with a packet of blasting caps—and the location of a stash of dynamite. Better was the fact it was recently made; predark dynamite would have long since grown so unstable that thinking about it from across the room would set it off.

J.B. had been a little freaked out by Jak's carrying the caps and the sticks of explosive so close together, but since Jak had made it there without spontaneously blowing up, the Armorer figured in the long run it was okay.

While Jak had snuck out of the little camp to work his incendiary mischief back in the Wild, J.B. and Ricky had slipped off to the east to plant some hastily assembled charges. Then they'd returned to the camp site to prepare to stand off the sec men lurking among the vines.

Meanwhile, Jak was to try to get into position—just upwind of where he had set the fire line—in time to watch for the marshals' attack. It was his responsibility to use the radio detonator to trigger the charges J.B. and Ricky had hidden in caves in the red clay cliff when Cutter Dan led his men obliviously into the kill zone. It was a triple-iffy plan, but a more solid one required time and bodies they simply didn't have.

The blasts had momentarily stunned Ryan. He knew they were coming, or hoped they were. But he couldn't know precisely *when*. They were so tremendously powerful that nothing he could have done could have prepared him fully for them, anyway.

But he never lost consciousness. His focus just…wavered. Momentarily.

Then it snapped back and he returned to watching the red-earth knee. If any of the sec men had escaped the explosions and landslide, and still somehow had the balls and heart to press the attack, they'd come this way. It was his job to deal with them so there'd be no flank attacks on Ricky, Doc and J.B.

He was also keenly aware of the two scouts who had flashed through his field of vision and vanished. Of course, after the summary way Ryan had dealt with the trio of mercies who followed them, and the earth-shattering series of explosions that had just swallowed up much if not all of the force they were scouting for, they might well have decided that discretion was the better part of valor and chosen just to bug out while the bugging was good.

No, Ryan thought. He wasn't that lucky on his best day. And, if anything, he'd used up all the luck he had coming in the past twelve hours or so, plus enough to last for months to come.

A dark shadow detached itself from the dawn half-light to his right and flew toward him. Then Ryan rolled violently to his left side, bringing up his longblaster defensively. A dark figure landed on him like a chunk of the great red cliff.

THE SAVAGE MODEL 110 cracked and kicked Ricky's right shoulder.

The report wasn't currently bothering him, but only because his ears were still ringing so badly from the dynamite packets going off moments before. The recoil took some getting used to, though. The .270 Winchester cartridge was way more powerful than the pistol-caliber De-Lisle he was accustomed to shooting, and had a sharp recoil for its power. At least, for him.

A bullet cracked over his head, and he winced, but he still jacked the bolt as the blaster came back down.

Ricky had fired only a few shots and his shoulder already stung. He wondered if it was separating. He didn't know what that meant, exactly. He hoped he wouldn't have to find out.

To Ricky's right lay J.B., who was cranking the action of a .30-30 Marlin. He was a decent sniper, but his real role would come when the attackers got close enough for him to take them out with bursts from his 9 mm Uzi machine pistol, which was laid out by his right leg. His Smith & Wesson M-4000 shotgun lay by his left leg, but if the marshals got close enough for that, he, Doc and Ricky were probably as good as staring up at the slowly disappearing stars overhead anyway.

Doc had scavvied a Remington 700 in 7.62 mm, the same cartridge Ryan's Steyr Scout used. The old man was normally content with his massive replica LeMat handblaster, but he was a fair shot with a longblaster when he had to be.

And he did. The bulk of the sec men waiting in the Wild had been flushed out by the blaze Jak set, and now they were coming fast, shooting as they ran.

The dawn was still not fully blown, but it was no longer cellar dark. The wall of fire had already passed beyond the enemies immediately to the front of the three defenders.

There were no consecrated priests back in Ricky's peaceful coastal ville on Puerto Rico's southern coast, but the self-styled Catholic padre who held sway in the ville hadn't liked to talk about hell. He said there was a sort of hell on Earth nowadays, after the Big Nuke and skydark. He held that hell was only there to burn the sin out of the very worst, very most deliberately self-lost souls. Like the coldhearts who had destroyed Ricky's ville, murdered his family before his eyes and carried his adored older sister, Yamile, off to slavery. When Ricky thought about hell at all, which was seldom, he thought those slavers would be in the darkest, hottest corner, burning for all eternity.

The sounds that had come from the roaring heart of that fire had brought those awful memories to life with a vividness Ricky had never before experienced. He knew he'd experience it over and over now, though. In his dreams.

If he lived.

The infernal wave was dwindling, already three hundred yards or so to the east, as the predawn west wind that had propelled it so lethally fast died back. Its orange glare, and the lights of the scattered fires that burned in the blackened tangle its passing had left, combined with the faint but perceptibly growing sunlight to render the attacking sec men as distinct man-like blobs. It was more than enough to shoot by.

Ricky lined up on the closest man. He was no more than a hundred yards off. He couldn't make out any details of the man's face; it was just a gray blur above the darker blur of his body. But just the hunch of his body as he ran told Ricky he was driven by confusion and desperation as much as anything else, as if he didn't have any idea of what to do right now except charge straight at the foe.

Just as Ricky squeezed the trigger, the man turned his body right, still running, to fire a shot from the hip from his carbine. Ricky's 130-grain slug, which he'd aimed for the center of mass, caught his target on the right side of the chest instead, or perhaps in the shoulder, from the way he spun as he went down.

Ricky was already looking for new targets as he worked the action of his longblaster again. Too many enemies were still on their feet and still coming fast to waste time on a wounded enemy, especially one who'd dropped completely out of sight in front of the gradual slope of fallen dirt that led to the camp.

From the right came a strobing muzzle flare, seeming disproportionately bright. Bullets kicked up dirt and bits of vegetation right in front of Ricky. Someone was firing a longblaster fullauto at him, and from the sound and the size of the flames, the shooter couldn't be any farther than fifty yards out.

Ricky couldn't help trying to scrunch himself down harder into the ground. The clay was held firmly by the roots of the brush and grasses that screened him, and well compressed by the boots and bodies of the four men who had camped on the ledge for two days. It didn't give any more than concrete would.

The blaster's jittery fire dance ended. Almost immediately it commenced again.

Now Ricky successfully got control of his brain and body. Mostly. It was enough. He tried to shift aim to the automatic rifleman. From the sound of his weapon, he was shooting the Heckler & Koch G3. J.B. had identified the blaster last sunset, when Cutter Dan used it to call attention to his ultimatum.

The fresh burst kicked dirt directly into Ricky's eyes. He cried out, blinking furiously to clear the stinging fragments. Bullets cracked overhead.

Nuestra Señora, pray for me, he thought. He realized his own most recent shot had given his position away to the shooter.

The burst ended and a third began. The earth shook beneath Ricky as bullets hit the slope directly in front of him. They began to walk inexorably upward toward him, and his vision was still too tear-misted for him to sight on the man who was about to chill him.

A nearby longblaster roared and the distant shooter fell back.

"Even I could see you, lighting yourself up like that, you stupe son of a bitch," J.B. said in satisfaction.

"By the Three Kennedys, they're running!" Doc yelled,

his voice crazily exultant. "They're broken! Flee you cai-
tiff dogs! Flee the wrath to come!"

The old man cranked off the last three shots in his
blaster's internal magazine. Ricky's eyes finally cleared
up enough to see that Doc was wasting ammo—a cardi-
nal sin in Ryan's rule book. The Second Chance marshals
were, indeed, turning away, mostly racing off to the east
as fast as they could, so Ricky couldn't find it in his heart
to blame the old man.

Now that it looked as if he'd live and all, Ricky realized that what was amazing wasn't that the sec men broke
when they did.

Given the terrible blazing death they'd so narrowly escaped, and the fate of their commander and dozens more
of their comrades, and after they'd run straight into blasterfire aimed from a powerful defensive position, it was
amazing that they had pressed the attack as long as they
had.

Ricky jumped slightly when J.B. slapped him on the
shoulder. He turned to see the Armorer squatting over
him and grinning.

"Time to shift out of here, kid," J.B. said. "Time to go
hunt up Ryan and then head back to Second Chance to
rescue Millie and Krysty, since it looks like we're going
to live a little longer."

Chapter Thirty-Three

Dawn light broke against a bright blade and glanced into Ryan's eye. He smelled sweat and old wool. Two dark eyes glared down at him from a dark, determined face. He had an impression of a hat rolling away on its brim.

He never knew how he'd spotted the Indian just on the raw, ragged edge of too late to do any good. It might have been peripheral vision—the man had made no more noise than even the loudest daybreak. Or it might just have been a seasoned warrior's sense for the approach of danger.

His assailant's full weight was lying angled across his Scout longblaster. The man had one hand clamped on the weapon and the other raised over his head with the saw-backed KA-BAR-style blade jutting downward.

Pushing hard with his right boot, Ryan continued with his counterclockwise roll. At the same time, he shoved up forcefully with his right hand, throwing the man off him to the left.

As he bounced off the clay wall, Ryan jackknifed forward. He managed to get into a kneeling position before his attacker recovered and started to get up. He swung the carbine hard left, trying to slam the man across the side of the head with the buttstock.

The man caught it with his left hand and held on tight. He threw his weight back down, trying to drag Ryan into reach of his fighting knife.

Ryan let go of the longblaster, slipped the sling, and

jumped to his feet. He drew his panga, simply because his hand was closer to its hilt than to the butt of his SIG and fractions of seconds counted.

The man threw down the weapon and launched himself at Ryan's midriff. The man was a good six inches shorter than the Deathlands warrior but low-slung and wide across the shoulders. Ryan reckoned he didn't outweigh his attacker by much.

He didn't like not knowing where the man's older partner was, but right now he had his hands too full to distract himself with side issues.

The guy was trying for a takedown, not a stab. The angles were all wrong for that, anyway. Ryan, on the other hand, wasn't in position to hack with the panga. Instead, he threw himself to meet the other, bringing his left hand and the butt of weapon down on his shoulders.

The sprawl defense worked. The Indian slammed to the hard clay of the trail with Ryan's stubbled cheek rasping his. He grunted as air was driven out of his body.

The attacker had put his hands down to break his fall. Now he pushed furiously upward to throw Ryan off. The move didn't take Ryan by surprise. He was already pushing off himself, stealing momentum from his enemy to thrust himself up to a crouch and on over onto his butt. As the shorter man got to his knees, Ryan rolled hard left again, swinging up his right leg. His shin caught the side of the man's head and knocked him sideways off the trail.

The downhill slope wasn't steep there, and the scrub that had helped the scout sneak up on Ryan slowed him. He rolled over twice before he caught himself and sprang back up.

But Ryan was ready for him. He leaped down and was swinging his panga in an overhand arc as the Indian rose. The wide, heavy blade of the knife caught the upper-right-hand side of the man's head. It split his skull clear to the left eyebrow with a crack and a moist crunch. Brown eyes rolled up in the scout's head, and he collapsed, an instant chill.

Ryan wrenched the panga free as he slumped. He straightened to stand over his opponent, breathing heavily.

Not twenty feet away, as if magically materializing out of the smoke-laden air, a figure rose from the weeds beside the trail.

A figure holding a longblaster.

EDWARDS LAY IN a clump of skunk bush and watched the remnants of the Second Chance sec force head east, between the Red Wall and the Wild.

A heartbeat after Yonas got his stupe head blown off, Edwards had uttered a grunt as if hit and flopped to the ground. He thought he'd done a good job of acting, but as far as he could tell nobody had so much as glanced in his direction. So that was wasted.

For some stupe reason they'd kept right on charging, when it was plain as a mole on a gaudy-slut's cheek that the whole nuking endeavor was snake bit on the ass and going to fail, anyway. But no, they had to go racing across the mostly clear ground toward the slope that led up to the enemy position. That, at least, was easy to spot now, since there were three longblasters blazing away at them from there.

He climbed to his feet and dusted himself off.

"Well, that worked for shit," he said disgustedly. Even he wasn't sure if he meant the chief marshal's cunning sure-fire plan to bring down the elusive fugitives, or his whole entire career as a so-called U.S. Marshal.

Both, he reckoned.

"Screw a bunch of this," he said, and set off walking

briskly west into the rising sun. The deathbirds wouldn't bother him, he knew. They hated to leave the cover of the thorn thicket.

All he knew was, whichever way the rest of the sec men were going, he wanted to go the opposite direction.

"Easy," the newcomer said in an age-cracked voice.

Ryan caught himself as he was about to start a desperate dive for the dirt. It had penetrated his awareness that the longblaster was cradled across the man's chest, not aimed at Ryan. And anyway, if the man had wanted to blast him, he would have. It was as simple as that.

"You're the other scout," he said, straightening again. If he wasn't going to dive for cover, draw his SIG and start blasting, he was nuking well going to show a little dignity.

"I am," the oldie said. He had iron-colored hair hanging from under a green turban to frame a deeply furrowed face. He wore a well-kept Remington Model 1858 Army revolver, presumably a replica, in a flapped cavalry holster diagonally before his left hip. At his right hip a steel hatchet rode in a carrier. Its fancy beadwork told Ryan which weapon the man favored.

Ryan gestured at the longblaster, a Winchester lever-action carbine. "He was carrying that blaster."

"He was."

"Why'd he jump me with a knife, then, instead of blasting me?"

"He wanted to count coup on his opponent." He patted the Winchester. "Even left his piece with me."

Ryan raised a skeptical eyebrow.

The oldie shrugged. "Boy never did have good judgment. That's why he's here, pretty much."

Something about his tone and manner made Ryan ask, "He yours?"

"My daughter's son. His name was Mort. They call me Old Pete."

"We got a beef over this?"

The oldie shook his head. "There is no blood between my family and yours, Ryan Cawdor."

"You know who I am?"

"I know many things, One Eye Chills. It's my job."

"So, why not a blood debt? Not that I'm complaining. I've got problems enough on my hands."

He gave the panga a couple of hard, quick shakes to the side. He didn't feel quite right standing there talking to a man with his nephew's blood and brains drying on the blade.

"We were not willingly helping the sec men from Second Chance," Old Pete said. He waved a hand down the slope, where the sec men who had been attacking Ryan's friends were running east in an obvious rout. "My nephew performed an indiscretion. He ran up debts gambling at a gaudy owned by a man from there named Myers."

"Is he was one of the fat cats who run the place?"

"He is one who thinks they do. Santee is true baron in Second Chance. He rules the others. He lets them help out, so long as they serve his interests. But yes. That is Myers."

"I would've thought Santee was too uptight to let gambling go on in his ville."

"He is. Myers operates a roadhouse south of Second Chance. Santee knows of it, of course, but he permits it to continue for his own reasons."

Old Pete shook his head. "He is a bad man, and a mad one. Anyway, the game was probably rigged. But a debt of honor is a debt of honor, and Mort's parents warned him many times about what he was getting himself into."

"So he got stuck working for Cutter Dan whether he wanted to or not?"

"He most certainly did not want to, but he also did it to prevent bad blood between our people and Santee's. That Judge is crazy and evil, but very powerful. My nephew came late to a sense of duty. But he did."

"What about you, then? You along to look out for him?"

"In a manner of speaking. I was asked to accompany my sister's son to help him find a warrior's death."

He gazed down sadly at his nephew, lying on his back with his brains leaking into the grass, staring up at the pink-streaked blue sky.

"Struck down by the hand of One Eye Chills himself," he said. "A death any warrior might envy."

"And you don't?" Ryan asked cautiously. The scout's story made sense, and very little else did, given that he hadn't shot Ryan. But Ryan didn't feel like making any assumptions, here.

"It is not my path to be chilled by you, nor you by me. Our paths diverge here. I shall return my nephew's body to his people, and tell Bluebird the glad news of her son's death."

Even Ryan had to blink his eye at that. Trying not to sound as nonplussed as he felt, he said, "So what about Cutter Dan and Second Chance?"

Old Pete stood and silently thought about that for what seemed like a whole minute. Ryan kept his head turning from side to side, in case any bitter marshals might be taking advantage of their palaver to creep up for a shot at a little vengeance.

"Fuck them," the old man said, at last.

DRIVEN BY HATE, sustained by the last of the foul air trapped in the small pocket with him, Cutter Dan struggled to break free of the grave that enveloped him. The weight of the world seemed to by lying on his back. His whole body ached, and his lungs felt as if they were being shredded by the struggle to breathe.

By some instinct, or simply by blind luck, a hand broke free. The open air was like a warm kiss after the cold, enclosing earth.

His failing strength renewed, he clawed away the clay and rocks until the air flooded down into his upturned face to fill his nose and lungs. Even though it was rank with the fumes of spent explosives, smoke and the stench of burned bodies, it was the sweetest smell he'd ever known.

The light blinded him. He struggled into it anyway.

Then he fell to lie exhausted on the mound of soil.

When Cutter Dan regained some strength, he raised his head to utter devastation. A fifty-yard section of the Red Wall had fallen, burying his entire force. Only because he was in the very lead, at the western fringe of the fall, had he survived.

To the east a dozen or so bodies lay scattered between the Wild and the Wall, or rather the bizarre blackened-wire sculpture that the burned-over thorn vines resembled now.

The rest of that group, the ones who hadn't died in the flames or the blasterfire, were gone, as completely as if they, too, were chills.

If nothing else, not a man jack of the yellow bastards wanted to run the risk of Santee's marshals ever laying eyes on them again. They knew the fate that awaited deserters.

The chief marshal stood. He still had his handblaster and his trademark Bowie knife. They had been safely holstered when the boobie charges went off.

His legs weren't very steady beneath him. His body felt like one big bruise, his head as if a blacksmith was hammering it on an angle. His left ear heard only faintly. The right, the one nearer the shattering explosions, could hear nothing at all. A quick exploration of his fingertips came away with a mix of red mud and congealed blood that told the story: burst eardrum.

None of which mattered a hot steaming dump on a fresh tortilla.

I'm alive, he thought. That's all that counts.

That's all I need.

All that he had left was vengeance, and he knew just where to go to get it.

"I'm not done yet. You're gonna see me again, One Eye," he told the red risen sun. "And when you do, it'll be the very last thing you ever see!"

Chapter Thirty-Four

"We have a pretty sparse turnout this morning, it looks like, Judge," Marley Toogood announced.

He stood at the rear of the scaffold, behind the four miserable hostages awaiting execution. Though there were at least a hundred ville folk clustered before the gallows, that was nothing like the turnout such an event should have drawn.

It was not as if Toogood cared. Stir the pot, stir the pot, he thought.

"My employees weren't turning out for work this morning, either," Gein complained from the VIP box behind the platform. "My mills won't run themselves."

Seated while the two rich folk with him preferred to stand for the moment, Judge Santee uttered a caw of laughter.

"Well," he said, "we'll have plenty of object lessons to teach them. If the ringleaders and coldhearts who broke out of my jail do turn themselves in, we can still keep hanging our hostages until their friends and relatives come out of the woodwork to do their civic duty and watch."

Myers made a face as if someone had smeared fresh shit on his red mustache. "That's a good way to deplete our workforce," he stated.

"No matter," Santee said. "We can execute every last shiftless, ungrateful ne'er-do-well in this whole ville, come to that."

"What do you mean, Your Honor?" Toogood asked, feeling genuine alarm.

"I expect Cutter Dan to return directly with those fugitive coldhearts he's been pursuing. And then we can commence to rapidly expand the rule of these re-United States!"

"Where will you get the men," Myers asked, his piping voice sour, "when we've already sent so many marshals out of Second Chance for this manhunt? And please allow me to remind you that Chief Marshal Sevier reports taking numerous casualties."

"That's funny," Gein said. "There's at least a score of sec men in view. Not all of them even have armbands, I see."

He looked sideways at the Judge. "I can only presume they haven't been issued them yet? Since otherwise, of course, the sworn marshals would arrest them on sight for bearing arms."

"They are mercenaries," Santee said, "as well as recruits. More are on the way." He sounded pleased to the point of smugness. "Many more are on their way, I can assure you, gentlemen."

"What on earth?" Myers asked. "I knew the chief marshal put out a call for extra manpower for the final phase of his manhunt, but mercies and untried outlanders guarding Second Chance and our fortunes? How can they be trusted?"

"My marshals keep keen eyes on them," Santee said. "Beyond that—the promise of being handsomely armed themselves. And paid."

"Armed?" Toogood asked nervously.

He glanced at the sky. It hadn't begun to lighten yet, but the deadline for the rebels to turn themselves in was fast approaching.

The *first* deadline.

"I have just concluded a deal with Mohandas the Merchie, in Broken Arrow," Santee said. "An arms caravan is on its way to us as we speak."

My word, Your Honor, Toogood thought. You have been busy, behind even my back. It did not seem to portend anything good.

"Arms caravan?" Gein asked in surprise.

"Where will all this jack come from?" Myers demanded. "To buy a whole caravan of weapons, not to mention paying men to use them?"

"From Bates's estate, to start with," Santee said.

"But it was meant to be paid out equally among the four of us!" Myers exclaimed. "That was our agreement!"

"Circumstances have dictated a change of arrangements. Opportunity has shown its shy face and must be seized by the neck! Bates's holdings are forfeit. And while we're on the subject, your contribution to ville security has been doubled, effective immediately."

"What?" Toogood yelped.

Myers and Gein jumped to their feet. "Absurd! Obscene! We won't sit still for it!" Gein exclaimed.

A throat was cleared. The men in the box with Santee looked around to note it was the impressive bullfrog throat of Suazo, acting chief marshal in Cutter Dan's absence.

It struck Toogood that he and his fellow local magnates were surrounded by armed men whose loyalty to the tall, cadaverous old man in black might safely be presumed to have been reinforced by a promise of increased pay.

"You can pay as you're told, gentlemen," Santee said, "and continue to sit here. Or you can refuse—" he stretched a long, black-sleeved arm toward the scaffold, past the mayor to where the first four victims stood on the traps with hands bound and nooses looped around their necks "—and stand there!"

They sat. Toogood took a handkerchief from his vest pocket and mopped his brow. Though the morning was by no means warm, his face ran with sweat.

Suazo leaned forward to murmur in the Judge's ear. No easy feat, since his paunch was even more impressive than his thick throat.

Santee rapped knuckles briskly on the rail before him.

"Gentleman!" he declared, his eyes fever-bright in his pale, withered old face. "It is time! Mr. Toogood, proceed with the executions."

The executioner cleared his own throat. "Uh, boss…" he said to Toogood.

A murmur ran through the crowd. The sec men hemming them in started to look over their shoulders.

Up the street from the right came a crowd of people. Down the street from the left came another crowd.

They seemed far more resolute than the usual miserable flocks herded to the courthouse by sec men to watch the hangings.

"What's this?" Gein demanded, craning forward in his seat and blinking near-sightedly.

"It's all right," Toogood announced heartily, to cover his dawning, horrid suspicion it was anything but. "Perhaps they're coming to watch the executions as they ought. Better late than never, right, Your Honor?"

But Santee was glaring furiously east, then west. "They are carrying implements!" he declared. "That's counter to regulations! And—wait, are some of them actually armed?"

He sprang to his feet. "Marshals! Take these mobs under fire at once. Show them that such disobedience will not be tolerated."

The sec men turned to face the two approaching groups. They started drawing handblasters to augment the truncheons they already held in their hands.

Suddenly onlookers who were clustered around the gallows started jumping on the sec men from behind and wrestling with them. Six or seven others began to clamber onto the gallows itself. Toogood shrank back in shocked disbelief.

"Shoot them!" Myers cried in a quavering tenor voice. "Shoot them all down like the rad-scum they are!"

"Wait!" Toogood said, turning and frantically waving his arms at the marshals in the box with Suazo. They were raising blasters toward the scaffold. Toward *him*. "Don't shoot!"

"Get me to safety first, Suazo!" Santee almost screamed. "It's an insurrection."

Suazo boomed orders to his men. They surrounded the Judge and started moving him bodily toward the steps at the rear of the box.

"Then shoot the rebels!" the Judge cried, shaking his fist. "But first—hang the prisoners!"

The executioner reached for the lever that would spring the traps beneath the condemned.

Then it seemed he stumbled, almost as if drunk.

The huge, burly man fell on his face. A dark pool began to spread out over the planks around him.

The rebels from the crowd gained the platform.

Toogood didn't wait any longer. Uttering a yelp of despair, he turned and jumped off the rear of the scaffold.

He twisted his left ankle sorely when he landed but scuttled off toward the nearest cover as if nothing had happened.

WISH I'D GOT a decent crack at that bastard Judge, Mildred thought. She twisted open the bolt of the longblaster and slammed a fresh cartridge home.

She was perched on the flat roof of a two-story building a block west of the gallows, on the far side of the street from the courthouse. It gave her a nice clean shot at the gallows and the semicircle of sec men holding the crowd in place around it. But, to her intense annoyance, it didn't offer an unobstructed line of fire to the box behind— where Santee and his partners in crime were sitting.

The plan, such as it was, hadn't allowed much leeway for scouting for an ideal sniper's nest. Or any scouting at all. They had to rely on the locals' knowledge of their own ville, which was fine; she figured they knew the damn place. But it left little margin for error if Suazo had thought to hide some of the newly arrived sec men in case of trouble.

And trouble had come to Second Chance. No question about that. The $64,000 Question was whom it was going to be the most trouble for.

Santee's sec men hustled him out of the VIP box and into the courthouse without giving Mildred anything resembling a shot. When she switched aim over the open sights back to the box itself, she didn't see any targets. She wondered what had happened to the pair of plutocrats who'd been perched there.

One of the people who'd climbed up onstage, as it were, turned forward and flung her broad-brimmed hat away. It was Sharleez.

"People of Second Chance," she cried. "Now is the time for your ville to live up to its name! Rise up and throw off the chains of those who so cruelly oppress you!"

It was a bold move, if a foolhardy one. But Mildred

guessed now was the best time to try to get as many of the citizens as possible to throw in with the insurrection. Not just the ones still milling around on the street by the gallows, mostly looking to get away without being spotted, but the ones undoubtedly watching and listening from behind closed doors and shutters. And the hundreds more cowering indoors throughout the ville, willing to defy the order to turn out to watch their innocent neighbors and friends be hanged, but too scared to take any more direct action.

Mildred expected shots from Santee's crowd control detail to knock Sharleez right off her soapbox. Then she saw they were too occupied with actually trying to control the crowd. Even the ones who hadn't been jumped from behind by revolutionaries who'd infiltrated the audience were now grappling with the majority of onlookers who were simply trying to get the hell out of there.

"Shit," Mildred said. She kept looking for targets, but there was too much confusion. Too many bodies were in the way.

The two approaching mobs were getting close to the gallows now. Mildred guessed that only a few people in either bunch had much stomach for a direct fight. The others were going along on the basis of feeling safety in numbers—like any mob.

Krysty was with the one coming in from the east. Though she wore a bandanna over her head to prevent the sec men from recognizing her distinctive flame-red hair, she was walking with the aid of a cane and had a ginormous bloody bandage wrapped around the thigh of her left leg, which was a complete fake. Her leg still pained her, she said, but it had healed up well enough for her to get around on it unaided. It wasn't likely to open up and start bleeding again. The blood had come from a spare rooster bound for the stewpot.

Word had naturally gotten out about Krysty's miraculous feat in breaking the prisoners out of Santee's jail. The story had also gone around how she'd fought against Cutter Dan's marshals to the very last, and had only been captured because she took a mutie spear to the thigh. Krysty and Sharleez had both thought they could play up those tales to help put some steel in the spines of their would-be street rioters.

Mildred looked back toward the struggle between the sec men and citizens around the gallows. Then she found out what had happened to at least one of the rich ville folk who'd been next to Santee. She heard a rebel who was helping free the noosed hostages cry a warning to Sharleez. She turned her head to see the little, fussily neat dude—Gein, she heard he was called—pop up and point a blaster at the firebrand's back.

Mildred swung her longblaster toward him, already knowing she'd be too late to do anything but avenge Sharleez. But the young woman wheeled rapidly. She had the Beretta M9 they'd taken from the leader of the sec squad they'd trapped the night before last.

She emptied the blaster in Gein's direction. He fell back into the box, discharging his own piece harmlessly into the air. Sharleez didn't seem to be a very good shot, and exhibited lamentable trigger control. But this time, at least, she'd gotten the job done.

Mildred was starting to feel antsy. She still hadn't got off a shot since the one that had dropped the fat bastard of an executioner.

But what really made her skin creep was the thought that kept ringing in her head: This is too easy.

And as if that thought had been a self-fulfilling prophecy, from up the street she heard longblasters being rack and shots fired.

Near Krysty, limping proudly along at the head of the mob, people began to fall to the ground, writhing.

Chapter Thirty-Five

"Take cover!" Krysty shouted, as blasterfire ripped into the crowd from the courthouse.

The red-haired beauty lost no time following her own advice. She dropped her cane and raced for the buildings on the south side of the street. She drew her revolver, a Ruger Security Six taken from an ambushed sec man.

Shots spattered the street. A woman right in front of Krysty gasped and fell. Krysty ran past her. She hated not being able to help, but she wouldn't *be* a help if she took a bullet too.

Her goal here, and Mildred's, was to do what they could to get themselves, their men and their friends free of the clutches of Judge Santee and his murderous sec men. Everything else was a side issue.

People were breaking into the buildings across the main street from the courthouse. The generally dilapidated state of the structures helped. Krysty spotted a window without glass and dived through.

The floor was mildew-splashed, warped hardwood. Dust and mold hung thick in the air from others who had barged in through the doors and windows ahead of her. Now they huddled by the baseboards, some still clutching ax handles and hoes they'd carried in brave defiance of Santee and his law. They didn't seem so brave now.

But then, neither did Krysty. And Sharleez had insisted *she* get one of the few blasters. Mainly because she knew how to use one better than almost anyone in the ville who wasn't already a sec man.

Shots occasionally cracked and whined in through the empty windows. The rotting walls would barely slow down a well-thrown rock, much less a bullet. But the marshals followed the usual pattern of shooting at openings when no actual targets presented themselves.

Krysty risked a quick look over the sill. The blasterfire was coming from the barricaded steps and upper windows of the gray stone courthouse across the street. Before she ducked she saw sec men dumping sandbags across the wide doorway to provide better cover. The jail annex—which Krysty now knew wasn't stout redbrick at all, but some kind of fake covering over cinder block—had no external windows, which meant the sec men couldn't shoot out of it.

The street was clear except for bodies that were rolling back and forth and moaning, and ones that lay still. The rest of the crowd of several dozen who had accompanied Krysty during the march toward the gallows had found shelter of their own. Or had simply run away.

The plan, such as it was, had been to try to lure Suazo's marshals into a battle in the streets. Sharleez and the volunteers who scaled the scaffold had been willing to expose themselves to close range blasterfire in order to keep Santee and his protectors in the open. Like the short-haired young firebrand, the others had lost close family members to those gallows, and with them at least some of their will to live. Though she hadn't said so, Krysty also knew Sharleez was hoping to get a shot at the Judge herself, and if that cost her her life, she reckoned it was worth it.

The sec men in the courthouse were numerous and cagey about popping up to shoot and then quickly ducking. If she had been a crack handblaster shot like Mildred,

Krysty might have been able to pick off some of them. As it was, she was reluctant to waste any of her handful of cartridges on targets she had scarcely any hope of hitting.

But nobody had counted on the Judge, who certainly projected the image of a man who cared about nothing but his obsession for watching people hang by the neck until dead, showing such a brisk regard for the sanctity of his hide. Krysty suspected that his Messianic complex was really the passion that ruled him, and the mass-murder thing was more by way of a hobby.

So now the plan had gone completely to shit. The mob from the east was completely dispersed and suppressed, including Krysty, at least for the present.

A young man holding a pickax risked a look around the frame of the busted-in door. A shot promptly hit him in the eye and dropped him. Some of the others in the room moaned.

Now it's up to Mildred and the rest to save the situation, Krysty thought. Or we're all in for a really long day.

MOST OF THE crowd that had been standing listlessly before the gallows had run off. Not that Mildred could blame them. The sec men were too preoccupied wrestling with the insurgents who'd struck from concealment among the onlookers to pay any attention to them.

Now that the bystanders had dispersed, the sec men quickly broke free and fell back into a clump. The ones who hadn't drawn blasters did so now. They then retreated back beneath the gallows to stand off their former assailants as well as the mob now racing to join them. Two sec men and four of the rebels were down.

Mildred smiled. "Thanks for the targets, boys," she said, raising the longblaster and aiming. She picked a kneeling figure, lined him up in her iron sights and squeezed the trigger.

The man's head jerked as his muscles spasmed in response to the bullet punching through his chest. He fell forward. Mildred wasn't a longblaster woman by preference, but she knew her way around one. And she knew how to shoot.

The other sec men didn't realize the shot had come from above. They yelled angrily and delivered a withering volley right into the faces of the mob coming at them from the west.

The rioters screamed and fell back. It looked to Mildred as if only a few were hit, but that didn't matter. The members of the mob, angry though they were, weren't tacticians. Few of them were even brawlers. And nobody was eager to get chilled, ever.

The grand adventure of freedom didn't seem so magic and alluring when somebody you'd known all your life was suddenly on the ground next to you, huddled in a ball of doomed, intolerable agony around a gutshot.

Meanwhile, Sharleez and four of her co-conspirators were still atop the gallows. The placement of the VIP box and the angle kept the defenders in the courthouse from being able to sweep the gallows with their fire. The prisoners had long been freed, and had understandably taken the opportunity to climb down the thirteen steps and hightail it out of there. That had left the five rebels unsure exactly how to proceed. So Sharleez had waved her blaster, which to Mildred's annoyance had the slide locked back in indication the fool girl hadn't reloaded it, and shouted inspiring slogans at the crowd. Her companions punched the air with their fists and cheered.

But now, with the sec men right beneath them and shooting at their friends, they found something mean-

ingful to do. At a command from Sharleez one yanked the
lever Mildred had prevented the executioner, now well on
his way to ambient temperature, from grabbing. The four
spring-loaded traps promptly snapped downward. One
comically hit a sec man square in the face and knocked
him on his butt.

Sharleez's four companions, all young men, promptly
dropped down through the traps to do battle with the knot
of sec men. The last paused momentarily to hold up a
hand to stop Sharleez from joining them. He evidently said
something convincing, because she turned away from the
traps, back toward the front of the scaffold. The youth let
himself down to start milling his fists with furious inef-
fectualness at the embattled sec men.

"Well, shit," Mildred said. There went her nice, neat
targets.

Much of the crowd was starting to coalesce again a couple blocks from the action—a block west of Mildred's own
vantage point. That was unusual. Mostly when a group
broke and ran the way they had from that first fusillade,
they kept on running until they were exhausted. Or found
what they thought was a promising place to dig a hole,
crawl in and pull it in after them.

These people are seriously pissed, she thought. And
they actually seemed to be responding favorably to Sharleez hopping up and down and waving encouragingly at
them from the gallows. She did cut a brave figure, Mildred had to admit. If a person was susceptible to that kind
of romantic nonsense.

She'd seen it get too many people killed, herself.

Some of the crowd started back toward the gallows
and the melee beneath it, only to start going down again
as fresh blasterfire pummeled them from an unexpected
direction.

Mildred looked up to see sec men crouched on the roofs of a couple of buildings on the south side of the street, next to the courthouse. They were firing on the crowd with an assortment of longblasters.

That was a bad sign. If the ville folk lost their nerve, they were done for the day. But at least Mildred had targets again. She shifted her Winchester hunting rifle around, lined up the sights on a man in a gray and black plaid shirt with an SKS, and shot him through the torso.

The sec men initially had no idea where the chill shot had come from. They were at a height disadvantage that made it harder to see her, since the roofs they were on were one story. They kept shooting down into the crowd. Some of the ville folk, however, realized that if they hugged the building fronts on the south side of the street, the sec men couldn't shoot at them.

As they ran for cover, Mildred picked off another marshal. One of the others spotted her. He yelled and pointed. Longblasters were raised to spit yellow fire at her through the dawn half light.

As shots cracked by her, Mildred shot the bright boy who'd seen her through the neck.

A weird moaning cry made her look back toward the gallows. A figure appeared as if from nowhere behind Sharleez. Mildred got the impression of a tall, wide-shouldered man whose big square face was a mask of dried blood, and whose blond hair was half dyed pink from blood and red mud.

She swung her longblaster toward him. Before she could draw a bead, the man was behind Sharleez. The rebel leader was so caught up in cheering her followers on, despite the prime target she was making of herself, that she didn't respond initially to the desperate warnings being shouted at her.

It was quickly too late. The tall blood-smeared man locked a brawny arm around her throat and held a humongous knife to her cheek.

"All right, you traitor scum!" he hollered in a voice that overrode the chaos, the shouts and groans and screams and even the blasterfire. "I'm Cutter Dan, back from hell to teach you bastards the meaning of pain! Now throw down your weapons and surrender or the bitch loses an eye."

Mildred started to back away from her position by the roof rampart so she could try to line up a shot on the mysteriously manifesting sec boss with minimal risk of being hit by fire from the snipers on the lower rooftops. But the bastard was cunning about ducking behind his hostage to spoil a rescuer's shot.

Sharleez's laudable fighting spirit wasn't doing her any favors. She fought back furiously, kicking wriggling, batting at the sec boss's arms and face, which made it was even harder to shoot her captor without hitting her.

Mildred glanced back to the sec men below her on the roofs across the street. She didn't want to get so hypnotized by a futile attempt to save Sharleez that she gave one of those boys a chance to nail her. She liked the girl well enough, but in the end, she was just another random encounter in an endless string that stretched across the Deathlands and around the world. Not one of Mildred's family.

She swept the roofs with a quick look. There were seven shooters by her count, four on the building to the west, which was slightly higher than the other, though still much lower than Mildred's vantage point.

Except—suddenly there were five on one roof, three on the other. A figure reared up behind a sec man who was kneeling to fire a riot gun, snapping its fists to out the sides from the sec man's throat.

Blood flew in a sheet, out over the edge of the roof to fall in fine red rain on the street. As the sec man collapsed, Mildred saw the figure who had slit his gullet clearly. A slight figure, with a camouflage jacket and a bone-white face under long white hair.

Her heart jumped. *Jak!*

The albino turned to the next sec man in the firing line. The man glanced over and momentarily froze in surprise as he saw his buddy slumping bonelessly over the edge of the roof. Jak waded into him in a double whirl of his knives. More blood flew.

Another sec man spun to blast Jak with a lever-action longblaster. Mildred shot him through the cheek. His face exploded in a shower of blood, bone and teeth.

Jak turned to another foe, dancing deftly forward to put the sec man's body between him and the man's last remaining companion.

And down the street out of the west rode four new arrivals on horses.

Chapter Thirty-Six

The crowd scattered before Ryan and his friends as they rode up at a lope on the horses Jak had helped them steal.

Ryan had already spotted sec men shooters on two roofs to their right, and as he looked that way again that changed to one roof. A body plummeted off the nearer, taller building to crash to the gutter. Jak gave his friends a big grin and a bloody thumbs-up as they went by.

From the back of the mare to Ryan's right, J.B. raked the other roofline one-handed with a burst from his Uzi. The horses tossed their heads and snorted but didn't shy away.

The sec men on the roof cried out in alarm and pulled back. A high-powered longblaster cracked from the other side of the street. Ryan heard a scream from an unseen marshal.

"Mildred, I bet," J.B. said in satisfaction, and ripped off another short burst at the now-untenanted roof edge.

"Show-off," Ryan said.

"Ryan Cawdor," a familiar voice boomed. "The very man I came all this way to see."

Another longblaster shot roared from the roof to the left.

"Cutter Dan?" Ricky yelped from the horse to Ryan's left, past Doc. *"No es posible!"*

"Fireblast! J.B., Ricky, try to keep those bastards on the roof from back-shooting me, if any take a mind to," Ryan said. "Doc, come with me and deal with the sec men under the gallows."

"Excelsior!" Doc shouted. He drew his rapier from its sheath, which he had stuck through his belt, and hauled out his LeMat with his left hand. Then he and Ryan booted their horses forward.

Doc pulled out in front of Ryan's big black gelding. He rode a huge pinto mare with a notched ear and an attitude.

There were four sec men huddled under the scaffold, surrounded by bodies, some of which clearly weren't their brothers in arms. They gaped wide-eyed at this fresh and unexpected attack.

One of them went down flailing as Doc loosed the short-barreled shotgun at them. He reared his mount to a halt and slid off on its far side to use its big black and white body for temporary cover. He swatted the mare's rump with his rapier. The horse neighed and bolted down the street. Doc waded into the stunned sec men, blasting and stabbing and chortling gleefully.

Ryan slowed the horse enough to climb up on the saddle and launch himself at the gallows. He made it and didn't die; that was the good part. But he was forcibly reminded that he wasn't the expert horseman the companions believed him to be when he landed hard and rolled across the platform almost into range of the captive young woman's wildly kicking boots.

"Cawdor," Cutter Dan said, gazing down at him from beside his hostage's furious face. "You'd have made a much more impressive entrance if you'd stuck the landing."

"You should be dead, with half the mountain falling on your bastard head," Ryan gritted.

If the sec boss of Second Chance and Chief Marshal of Judge Santee's phantom United States, hadn't been upright with his knife held to the young woman's face, Ryan wouldn't have been able to swear the man *wasn't* dead. He looked as if someone had upended a bucket of blood over his head and let it dry. His clothes were half torn from his rangy frame.

"I'm no easier to kill than a cockroach," Cutter Dan said. "Just like you, Cawdor. Now, put your hands up like a good little perp or the bitch dies."

"Chill her," Ryan said from his back. "She's nothing to me. I never saw her before."

"Wait!" the woman yelled. She had the remarkable presence of mind to jab a thumb backward at Cutter Dan's eye.

Ryan kicked the chief marshal's left shin, hard. His boot slid back. The leg buckled, dropping him to a knee.

Sharleez heaved her body frantically and broke loose. She fell sprawling to the scaffold.

Ryan jumped to his feet, drawing his panga. Beat to hell as he was, Cutter Dan got up as rapidly. The two men faced each other, big knives in their hands, chests heaving to suck down air.

Cutter Dan gave Ryan a big old grin. He was missing a top front tooth.

"And now, coldheart," the sec boss growled, "we settle it."

His brought up his Bowie and held out his left hand to ward off his opponent's knife hand.

"Right," Ryan said, and kicked him in the balls.

Breath exploded from Cutter Dan and he doubled over. Ryan straightened him with a jaw-cracking left uppercut.

Then he buried the panga almost to the hilt in Cutter Dan's belly.

It had to have hurt like nuke fire, but Cutter Dan only grunted. He tried to stab Ryan.

The one-eyed man caught his wrist. For a moment they stood locked together, straining, arm to arm, strength against strength.

But it was a one-way fight. The agony and rapid bleeding out meant Cutter Dan could only weaken. Slowly Ryan forced up the fist that held the Bowie knife.

The chief marshal's eyes blazed defiance. His broad jaw was set. The muscles stood out on his neck like steel cables.

Then Ryan forced him to cut his own throat with his own knife.

"WAIT!" THE OLD MAN's voice screeched. "Unhand me you insurgent traitor scum!"

The final battle of Second Chance was brief, bloody and entirely one-sided. At least as far as Ryan's band was concerned.

With the sec men on the streets either running away or rounded up and beaten bloody by the mob, it was easy for Ryan and Ricky to take up position in a building across from the reinforced courthouse. They had quickly sniped down the armed sec men who dared show themselves. J.B.'s Uzi had ripped the thrown-together barricade of sandbags and office furniture to make sure the marshals behind it kept their heads down. The vengeful mob had swarmed over it and done the rest, despite the fact they lost a good dozen of their own to marshals fighting like the trapped rats that they were.

Now, proudly escorted by Ricky with his DeLisle long-blaster at the ready, Mildred and Krysty emerged from the courthouse with their backpacks on. The barricades had been mostly kicked to the side, but the women had to step carefully between the bodies still heaped around it.

"No! This is anarchy! You can't!"

Dozens of hands held a wildly struggling Judge Santee over the heads of the crowd gathered around the gallows. His hands were bound behind his back. His long black coattails flew as he thrashed and raved.

Other ville folk were waiting on the scaffold. Some were hauling up the body of a sec man, hanging from his distended neck, using the pulley system Santee had thoughtfully built into the gallows. They left two others dangling for the moment, along with the stocky body of a red-bearded guy in what had once been a very nice suit by ville standards. He'd been one of the rich men who'd helped Santee run Second Chance.

If Ryan had heard his name, he didn't remember it. There wasn't much point in learning it now.

Another of Santee's ruling partners lay dead in the viewing box behind the gallows. The woman Ryan had rescued—quite incidentally—from Cutter Dan had apparently shot him. And good for her.

The last remaining cohort of Judge Santee, the fat and dumpy mayor, stood off to one side, watching. He was the one who'd shown the howling, vengeful mob where his fellow plutocrat was hiding. They'd either forgiven him or forgotten him in their zeal to string up the red-bearded man.

Krysty joined Ryan and wrapped him in a warm embrace. The one-eyed man grinned at her but didn't return the hug. He had both hands on his Steyr and meant to keep them that way. He didn't like a lynch mob, even when he was its hero of the moment.

If there was any monster in the Deathlands whose gratitude could be relied on less than a baron's, it was a mob with its bloodlust up. He didn't intend the companions to become its victims.

The Judge was passed up onto the scaffold. He was forced to stand upright as the recently vacated noose was settled over his scrawny neck. Then he was marched a couple of steps back onto the reset trapdoor.

"You can't do this, you animals!" he screeched, spittle flying from his mouth. "This is treason! I am the law! You are in rebellion against the United States of Am—"

The trap snapped open beneath his feet. As Judge Santee reached the end of his rope, his words died abruptly.

So did he.

Standing on a front corner of the scaffold, the woman Krysty had told Ryan was called Sharleez shook a long-blaster in the air.

"Justice!" she cried.

"Justice!" the mob screamed back.

The helpers on the gallows began to reel up the bodies of the two sec men. A group of captured sec men, around a dozen, knelt on the street nearby. Their arms were bound behind their backs. They had been beaten bloody. A couple had been so battered that they lay on their sides, though they were clearly still alive by the piteous way they moaned.

"Bring more of the bastards to face justice!" Sharleez commanded.

"Justice!" the mob shrieked.

"Girl's got a knack for this sort of thing, you gotta admit," J.B. said, rubbing his jaw. He stood at Ryan's side, his shotgun in hand and his Uzi slung. Doc, Ricky and Jak stood behind them. They were all eyeing the crowd warily and not being subtle about it.

"John!" Mildred exclaimed in outrage.

A pair of the captives were booted to their feet and prodded with pitchforks. They stumbled toward the gallows.

Eager hands reached out to grab them.

J.B. shrugged.

"Well," he said, "you know I like to see a thing well done. Leaving aside what that thing may be."

The nooses were removed from the most recent two

dead sec men. Their bodies were unceremoniously rolled off the back of the platform to join the pile growing there. The next pair was put into the nooses in their place.

Mildred turned away shaking her head. "I'm ready to go," she said. "Anybody else feel like we ought to just maybe slide on out of here?"

"Brought horses," Jak said, nodding to Krysty and Mildred. He jerked his thumb to where their mounts, as well as the ones the men had ridden to town, were tethered a couple of blocks down the street.

"Yeah," Ryan said, "that sounds like an ace idea. Nobody's paying us any mind, anyhow."

"Shouldn't we at least say goodbye to Sharleez?" asked Krysty, as Ryan began walking west.

He just looked at her.

"You're right," she said, and followed.

They'd barely gone a block—and only Ricky had looked back at the sound of two traps being sprung simultaneously—when a new voice rang out through streets.

"People of Second Chance." The ringing, deep baritone echoed between the shabby buildings. "A bright new day has dawned for all of us today. The mad tyrant's reign of terror has ended! We are delivered!"

Ryan glanced back. To his surprise, the fat mayor had gotten up on the scaffold, where he stood up front at the opposite corner from Sharleez. She was looking at him as if she had no idea what to do about him. Though his hair was standing up all any which way, his coat was torn and his collar hung open, he was addressing the crowd calmly and authoritatively.

To Ryan's amazement, they were actually listening to him.

"Isn't he the one used to do the ringside announcing

at Santee's hanging bees?" J.B. asked. "Why aren't they stringing him up?"

Jak made a nasty feral sound, like a cornered wildcat.

"Agreed," Mildred said. "Mayor freaking Toogood. We got an earful about him when we were hiding out with the resistance. They say he's a silver-tongued devil and could talk a bear sow away from her cubs."

Ryan grunted. He turned his head forward again. He had never stopped walking toward the horses.

The man's mellifluous harangue continued to follow them, though. He was getting his say.

When they reached the horses Ricky and J.B. helped tie Krysty's and Mildred's packs behind their saddles. Ryan stopped and turned back.

Toogood was still standing there, waving his arms. Ryan could still hear his voice, but he couldn't make out the words.

Mebbe it didn't matter, he thought. The crowd wasn't just listening to him. More kept coming, as if his voice was soothing and enticing those who'd hidden through the battle out into the open.

"It appears our erstwhile plutocrat is securing himself a leading role in this bright new day he preaches of," Doc said. "At this rate, he will not be 'erstwhile' at all."

"Looks like," Ryan agreed. He stuck his left arm through the loop of his sling.

"Krysty and Mildred's young friend Sharleez should learn to sleep with one eye open, I fear," Doc said.

Ryan raised the longblaster to his shoulder. The sling drew taut, snugging the steel buttplate of his Scout against his shoulder and giving him a stable firing platform. He aimed through the scope, inhaled, partially exhaled, caught his breath. Gently but firmly he squeezed the trigger.

When the longblaster came back down from recoil,

Mayor Toogood was toppling straight over backward, with his arms flung theatrically out to his sides.

"That is…symbolic," Doc said in a small voice.

"Mebbe she will have to watch her back," Ryan said, "but it won't be on account of him."

Faces were turned their way; arms began to point.

Ryan turned his back and slung his longblaster. The others were already mounted. Krysty held the reins of his horse for him.

"Reckon I owed your little friend one," he said to her as he swung aboard his black gelding. "For helping you and Mildred out."

He accepted the reins and a quick kiss.

"You think they'll be better off now?" Ricky asked.

"Who cares?" Ryan said. "Let's ride."

The companions kicked their heels into the flanks of their horses and rode out of the ville.

* * * * *

JAMES AXLER

DEATH LANDS®

End Program

Newfound hope quickly deteriorates into a fight to save mankind

Built upon a predark military installation, Progress, California, could be the utopia Ryan Cawdor and companions have been seeking. Compared to the Deathlands, the tortured remains of a nuke-altered civilization, Progress represents a fresh start. The successful replacement of Ryan's missing eye nearly convinces the group that their days of hell are over—until they discover the high tech in Progress is actually designed to destroy, not enhance, civilization. The companions must find a way to stop Ryan from becoming a willing pawn in the eradication of mankind....

Available May wherever books and ebooks are sold.

GDL116

... James Axler
Oüt[anders®

NECROPOLIS

When an all-consuming darkness enters Africa, even the fittest may not survive

As immortal god-kings continue to lay claim to the planet as their own, the epic fight to repossess Earth continues. Although the Cerberus rebels exist to protect mankind, nothing can prepare them for what lurks in vampire hell. From her hidden city beneath the African continent, Neekra, the vampire queen, emerges to stake her claim to blood power. As her minions swarm to outmaneuver her rival, the taint of the undead descends across Africa. The rebels race to contain an unfurling horror and escape a dreadful destiny as tortured ambassadors for the vampire kingdom.

Available in May, wherever books and ebooks are sold.

AleX Archer
GRENDEL'S CURSE

**A politically ordered excavation
unearths more than expected**

Skalunda Barrow, rumored to be the final resting place of the
legendary Nordic hero Beowulf, is being excavated, thanks to
charismatic—and right-wing extremist—politician Karl Thorssen,
and archaeologist Annja Creed can't wait. But with the potential to
uncover Hrunting and Nægling,
two mythical swords the politician
would kill to possess, the dig
rapidly becomes heated. As
Thorssen realizes the power of
possessing Nægling, he is quick to
show how far he will go to achieve
his rabid ambitions. And when
Thorssen marks Annja for death,
the only way she can survive is to
find a sword of her own.

*Available May wherever books
and ebooks are sold.*

GRA48

Don Pendleton

ATOMIC FRACTURE

Innocence becomes collateral damage as civil war spills into terrorism

A civil war in the Middle East is the perfect breeding ground for Al-Qaeda's brand of terror. Taking advantage of the chaos, Al-Qaeda's ultimate goal is to dominate the war-torn country. On the President's orders, Phoenix Force drops in to stop the attacks, while Able Team remains stateside to ferret out a rebel mole who has stolen nuclear weapons. With the lines between right and wrong beginning to blur, Stony Man is sure of one thing: their only cause is the millions of lives at stake.

STONY MAN®

Available in April, wherever books and ebooks are sold.

The Executioner
Don Pendleton's®
PATRIOT STRIKE

Superpatriots decide Texas should secede with a bang

After the murder of a Texas Ranger, Mack Bolan is called in to investigate. Working under the radar with the dead Ranger's sister, he quickly learns that rumors of missing fissile material falling into the wrong hands are true. The terrorists, die-hard Americans, are plotting to use the dirty bomb to remove Texas from the Union. As the countdown to D-day begins, the only option is to take the bait of the superpatriots and shut them down from the inside. You don't mess with Texas. Unless you're the Executioner.

GOLD EAGLE®

Available April wherever books and ebooks are sold.